Subterranean Worlds

THE
WESLEYAN
EARLY CLASSICS
OF
SCIENCE FICTION
SERIES

General Editor
Arthur B. Evans

Invasion of the Sea
Jules Verne

The Mysterious Island
Jules Verne

Lumen
Camille Flammarion

The Battle of the Sexes in Science Fiction
Justine Larbalestier

The Last Man
Jean-Baptiste Cousin de Grainville

The Mighty Orinoco
Jules Verne

The Yellow Wave
Kenneth Mackay

Cosmos Latinos
Andrea L. Bell and
Yolanda Molina-Gavilán

Deluge
Sydney Fowler Wright

Caesar's Column: A Story of the Twentieth Century
Ignatius Donnelly

Star Maker
Olaf Stapleton

The Moon Pool
A. Merritt

The Twentieth Century
Albert Robida

Subterranean

A Critical Anthology

Edited by PETER FITTING

WESLEYAN UNIVERSITY PRESS

Middletown, Connecticut

Published by
Wesleyan University Press
Middletown, CT 06459

This collection © 2004 by
Wesleyan University Press
Introduction and Critical Materials
© 2004 by Peter Fitting
All rights reserved
Printed in the
United States of America
Set in Galliard type by BW&A Books, Inc.
Library of Congress
Cataloging-in-Publication Data
Subterranean worlds : a critical anthology /
Peter Fitting
p. cm. — (The Wesleyan early classics of
science fiction series)
Includes bibliographical references (p.)
and index.
ISBN 0-8195-6723-x (cloth : alk. paper)
1. Science fiction. 2. Civilization,
Subterranean—Fiction. 3. Underground
areas—Fiction. 4. Earth—Core—Fiction.
5. Utopias—Fiction. 6. Voyages, Imaginary. I. Fitting, Peter. II. Series.
PN6071.S33S84 2004
808.83'8762—dc22
2004045151
5 4 3 2 1

To the memory of my mother,

ELIZABETH (1917–1992), and

my father, PAUL (1913–1990)

Contents

Acknowledgments

This book should be considered as somewhere between a hobby and an obsession, and it has taken up much of the past ten years. My interest in subterranean worlds grows out of an attempt to reconcile my fascination with English language science fiction and utopian literature with my formal identification as a professor of French literature. I began to look at earlier works of the utopian tradition and at works in French, in the hope of finding pre-twentieth-century novels which would capture my imagination the way that science fiction did; and colleagues working in French—Lise Leibacher, Aubrey Rosenberg, and Nadia Minerva—spoke to me about eighteenth-century French utopias with underground settings. It was the discovery of Charles-Georges-Thomas Garnier's anthology, the thirty-six volumes of the *Voyages imaginaires, songes, visions, et romans cabalistiques* (Paris, 1787–1789) at the Bibliothèque nationale that opened the doors of wonder for me: these volumes constitute a treasure chest of mostly eighteenth-century fantastic voyages and other strange and often forgotten works. Although there was little "true" science fiction in these early works, I became engrossed by the recurrence of the underworld as a setting for many of these adventures, and by the sheer oddity of this location. In this book, I have not addressed my own fascination, nor why this setting may have caught the fancy of various writers. Instead, I have tried to track the permutations of this idea during the eighteenth and nineteenth centuries, and to set the record straight in terms of why some works have been mistakenly classified as set in the underworld.

My thoughts on some of these works have been presented in various places, most especially at meetings of the Society for Utopian Studies. Here I would like to thank one of the key figures in the development and success of the society for his support and advice. As a past president of the society and as the founding editor of the journal

Utopian Studies, Lyman Tower Sargent has played a key role in making the society a "cooperative and non-competitive environment" for intellectual interchange across a range of disciplines. He has always been generous in his encouragement and advice, and I am honored to consider him a friend. Nor has he been alone. The Society for Utopian Studies provides a supportive atmosphere in which to work, and the encouragement of many of my colleagues in the society has been invaluable over the years, including that of Jack O'Connor, Tom Moylan, Jeannie Pfaelzer, Naomi Jacobs, Phil Wegner, Ken Roemer, and many others too numerous to mention. At the same time, though this anthology may show little evidence of his influence, or of the political concerns that have driven much of my writing on utopia, I would like to thank Fredric Jameson for years of support and encouragement for many of my less conventional interests.

The French department here at the University of Toronto has always supported my work, however far my interests may have strayed from strictly French concerns. More generally, Toronto provides me a community of like-minded friends and colleagues who, though they were not always prepared to follow me into the underworld, have always encouraged my work—David Galbraith, Eric Cazdyn, Ian Balfour, Frank Cunningham, and Gavin Smith among them, although this only scratches the surface of supportive friends and colleagues. I should also like to thank my colleague John Fleming, who lent me some volumes of the Garnier at a crucial moment.

Thanks, too, to Arthur Evans, who first approached me about a book on these subterranean worlds in this format—without his suggestion I would have gone on looking for other examples for another ten years! I would also like to thank my editor, Maura High, for guiding me through the process.

Finally, thanks to my partner, Barbara Lampert, for her support and encouragement, and for her patience.

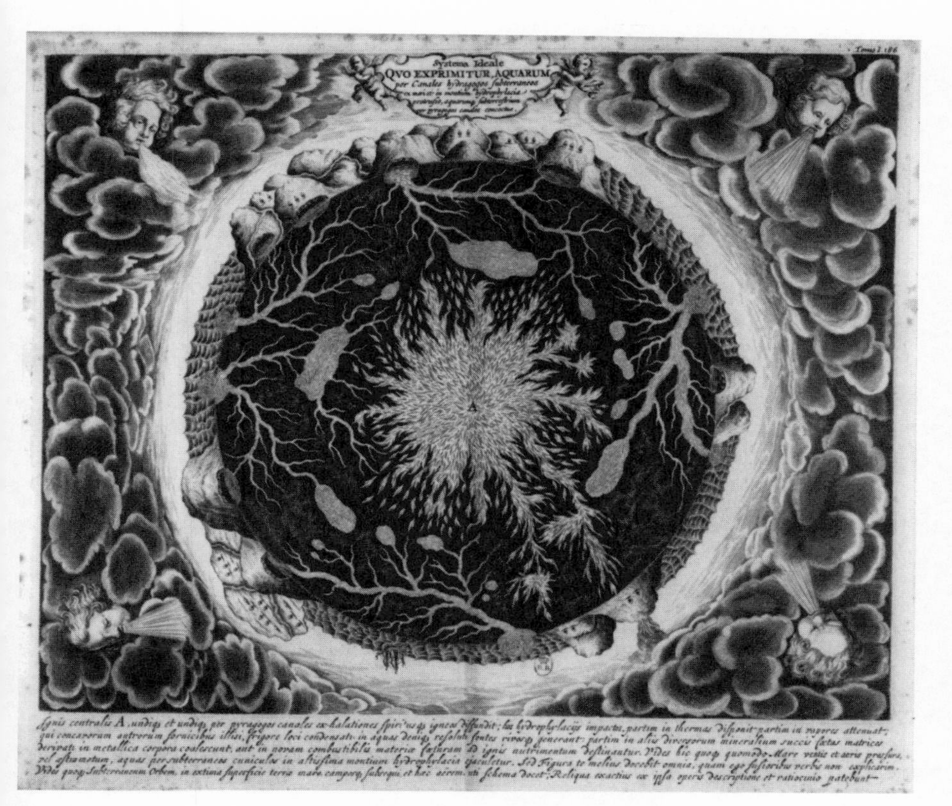

Athanasius Kircher, *Mundus Subterraneus* (1665)
(courtesy of the Bibliothèque nationale)
Athanasius Kircher's proposed model of the workings of the elements of the Earth, bound together in "an intricate system of intercommunicating cavities" beneath the planetary crust, the most important of which was a subterranean channel of water running "through the earth from the north pole to the south" (Collier, *Cosmogonies*, 372).

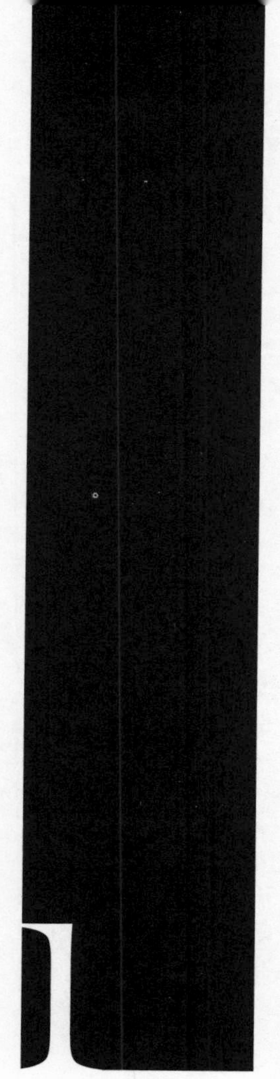

A Bluffer's Guide to the Underworld: An Introduction to the Hollow Earth

To the Future Explorers of the New World that exists beyond North and South Poles in the hollow interior of the Earth. Who will Repeat Admiral Byrd's historic Flight for 1,700 Miles beyond the North Pole and that of his Expedition for 2,300 Miles beyond the South Pole, entering a New Unknown Territory not shown on any map, covering an immense land, areas whose total size is larger than North America, consisting of forests, mountains, lakes, vegetation and animal life.
—Raymond Bernard, *The Hollow Earth*

Every schoolboy knows that the earth is a solid ball, slightly flattened at the poles, and surrounded by a cosmos of inconceivable immensity. Since Magellan sailed around the globe in 1519, few have doubted that the earth is round. Yet it is precisely because these views are universally accepted that the shape of the earth is such a happy field of speculation for the pseudo-scientist.
—Martin Gardner, "Flat and Hollow"

In 1999 a science fiction novel appeared with the simple title *Subterranean* (James Rollins [New York: Avon, 1999]). A cross between Jules Verne's *Journey to the Center of the Earth* (1864) and the film *Jurassic Park* (1993), the novel is poorly written, but it exemplifies a continuing tradition. For the idea of a vast subterranean world is still alive, at the beginning of this new millennium, in fiction and in various New Age writings, and also—perhaps in a more sinister form—in the works of Holocaust deniers such as Ernst Zundel.[1] How could such an idea, such a setting, still be given credibility, when science seems clear on the subject? Critics have pointed out that the emergence of extraterrestrial settings in earlier fiction corresponded to the gradual exploration and mapping of the uncharted areas of the globe (uncharted by Westerners, that is to say), and it is certainly seems to be the case that there are few SF or fantastic novels written today—Michael Crichton's *Jurassic Park* aside—which propose an unexplored area of the Earth in which to situate their adventures. There are no longer any "lost civilizations" left to discover, no hidden valleys or uncharted islands where dinosaurs and other creatures from our geological past have managed to survive. And yet Rollins's novel does exactly that, situating a vast underground civilization beneath the continent of Antarctica—a continent that, however remote and unfriendly, can hardly be described as uncharted or unexplored. While I cannot fully explain the continuing acceptance of this belief in an underground world, I intend in this first chapter to explore the prehistory of the genre, up to the end of the nineteenth century.

History of an Idea

In 1836 the United States Congress passed a bill establishing what would become the first and most famous American naval scientific exploration, the "United States Exploring Expedition" which lasted from 1838 to 1842 and which led to the establishment of a national museum of natural history—the Smithsonian Institution—to house the more than 50,000 specimens collected. This expedition began in what the historian William Stanton has called the "fervent foolishness" of one man, John Cleves Symmes Jr., a self-educated former soldier who in 1818 issued his "Circular Number 1," "sending copies to 'each notable foreign government, reigning prince, legislature, city, college, and philosophical society, quite around the earth'" (Stanton, *Expedition,* 8):

> I declare that the earth is hollow and habitable within; containing a number of solid concentric spheres, one within the other, and that it is open at the poles twelve or sixteen degrees. I pledge my life in support of this truth, and am ready to explore the hollow, if the world will support and aid me in the undertaking. (Symmes, "Declaration")

Symmes's theories led to a number of fictional visions of the "world within," beginning with Adam Seaborn's 1820 *Symzonia*—a work which has often been attributed to Symmes himself—as well as providing the "proof" for various defenders of the idea. Symmes was not, however, the first to argue that the Earth was hollow; nor is *Symzonia* the first novel set in the hollow Earth. Although there are of course, numerous narratives—dating back to Greek and Roman texts—of mysterious caverns and descents into the underworld, the theory of a vast cavity inside the Earth appears to be much more recent and was advanced by some European thinkers in the seventeenth and eighteenth centuries as a scientific explanation of the Earth's structure. This period is filled with a variety of now discarded cosmological hypotheses, many inspired by the attempt to reconcile scriptural accounts of creation with scientific observation: hypotheses about the movement of the sun, the Earth and the stars, about the universality of the great flood, about creation and the origins of life, and about the Earth's own formation and composition.

Many critics identify the emergence of the idea of the hollow Earth with the writings of the Jesuit priest Athanasius Kircher (called by one biographer "the last of the polymaths" [Godwin, *Kircher*, 5]), who poured his encyclopedic knowledge into a variety of treatises, including the *Mundus Subterraneus* (1665). This illustrated treatise was intended to serve as a refutation of alchemy as well as a general overview of the new sciences, with particular attention to the "workings of the elements of the earth" (Godwin, *Kircher*, 84). Kircher did not really propose that the Earth was hollow, but rather that it was composed of the four elements, bound together in "an intricate system of intercommunicating cavities" beneath the planetary crust, the most important of which was a subterranean channel of water, running "through the earth from the north pole to the south" (Collier, *Cosmogonies*, 372).

The selections in the first section have been chosen to illustrate the purported scientific and theoretical descriptions of an inner world which may have led to the various fictions under consideration. While some early descriptions of the Earth's interior describe a globe riddled with interior channels and passageways (some empty, some filled with water or fire), the renowned British astronomer Edmund Halley went further, describing the interior of the Earth in terms of something like the "concentric spheres" of Symmes's theory (see frontispiece).

In 1947 Conway Zirkle presented a very convincing genealogy of this idea in his "Theory of Concentric Spheres: Edmund Halley, Cotton Mather, & John Cleves Symmes." Zirkle traces Symmes's theory of concentric spheres to Halley's 1692 "Account of the Cause of the Change of the Variation of the Magnetical Needle with an Hypothesis of the Structure of the Internal Parts of the Earth: As It Was Proposed to the Royal Society in One of Their Later Meetings." According to Zirkle, these ideas were further elaborated by Cotton Mather in *The Christian Philosopher* (1721). As Walter Kafton-Minkel points out, while Symmes may not have known Halley's original paper, "we can be fairly certain that one of the books he read was Cotton Mather's *Christian Philosopher*, with its description of Halley's concentric-Earths idea. Coming as he did from an educated family with a Puritan background—Mather had mentioned one of Symmes's ancestors in another of his books—the *Philosopher* could not have been unknown to him" (Kafton-Minkel, *Subterranean Worlds*, 58).

Subterranean Worlds before Symmes

In this collection, I will concentrate on works written prior to Jacques Collin de Plancy's *Voyage au centre de la terre ou Aventures diverses de Clairancy et de ses compagnons dans le Spitzberg, au Pôle-nord, et dans des pays inconnus* (1821), since the later works have been discussed in some detail by scholars writing about subterranean fiction (Becker, Guillaud, Kafton-Minkel, and Minerva);[2] and indeed, most of these works are readily available. Moreover, it is relatively easy to follow the traces of this idea in the wake of the publication of *Symzonia* in 1820, from Edgar Allan Poe's "Ms. Found in a Bottle" (1833) and his unfinished "Narrative of A. Gordon Pym" (1837) to Jules Verne's *Voyage au centre de la terre* (1865).[3] I will, however, take a few examples of works written after Verne to give a sense of the continuity in themes and motifs as much as of the inventiveness of many of those early writers.

Previous attempts to investigate how the idea of a hollow Earth developed in fiction have been complicated by the fact that many of the early works to which critics refer are not readily available. Another complicating factor in the development of an inventory of novels and stories with subterranean settings is to be found in Régis Messac's pioneering article "Voyages modernes au centre de la terre" (1929), where his list of works established those that are key to this subgenre of the fantastic—a list subsequent critics have often taken to be definitive without checking the works themselves. It is difficult enough to know how widespread the idea of a hollow Earth was in the eighteenth century, but the situation is further complicated by questions about the appropriateness of some of the works Messac includes, as well as by the existence of other fictions with subterranean settings of which he was not aware. Messac's trailblazing effort begins with his description of three eighteenth-century texts that will be cited again and again: the anonymous *Relation d'un voyage du Pôle Arctique au Pôle Antarctique par le centre du monde, avec la description de ce périlleux passage, et des choses merveilleuses et étonnantes qu'on a découvertes sous le Pôle Antarctique* (1721), Fieux de Mouhy's *Lamékis ou Les voyages extraordinaires d'un Egyptien dans la terre intérieure; avec la découverte de l'Isle des Sylphides* (1735–1738), and Ludvig Holberg's *Journey of Niels Klim to the World Underground* (1741). Messac then turns to the more familiar works of Poe, Verne, Bulwer-Lytton, and Burroughs, and he briefly mentions some forgotten early-twentieth-century French novels. Although he does mention *L'Icosameron* (1788), he admits that he knows little about it since he was not able to locate a copy of Casanova's subterranean utopia. But his most glaring oversight is the omission of John Cleves Symmes and of Seaborn's *Symzonia*; nor does he mention the anonymous *Voyage to the World in the Center of the Earth* (1755), or Jacques Collin de Plancy's *Voyage au centre de la terre* (1821)—both works that seem much more pertinent to an inventory of hollow-Earth fiction than do the anonymous *Relation* or the Chevalier de Mouhy's *Lamékis.*

Even before Messac's article, however, one finds that the choice of these three eighteenth-century novels (the *Relation* and the novels of Holberg and Mouhy) had already been featured in the "subterranean worlds" section of the great French astronomer Camille Flammarion's popularizing look at imaginary worlds and the possibility of life elsewhere, first published in 1865 and titled *Les mondes imaginaires et les mondes réels: voyage pittoresque dans le ciel et revue critique des théories humaines scientifiques et romanesques, anciennes et modernes sur les habitants des asters* (459–469). In turn, although neither identifies his sources, it is likely that Flammarion and Messac took this subterranean trio from Charles-Georges-Thomas Garnier, who published these three works as the "Voyages to the Underground" section of his thirty-six-volume anthology of fantastic fiction, the *Voyages imaginaires, songes, visions, & romans cabalistiques* ("aux entrailles de la terre": vols. 19–21).[4]

Types of Subterranean Worlds

These three imaginary voyages nonetheless illustrate the most important aspects of the subterranean domain. The *Relation* is probably the first fictional example of what is sometimes referred to as the "holes at the poles" version of the hollow-Earth theory; *Lamékis,* though it does not really belong to the genre, includes several underground settings (crypts and caverns); and Holberg's *Niels Klim* is almost certainly the first fictional depiction of the hollow Earth.

Pierre Versins was the one of the first critics to point out that there were two basic subsets of fictional hollow-Earth settings, which he humorously labels *gruyère* and *calebasse* (gourd). The first refers to descriptions that depict the interior of the Earth in terms of a Swiss cheese, that is, as containing one or more immense caverns in its crust; in the second, the Earth is hollow (874–877). Versins's distinction is a useful one, although it is possible to divide the second hollow-Earth classification into a number of further subsets. As we shall see, some versions of the hollow Earth depict a vast chasm inside the Earth, "adorned [as Klim puts it] with lesser sun, stars, and planets." In Holberg's novel, however, in addition to the planet floating inside the Earth, the underside of the Earth's crust—what he calls the "firmament"—was also inhabited. This world is even more vast than the surface of the subterranean planet.

Finally, a third type of the hollow-Earth setting describes not a hollow Earth per se, but—following Kircher—a subterranean passage. This is exemplified by the second of Messac (and Garnier's) three subterranean works: the anonymous and relatively short *Relation d'un voyage du Pôle Arctique au Pôle Antarctique par le centre du monde* (1721), which tells of a traveler whose ship is caught in a whirlpool at the North Pole, rushed through the Earth, and ejected at the South Pole. It also introduces several other variants: the question of how one enters the inner world (caves, whirlpools, volcanoes and so on) as well as that of whether the inner world is (or was) inhabited. The *Relation* is one of the few subterranean works that does not put any humans in the underworld, although when the crew emerges at the South Pole, they find signs of a vanished culture.

Leaving aside various journeys to the land of the dead, there are no major examples of Versins's "Swiss cheese" model until we descend into the inner worlds of Verne and Bulwer-Lytton. In *Le voyage au centre de la terre*, Verne describes the inner world as a vast cave, "capable of containing an ocean." At the same time, insofar as Liedenbrock and Axel are described as entering this cavern through an extinct volcano in Iceland and, descending diagonally in a southeasterly direction, being eventually ejected from a volcano in Sicily, Verne's novel suggests a much more extensive and complex cave world than do some others with similar settings, and it continues the familiar idea of Kircher's communicating subterranean passageways between volcanoes and the like.

The descent into the "bowels of the earth" is the logical extension of another type of voyage that is often associated with this descent: the "subterraneous" or subterranean voyage, as first discussed by Alexander Krappe in his article "The Subterraneous Voyage" (1941). As Krappe points out, the model for this type of narrative lies in the "Voyages of Sinbad the Sailor" in the *One Thousand and One Arabian Nights* (which Galland translated into French between 1704 and 1717).[5] The subterranean voyage is epitomized by the El Dorado section of *Candide*, or rather by the manner in which Candide and Cacambo arrive in El Dorado: in a boat rushing down a river that runs through "a vault in frightening rocks which reached up to the skies" (cited in Krappe, "Subterraneous Voyage," 119). Krappe then ties the subterraneous voyage to some older traditions, beginning with a similar passage in Sinbad's sixth voyage (and including the *History of the Forty Vezirs* and the medieval Alexander romances).

> Two main variants of our theme thus stand out: in the one (A) the hero in the course of his wanderings ascends or descends an unknown river, passes through a tunnel, and arrives in a sort of Terrestrial paradise or El Dorado. . . . In the other (B) the hero, after a shipwreck, descends a river, passes through a tunnel, and reaches a known country or a known sea, from which he manages to return home safely. (124)

According to Krappe, there is another, even older version of this theme in the tradition of the terrestrial paradise (found in Philiostorgios, Pliny the Elder, and the Koran), which revolves around the search for the headwaters of the Tigris. This leads him to conclude that his group A derives from "the land of its origin, the region of the Tigris tunnel in Armenia." It is thus "the original version of the story [while] B, which combines the theme with a story of shipwreck and sea adventures, is merely a derivative due, probably, to Arabic storytellers and hardly older that the time of the maritime expeditions of the Arabs" ("Subterraneous Voyage," 129).

This sort of subterranean journey can be found in a number of other well-known eighteenth-century works that, because they describe this passage to another world, are sometimes mistakenly labeled "subterranean novels." They include Tyssot de Patot's *Les voyages et aventures de Jacques Massé* (1710)[6] and Robert Paltock's *Life and Adventures of Peter Wilkins* (1750). Like those two novels, Margaret Cavendish's *Blazing World* (1666) was also set in the polar regions and has also been called a subterranean utopia (e.g., Trousson refers to it as a "vaste cité sous les glaces . . . la première utopie souterraine"; *Voyages*, 96), although a close examination of the passage to the utopian society suggests that this is not the case:

> Those few men which were in [the boat] were all frozen to death, the young Lady only, by the light of her beauty, the heat of her youth, and protection of the gods, remaining alive: neither was it

a wonder that the men did freeze to death; *for they were not only driven to the very end or point of the Pole of that world, but even to another Pole of another world,* which joined close to it; so that the cold having a double strength at the conjunction of those two Poles, was insupportable: *at last, the boat still passing on, was forced into another world,* for it is impossible to round this world's globe from Pole to Pole, so as we do from East to West; because the Poles of the other world, joining to the Poles of this, do not allow any further passage to surround the world that way; *but if any one arrives to either of these Poles, he is either forced to return, or to enter into another world.* (125–126; emphasis mine)

I think that this rather confusing description is invoking not a world "under" or "inside" the Earth, but what might in science fiction be called a "parallel world."[7] There is nothing in subsequent descriptions of the setting of Cavendish's utopia to suggest the subterranean locale, and it is simply a background for the action; the pole is a conveniently mysterious and unknown place—like the Americas and Australia in so many utopias of the time—in which to situate the unusual society.

Although the idea of an inner world, and of the hollow Earth in particular, has been thoroughly discredited in contemporary scientific accounts of the make-up of our planet, some people continue to be--lieve in various forms of the subterranean world. They claim there are tunnels connecting such esoteric places as Shambala, Agarthi, and Mount Shasta as well as the lost kingdom of Lemuria; or that Admiral Byrd discovered an opening at the South Pole, a discovery that has been concealed by the U.S. government, like that of the alleged aliens at Roswell. Indeed, it is no coincidence that in some of these theories, the underground caverns are used by various aliens to conceal their spacecraft. Books still appear insisting that the Earth is hollow, and that this truth is being covered up by various government agencies—books with titles such as *The Hollow Earth: The Greatest Geographical Discovery in History; Made by Admiral Richard E. Byrd in the Mysterious Lands Beyond the Poles—The True Origin of the Flying Saucers.*[8] The persistence of these beliefs might be seen as a restaging of the clash of rationalism versus hidden explanations of human activities, a credulity that is overdetermined by growing skepticism of the actions of governments, on the one hand, and by the mythical and symbolic power of the underground itself, of buried and repressed knowledge and fears, of the experiences of birth and death. A full explanation of the mythological power of the subterranean world still awaits its Bachelard or its Campbell.[9]

The purpose of this anthology is to give the reader a sampling of the richness and diversity of one particular aspect of the prehistory of science fiction, namely the fortunes of the underworld location. To this end, I have included a range of selections from the many eighteenth- and nineteenth-century texts that used this setting, beginning with the various explanations for the existence of the subterranean world or with accounts of the actual passage to that world. In addition to the different types of underground worlds and the question of how the visitors get there (through a cave or volcano, or caught in a whirlpool, or through a hole somewhere near the pole), there is also the question of how they return—a passage that in many cases depends on chance (such as Klim's falling into the same hole through which he originally reached the underground world). I have also selected passages that describe that world and its inhabitants (which are not always human or intelligent). And in this context, I have looked for examples of the strange and fantastic. At the same time, many of these works have used the subterranean setting as a location for social satire and utopian imagining. The discovery of a hidden or lost civilization inside the Earth is an opportunity to describe some other society as a way of critiquing one's own and of imagining an alternative to it. In some cases, I have sketched in the principal features of the utopian society, which may involve its general outlines, as well as such features as government, private property, gender relationships, living arrangements, and the like. Of course, this raises the question of how the people living inside in the Earth themselves got there, a question that is often not answered—although, as we shall see, Casanova gives an intriguing explanation based on the book of Genesis, while Seaborn goes so far as to suggest that the inhabitants of the upper Earth are in fact the descendants of exiles from the subterranean world. Finally, in terms of the early history of science fiction, these worlds occasionally contain new technologies, although they appear infrequently until well into the nineteenth century. This raises another interesting question: how are these inner worlds illuminated? The answers range from the internal suns of Holberg and Casanova to the light from our sun shining through holes in the Earth's crust (in Seaborn and Collin de Plancy). On the other hand, the cave worlds of Verne and Bulwer-Lytton are illuminated in diametrically opposed ways, since the former posits an internal electricity (like the aurora borealis) while the latter describes a system of artificial lighting.

One example of a utopia set in a vast underground cavern I have excluded from this collection. It is exemplified by Tyssot de Patot's *La vie, les aventures et le voyage de Groenland du Réverend Père Cordelier Pierre de Mésange; avec une relation bien circonstanciée de l'origine, de l'histoire, des moeurs et du Paradis des habitans du Pole Arctique* (1720). This novel shows people living in underground cities in an immense cavern beneath the North Pole; but it is a constructed underground city, built by a people who fled their home in a land somewhere between Europe and Africa many centuries before. As they explain to the narrator, after they arrived "we began digging, and then building; and little by little, over God knows how many centuries, we built this superb city" (86). (One might exclude Verne's *Indes noires*, with its underground Coal City, for the same reasons.) Another type of story, while it does not depict the inner world, should nonetheless be included: stories set on the edge of or at the entrance to the inner world, epitomized by the ending of Poe's "Narrative of Arthur Gordon Pym." Although the novel breaks off abruptly, Poe's critics are almost unanimous in not considering the story incomplete. They see this breaking off as a deliberate act which heightens the mystery and sense of foreboding that pervades this and so many of Poe's tales (and there are certainly many other examples in literature). Such works belong in this anthology because of their ability to inspire various sequels (including Jules Verne's *Le sphinx des glaces* [1897]).

These are some of the wonders of the internal world that await the reader.

Athanasius Kircher, *Mundus Subterraneus* (1665)
(courtesy of the Bibliothèque nationale)
"This drawing portrays the compartments of heat or fire, or what is the same thing, the fire cells, throughout all the bowels of the Geocosm, the wonderful handiwork of GOD! These are variously distributed so that nothing be lacking which is in any way necessary for the preservation of the Geocosm. Also it is not believed that the fire is located exactly in the way the drawing shows, nor the channels placed exactly in this order. For who has examined this? Who among men ever penetrated down there? By this drawing we only wished to show that the bowels of the earth are full of channels and fire chambers, whether placed in this way or in another" (cited in Mather and Mason, *A Source Book in Geology*, 18–19).

THEORIES AND DESCRIPTIONS OF THE INNER EARTH, FROM KIRCHER TO SYMMES

■ Athanasius Kircher, *Mundus Subterraneus* (1665)

This drawing portrays the compartments of heat or fire, or what is the same thing, the fire cells, throughout all the bowels of the Geocosm, the wonderful handiwork of GOD! These are variously distributed so that nothing be lacking which is in any way necessary for the preservation of the Geocosm. Also it is not believed that the fire is located exactly in the way the drawing shows, nor the channels placed exactly in this order. For who has examined this? Who among men ever penetrated down there? By this drawing we only wished to show that the bowels of the earth are full of channels and fire chambers, whether placed in this way or in another. In the end we trace fire from the center through all the paths of the subterranean world clear to those volcanic mountains out on its surface. The letter A indicates the central fire. The rest are glory-holes of Nature, marked B. Fire-conducting channels C are not conduits; they are fissures of the earth through which the gusts of fire make their way.

The central fire, A, pours out surging and burning exhalations to each and every part by fire-carrying channels. Striking the water chambers, it forms some into hot springs. Some, it reduces to vapors which, rising to the vaults of hollow caves, are there condensed by cold into waters which, released at last, give rise to fountains and rivers. Among others, some, drawing the juice of various minerals from the source matrices, coalesce into metallic bodies or into new formations of combustible material destined to nourish the fire. Here you will also see the manner in which the sea, by pressure of air and wind or movement of the tide, pushes the waters through subterranean passages to the highest water chambers of the mountains. But the Figure will show you all this better than I could describe it with a profusion of words. You see also that the subterranean globe conforms to sea and to lands on the uppermost extent of the earth, and these to the atmosphere, as the drawing shows. The rest will be clearer from the very description of the effects and from reasoning. [Quoted in Mather and Mason, *A Source Book in Geology,* 18–19]

■ Thomas Burnet, "The Deluge and Dissolution of the Earth," from *The Sacred Theory of the Earth* (1691)

The first set of page numbers refers to the Osborne edition; the second, to the Centaur edition.

We will speak first of Subterraneous Cavities and Waters, because they will be of easier dispatch, and an introduction to the rest. That the inside of the Earth is hollow and broken in many places, and is not one firm and united mass, we have both the Testimony of Sence and of easie observations to prove: How many Caves and Dens and hollow passages into the ground do we see in many Countries. . . . It would be very pleasant to read good descriptions of these Subterraneous places, and of all the strange works of Nature there. [191–193; 93–94]

The subterraneous Cavities that we have spoke of hitherto, are such as are visible in the surface of the Earth, and break the skin by some gaping Orifice; but the Miners and those that work under ground, meet with many more in the bowels of the Earth, that never reach to the top or it: Burrows, and Chanels, and Clefts, and Caverns, that never had the comfort of one beam of light since the great fall of the Earth. And where we think the ground is firm and solid, as upon Heaths and Downs, it often betrays its hollowness, by sounding under the Horses feet and the Chariot-wheels that pass over it. We do not know when and where we stand upon good ground, if it was examin'd deep enough; and to make us further sensible of this, we will instance in two things that argue the unsoundness and hollowness of the Earth in the inward recesses of it, though the surface be intire and unbroken; These are *Earthquakes* and the communication of *Subterraneous waters and Seas.* [147–148; 96–97]

Nay, I believe the very Ocean doth evacuate it self by Subterraneous out-lets; for considering what a prodigious mass of water falls into it every day from the wide mouths of all the Rivers of the Earth, it must have out-lets proportionable; and those *Syrtes* or great Whirlpools that are constant in certain parts or Sinus's of the Sea, as upon the Coast of *Norway* and of *Italy,* arise probably from Subterraneous out-lets in those places, whereby the water sinks, and turns, and draws into it whatsoever comes within such a compass; and if there was no issue at the bottom, though it might by contrary currents turn things round, within its Sphere, yet there is no reason from that why it should suck them down to the bottom. Neither does it seem improbable, that the currents of the Sea are from these in-draughts, and that there is always a submarine inlet in some part of them, to make a circulation of the Waters. But thus much for the Subterraneous communication of Seas and Lakes.

And thus much in general concerning subterraneous Cavities, and concerning the hollow and broken frame of the Earth. If I had now magick enough to show you at one view all the inside of the Earth, which we have imperfectly describ'd; if we could go under the roots of the Mountains, and into the sides of the broken rocks; or could dive into the Earth with one of those Rivers that sink under ground, and follow its course and all its windings till it rise again, or led us to the Sea, we should have a much stronger and more effectual *Idea* of the broken form of the Earth, than any we can excite by these faint descriptions collected from Reason. The Ancients I remember us'd to represent these hollow Caves and Subterraneous Regions in the nature of a World under-ground, and suppos'd it inhabited by the *Nymphs,* especially the *Nymphs* of the waters and the Sea Goddesses; so *Orpheus* sung of old; and in imitation of him Virgil hath made a description of those Regions; feigning the Nymph *Cyrene* to send for her son I come down to her, and made her a visit in those shades where mortals were not admitted. . . .

If we now could open the Earth as this *Nymph* did the Water, and go down into the bosom of it, see all the dark Chambers and Apartments there, how ill contriv'd, and how ill kept, so many holes and corners, some fill'd with smoak and fire, some with water, and some with vapours and mouldy Air; how like a ruine it lies gaping and torn in the parts of it; we should not easily believe that God created it into this form immediately out of nothing; It would have cost no more to have made things in better order; nay, it had been more easie and more simple; and accordingly we are assured that all things were made at first in Beauty and proportion. And if we consider Nature and the manner of the first formation of the Earth, 'tis evident that there could be no such holes and Caverns, nor broken pieces, made then in the body of it; for the grosser parts of the Chaos falling down towards the Center, they would there compose a mass of Earth uniform and compact, the water swimming above it; and this first mass under the water could have no Caverns or vacuities in it; for if it had had any, the Earthy parts, while the mass was liquid or semiliquid, would have sunk into them and fill'd them up, expelling the Air or Water that was there; And when afterwards there came to be a crust or new Earth form'd upon the face of the Waters, there could be no Cavities, no dens, no fragments in it, no more than in the other; And for the same general reason, that is, passing from a liquid form into a concrete or solid leisurely and by degrees, it would flow and settle together in an mass; There being nothing broken, nor any thing hard, to bear the parts off from one another, or to intercept any empty spaces between them.

'Tis manifest then that the Earth could not be in this Cavernous form originally, by any work of nature; nor by any immediate action of God, seeing there is neither use nor beauty in this kind of construction: Do we not then, as reasonably, as aptly, ascribe it to that desolation that was brought upon the Earth in the general Deluge? When its outward frame was dissolv'd and fell into the great Abysse: How easily doth this answer all that we have observ'd concerning the Subterraneous Regions? That hollow and broken posture of things under ground, all those Caves and holes, and blind recesses, that are otherwise so Unaccountable, say but that they are a *Ruine,* and you have in one word explain'd them all. For there is no sort of Cavities, interior or exterior, great or little, open or shut, wet or dry, of what form or fashion soever, but we might reasonably expect them in a ruine of that nature. And as for the Subterraneous waters, seeing the Earth fell into the Abysse, the pillars and foundations of the present (exteriour) Earth must stand immers'd in water, and therefore at such a depth from the surface every where, there must be water found, if the soil be of a nature to admit it. 'Tis true, all Subterraneous waters do not proceed from this original, for many of them are the effects of Rains and melted Snows sunk into the Earth; but that in digging any where you constantly come to water at length, even in the most solid ground this cannot proceed from these Rains or Snows, but must come from below, and from a cause as general as the effect is; which can be no other in my judgment than this, that the roots of the exteriour Earth stand within the old Abysse, whereof, as a great part lies open in the Sea, so the rest lies hid and cover'd among the fragments of the Earth; sometimes dispers'd and only moistning the parts, as our bloud lies in the flesh, and in the habit of the body; sometimes in greater or lesser masses, as the bloud in our Vessels. And this I take to be the true account of Subterraneous waters as distinguished from Fountains and Rivers, and from the matter and causes of them.

Thus much we have spoke to give a general *Idea* of the inward parts of the Earth, and an easie Explication of them by our *Hypothesis;* which whether it be true or no, if you compare it impartially with Nature, you will confess at least, that all these things are just in such a form and posture as if it was true. [153–157; 99–101]

■ Edmund Halley, "A Theory of the Magnetic Variations" (1692)

These *Phænomena* being well understood, and duly consider'd, do sufficiently evince, that the whole Magnetical System is by one, or perhaps more Motions translated: That this moving thing is very great, as extending its Effects from Pole to Pole; and that the Motion thereof is not *per saltum*, but by a gradual and regular Motion.

Now considering the Structure of our *terraqueous* Globe, the only way to render this Motion intelligible and possible, is, to suppose it possible to turn about the Center of the Globe, having its Center of Gravity fixt and immovable in the same common Center of the Earth: And there is yet required that this moving internal Substance be loose, and detached from the external Parts of the Earth whereon we live. So then the External Parts of the Globe may well be reckoned as the Shell, and the Internal as a *Nucleus* or inner Globe included within ours, with a fluid Medium between. Which having the same common Center and Axis of diurnal Rotation, may turn about with our Earth each 24 Hours; only this outer Sphere having its turbinating Motion, some small matter either swifter or slower than the internal Ball; and a very minute difference in length of time, by many Repetitions becoming sensible, the internal Parts, will, by degrees, recede from the external, and not keeping pace with one another, will appear gradually to move either Eastwards or Westwards by the difference of their Motions. So that if this exterior Shell of Earth be a Magnet, having its Poles at a distance from the Poles of Diurnal Rotation; and if the Internal *Nucleus* be likewise a Magnet, having its Poles in two other Places distant also from the Axis, and these latter by a gradual and slow Motion change their place in respect of the external, we may then give a reasonable Account of the four Magnetical Poles, as likewise of the changes of the Needle's Variations, which, till now, hath been unattempted. [616–617]

I doubt not but this Hypothesis of an Internal *Nucleus* will find Opposers enough: But the Globe of *Saturn* being environ'd with his Ring, is a notable Instance of this kind, as having the same common Center, and moving along with it, without sensibly approaching one side of it more than another: And if this Ring were turned on one of its Diameters, it would then describe such a Concave Sphere as I suppose our External one to be. And since the Ring, in any Position given, would in the same manner keep the Centre of *Saturn* in its own, it follows that such a Concave Sphere may move with another included in it, having the same common Center. Nor can it well be supposed otherwise, considering the Nature of Gravity: For should these Globes be adjusted once to the same common Centre, the gravity of the parts of the Concave would press equally towards the Centre of the internal Ball, which Equality must necessarily continue till some external Force disturb it; which is not easy to imagine in our Case. This perhaps I might more intelligibly express, by saying, That the inner Globe being posited in the Centre of the exteriour, must necessary ascend, whatsoever way it move; that is, it must overcome the force of Gravity pressing towards the common Centre, by an Impulse it must receive from some outward Agent: But all outward Efforts being sufficiently senced against, by the Shell that surrounds it, it follows, that this *Nucleus* being once fixt in the common Center, must always there remain.

It may be objected, that the Water of the Sea would perpetually leak thro this Shell, unless we suppose the Cavity full of Water: But when we consider how tightly great Beds of Chalk or Clay, and much more Stone, do hold Water, and even Caves arched with Sand, no Man can doubt but the Wisdom of the Creator has provided for the *Macrocosm,* by many other Ways than I can either imagine or express. We cannot think it a hard supposition that the internal Parts of this Bubble of Earth should be replete with such Saline and Vitriolick Particles as may contribute to Petrefaction, and dispose the transuding Water to shoot and coagulate into Stone, so as continually to fortify, and, if need were, to consolidate any breach or flaw in the Concave Surface of the Shell. And this perhaps may, not without Reason, be supposed to be the final Cause of the Admixture of the magnetical Matter in the Mass of the terrestrial parts of our Globe, *viz*. To make good and maintain the Concave Arch of this Shell: For by what the excellent Mr. *Newton* has shewn in his *Principia Philosophia*, it will follow, That according to the general Principle of Gravity, visible throughout the whole Universe, all those Particles that by length of time, or otherwise, shall moulder away, or become loose on the Concave Surface of the external Sphere, would fall in, and with great force descend on the internal, unless those Particles were of another sort of Matter capable, by their stronger tendency to each other, to suspend the Force of Gravity: but we know no other Substances capable of supporting each other by their mutual Attraction, but the Magnetical; and these we see miraculously to perform that Office, even where the power of Gravity has its full Effect, much more within the Globe where it is weaker. Why then may we not suppose these said Arches to be lined throughout with a Magnetical Matter, or rather to be one great Concave Magnet, whose two Poles are the Poles we have before observed to be fixt in the Surface of our Globe? [618–619]

It must be allowed indeed, that these included Globes can be of very little service to the Inhabitants of this outward World, nor can the Sun be serviceable to them, either with his Light or Heat: But since we see all the parts of the Creation abound with animate Beings, why should we think it strange that the prodigious Mass of Matter, whereof this Globe does consist, should be capable of some other Improvements, than barely to serve to support its Surface? Why may we not rather suppose that the exceeding small Quantity of solid Matter in respect to the fluid Æther, is so disposed by the Almighty Wisdom, as to yield as great a Surface for the use of Living Creatures, as can consist with the Conveniency and Security of the whole?

And tho without Light there can be no Living, yet there are many ways of producing Light which we are wholly ignorant of: The Medium itself may be always luminous after the manner of our *Ignes fatui;* The Concave Arches may in several Places shine with such a Substance as invests the Surface of the Sun; nor can we without a Boldness unbecoming a Philosopher, adventure to assert the Impossibility of peculiar Luminaries below, of which we have no sort of Idea.

Thus I have shewed a Possibility of a much more ample Creation, than has hitherto been imagin'd: A Notion till hitherto not so much as started in the World, and of which we could have no Intimation from any other of the *Phænomena* of Nature. [619–620]

■ Cotton Mather, *The Christian Philosopher* (1721)

Behold, the Disposition of the *magnetical Vertue*, as it is throughout the whole globe of the *Earth* at this day:

But now to solve the *Phoenomena*!

We may reckon the external Parts of our Globe as a *Shell*, the internal as a *Nucleus*, or an *inner Globe* included within ours; and between these a *fluid Medium*, which having the same common Center and Axis of diurnal Rotation, may turn about with our Earth every four and twenty Hours: only this outer Sphere having its turbinating Motion some small matter either swifter or slower than the internal Ball, and a very small difference becoming in length of Time sensible by many Repetitions; the internal Parts will by degrees recede from the external and not keeping pace with one another, will appear gradually to move, either Eastwards or Westwards, by the difference of their Motions. Now if the exterior Shell of our Globe should be *a Magnet*, having its Poles at a distance from the Poles of diurnal Rotation; and if the internal *Nucleus* be likewise a *Magnet*, having its Poles in two other places, distant also from the Axis, and these latter, by a slow and gradual Motion, change their place in respect of the external, we may then give a reasonable account of the four *magnetical Poles*, and of the *Changes of the Needle's Variations*. *Who* can tell but the *final Cause* of the Admixture of the *magnetical Matter* in the Mass of the terrestrial Parts of our Globe, should be to maintain the concave Arch of this our Shell? Yea, we may suppose the Arch lined with a *magnetical Matter,* or to be rather one great *concave Magnet,* whose two Poles are fixed in the Surface of our Globe? Sir Isaac Newton has demonstrated the Moon to be more solid than our *Earth,* as nine to five; why may we not then suppose four Ninths of our Globe to be Cavity? *Mr. Halley* allows there may be Inhabitants of the lower Story, and many ways of producing *Light* for them. The Medium itself may be always luminous; or the concave Arch may shine with such a Substance as does invest the Surface of the Sun; or they may have peculiar *Luminaries,* whereof we can have no Idea: As *Virgil and Claudian* enlighten their *Elysian Fields* . . . The Diameter of the Earth being about eight thousand *English* Miles, how easy 'tis to allow five hundred Miles for the Thickness of the Shell! And another five hundred Miles for a Medium capable of a vast Atmosphere, for the Globe contained within it!

But it's time to stop, we are got beyond *Human Penetration;* we have dug as far as 'tis fit any *Conjecture* should carry us! [Quoted in Zirkle, "The Theory of Concentric Spheres," 156]

■ Alexander von Humboldt, *Cosmos: A Sketch of a Physical Description of the Universe* (1848)

Leslie has ingeniously conceived the nucleus of the world to be a hollow sphere, filled with an assumed "imponderable matter, having an enormous force of expansion." These venturesome and arbitrary conjectures have given rise, in wholly unscientific circles, to still more fantastic notions. The hollow sphere has by degrees been peopled with plants and animals, and two small subterranean revolving planets—Pluto and Proserpine—were imaginatively supposed to shed over it their mild light; as, however, it was further imagined that an ever-uniform temperature reigned in these internal regions, the air, which was made self-luminous by compression, might well render the planets of this lower world unnecessary. Near the North pole, at 82 degrees latitude, whence the polar light emanates, was an enormous opening through which a descent might be made into the hollow sphere, and Sir Humphrey Davy and myself were even publicly and frequently invited by Captain Symmes to enter upon this subterranean expedition: so powerful is the morbid inclination of men to fill unknown spaces with shapes of wonder, totally unmindful of the counter-evidence furnished by well-attested facts and universally acknowledged natural laws. Even the celebrated Halley, at the end of the seventeenth century hollowed out the earth in his magnetic speculations! Men were invited to believe that a subterranean, freely-rotating nucleus, occasions by its position the diurnal and annual changes of magnetic declination. It has thus been attempted in our own day, with tedious solemnity, to clothe in a scientific garb the quaintly devised fiction of the humorous Holberg. [1:163–164]

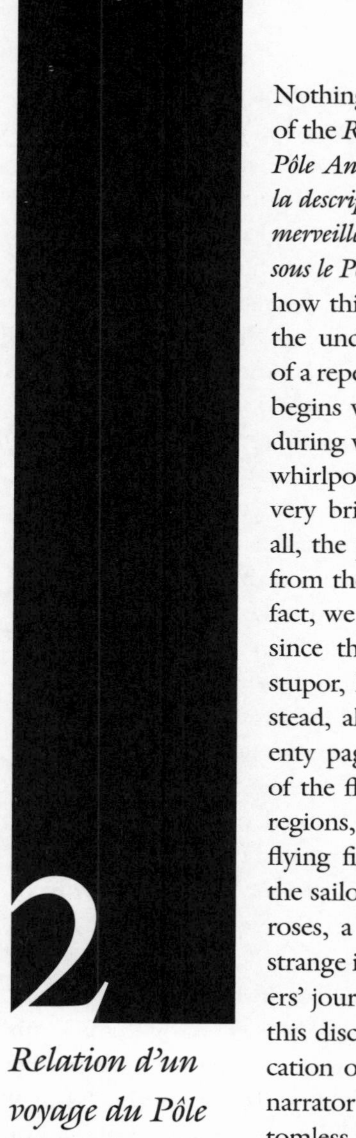

2

Relation d'un voyage du Pôle Arctique au Pôle Antarctique (1721)

Nothing is known of the anonymous author of the *Relation d'un voyage du Pôle Arctique au Pôle Antarctique par le centre du monde, avec la description de ce périlleux passage, et des choses merveilleuses et étonnantes qu'on a découvertes sous le Pôle Antarctique*.[1] What is interesting is how this early text passed into the canon of the underground-world novel on the basis of a repeated mistake. Set in 1714, the *Relation* begins with a whaling voyage off Greenland during which their ship is caught in a terrible whirlpool. The narrator's account describes very briefly, or rather does not describe at all, the passage through the Earth's interior, from the North to the South Pole: in actual fact, we learn nothing of the Earth's interior, since the crew spends the entire trip in a stupor, huddled in the hold of the ship. Instead, almost sixty of this short novel's seventy pages contain imaginative descriptions of the flora and fauna of the southern polar regions, whose wonders include some giant flying fish (which attack and kill several of the sailors); and, in a warm valley filled with roses, a white stone structure covered with strange inscriptions (although, like the travelers' journey through the center of the Earth, this discovery is simply noted, with no indication of what it might mean.) Because the narrator describes the whirlpool as "a bottomless pit into which the waters of the sea flowed through to the center of the earth and out to the Antarctic" (Garnier, *Voyages imaginaires*, 370), some commentators think the events take place inside the Earth.[2] The confusion may stem from the repeated use of the expression "sous le pôle antarctique," as for instance in the summary at the beginning of chapter 2: "How their ship was swallowed up by the whirlpool; how they found themselves unexpectedly beyond [*sous*] the Antarctic pole; and how they recognized that they were no longer under northern skies" (373). The simplest way to understand *sous* in this context is "beyond" or "on the other side of" the South Pole. On their arrival, the pilot immediately takes a sighting: they are at 71 degrees, 8 minutes southern latitude, a sighting "which made us realize that we were on the southern seas, beneath [*sous*] the Antarctic pole" (375). Since the South Pole is located at 90 degrees, almost anywhere at 71 degrees in the southern latitude would put them on the continent of Antarctica. Similarly, most of the wildlife is familiar—bears, birds, fish, seals and so on—while the lights in the sky are part of the mystery surrounding the aurora borealis. Finally, the absence of the sun is explained quite simply, in a way that confirms that they are in the Antarctic: "Wise Providence, to make up for the sun which is absent for such a long time in these sad climes, moderates the extreme cold with warm exhalations which conserve the grasses, plants and bushes that we saw there" (375).[3] Finally, at several points in the text the narrator points out that the view toward the south is obscured by clouds, in language which also makes clear that they are not inside the Earth: "Ever since we had anchored, our view to the south, that is to say, *towards* [*du coté de*] the Antarctic Pole, had always been obscured by large, thick clouds which were now dissipated by one of those wonderful, luminous exhalations so frequent *in the Polar regions* [*sous les Pôles*]" (384).[4]

The *Relation* is continually cited as one of the earliest depictions of a subterranean world, and the idea of a passage through the Earth linking the poles was to become a staple of later writing, for example in Rudy Rucker's *The Hollow Earth: The Narrative of Mason Algiers Reynolds of Virginia* (1990), which is both a continuation of Poe's "Narrative of A. Gordon Pym" and the depiction of a voyage through the Earth. As for the white stone structure, this is the most intriguing part of the narrative since it hints at a lost civilization, but living where?[5]

The Whirlpool

An old sailor told us that he had heard from a famous pilot that under the north pole there was a terrifying whirlpool, with a circumference of seventy or eighty leagues and which was the most perilous danger in the world, and in the middle of which there was a bottomless pit into which the waters of the sea flowed through to the center of the earth and out to the Antarctic. His story made our blood run cold, for we saw that the current was pulling us towards it and that it was impossible to reverse our course. Consulting among ourselves, we decided that although there was little hope of being saved, we should take every safety measure, quickly closing up all the openings in the boat so that the water could not get in. We then went onto the deck to see if there was any way to avoid the hideous peril which threatened us. The sun was no longer going down, but seemed to be turning around us on the horizon. . . . Against our will, the boat continued its downward course when it suddenly swung around. As it began to turn in slow circles we realized that we were now in the whirlpool . . . and we descended into the hold to await what the heavens would decide to do with us.

Only ten or twelve minutes had passed when we felt that we were rushing into the abyss at an incredible speed. The horrible whistling and roaring that we could hear around us filled our souls with fear and trembling and we fell into a kind of faint which prevented us from keeping track of how long we were caught in these terrifying torrents which were rushing us through the subterranean passages. When we awoke, no longer sure if we were dead or alive, we could no longer hear anything and it felt like our boat was no longer moving. Our pilot, the bravest amongst us, went up on deck and we followed him where we saw a becalmed sea, covered in a fog so dense that we could not see anything. The sea and the fog were the same color so that it seemed as if we were floating in the air. [370–374]

■ Flying Fish

Here there were some large flying fish with four wings: the front wings were quite large, and similar to a bat's wings; the wings at the back were much smaller. Three of these fish came towards our boat, diving and swooping back up. Although they were much larger and heavier than even a very large cow, they were able to fly quite high, and to spend more than a minute before diving back into the water. They were very voracious and insatiable; and since they always flew with their mouths wide open, we could see two rows of short, but very sharp teeth. Two of our sailors were sitting on deck near the stern when suddenly one of the fish shot high into the air and then took them both from behind, knocking them into the water. The first to fall was immediately torn apart and devoured while the second swam around the ship. As we were throwing him a rope he was attacked by the two other fish; one taking his head, the other his feet, and then pulling him apart. [397–398]

■ Strange Inscriptions

We came upon a remarkable structure made of white stone: the top was a large, triangular flat rock placed on six columns, each about three feet high, standing on an oval base some four or five inches high. The triangular stone on top was covered in bizarre inscriptions, in a writing none of us recognized. The circumference of the base was also covered with similar inscriptions, but they were almost completely obliterated. This monument provoked a number of suppositions since we could see that this was not the work of chance. Still I will have to leave the explanation to someone more intelligent than I, and we soon left this place. [393]

Lamékis, ou Les voyages extraordinaires d'un Egyptien dans la terre intérieure (1735–1738)

At 650 pages and with numerous interwoven plots, *Lamékis, ou Les voyages extraordinaires d'un Egyptien dans la terre intérieure; avec la découverte de l'Isle des Sylphides*, by Charles de Fieux, the chevalier de Mouhy, is a forgotten but rather unusual and even original novel. Set in the distant past, the characters move from ancient Egypt through a number of fantastic countries in a series of adventures reminiscent of Lucian's *True History* or, more probably, Galland's translation of the *Thousand and One Nights* (1704–1717). The very complicated narrative follows very generally the adventures of Lamékis and consists of a number of different plots and subplots set in a mythical past, which may be reduced to five basic narratives. The novel begins with the title character's father and his adventures as a high priest in Egypt. We are then introduced to the intertwined stories of two exiles from the neighboring North African kingdoms of Abdalles and Amphicléocles—Princess Nasildaé and Prince Motacoa—who have been banished to the underground world and who befriend Lamékis after the death of his parents. The third narrative follows Lamékis to the now joined kingdoms of Abdalles and Amphicléocles and tell of his terrible jealousy; while the fourth describes Lamékis's exile, including his celestial voyage to the Island of the Sylphs. A fifth and concluding narrative relates his return to Abdalles and Amphicléocles. The novel also includes an account of its composition, beginning with a preface in which Mouhy explains that he was told this story by a mysterious Armenian.

At the same time, there are a number of elements in Lamékis that destabilize traditional narrative by introducing imaginative and fantastic elements into the actual narration of the story. Halfway through the novel, there is a lengthy scene in which the author is visited by various characters from the novel, who now complain to him about his inaccuracies. They are followed by the philosopher Dehahal—a character from the island of the Sylphs who had tried unsuccessfully to convince Lamékis to undergo a ritual of purification, and who again urges Mouhy to undergo this same initiation. After he declines, the author awakes in his bed clutching a mysterious manuscript that defies all attempts at translation until, six months later, his pen—on its own—starts to translate the conclusion to *Lamékis.*

In a more comic mode, there are also numerous depictions of strange and exotic customs that take the reader from the fantastic to a kind of delirium of textual play and vivid imaginings. As a manifestation of the king's grandeur, for instance, no one is allowed to look at him, nor speak to him, nor even breathe in his presence. (This leads to a number of amusing and ridiculous situations, although the interdiction against breathing in the king's presence is softened by the practice of putting a finger in one's mouth.) Given these restrictions, communications are rather complicated, although various stratagems have been devised to deal with this situation. At one crucial moment, the king takes off his left shoe and hands it to the eldest of his councilors. This signifies that he is to be carried at once to the temple. There the king acknowledges the gravity of the situation by dropping a brass ball, which signals that his subjects are allowed to breathe and indeed to look at him. This is such an exceptional event that most of his subjects have never seen their king before; that opportunity comes once in a lifetime, when the king is installed (20:235–237). Moreover, the king is provided with a number of brass balls with specific instructions inscribed on them, which he throws to various ministers according to the situation.

These examples are only a small sample of the ludicrous ceremonies in the novel, which seem to lack any purpose other than the exercise of the author's imaginative abilities. These weird rituals and observances are certainly not a model of some better way of doing things (as such descriptions would be read in the utopian novel), and any satirical purpose is overwhelmed by the bizarre description. Other types of fantastic customs include ritual punishments (of which the most terrible is to be tickled to death by the priestesses, 20:241n 7) and outlandish royal games, such as the Bil-gou-router, in which the king and a chosen few lie with their heads in a circle into which a large rat is placed. The winner is decided when the rat hides in someone's mouth (21:46–48).

In terms of the frequent classification of *Lamékis* as an underground novel, three episodes in particular may explain Garnier's original designation, although none of them goes beyond the depiction of caverns and subterranean temples. The first involves Lamékis's father, the high priest of a secretive, monotheistic religion in Egypt. When the queen demands to be initiated into its mysteries, he disguises her as a man, and they descend into a city hidden beneath the temple. But there is little description of this underground city, and this setting is quickly abandoned.[1] The second underground setting is the most interesting, for its depiction of a race of giant and intelligent worm creatures. This is the story of Motacoa, who, in a ritual probably taken from Sinbad's fourth voyage, is lowered with his mother into a bottomless pit and left for dead.[2] Here, in an underground cave world, a number of adventures befall them as they battle various fantastic underground creatures. Finally, the third subterranean episode is similar to the first: in Paris, when the author begins to think of abandoning the novel, he is visited by a large black dog that one night leads him through the Paris catacombs to an underground temple; there on the walls, in a series of murals, is the story of Lamékis. Again, this does not really constitute a subterranean world.

While *Lamékis* should not really be classified as a novel set in a subterranean world, the imagination that the author demonstrates goes beyond the fantastic inventions of any of his predecessors, and it merits inclusion here, even if it is only remotely connected to our concerns. Nonetheless, this is the most extreme case of mistakenly labeling a novel as subterranean. It probably happened when Charles-Georges-Thomas Garnier, wanting to include the novel in his collection because of its many fantastic elements, had to find a category in which to put it, and then chose the "Voyages to the Underground" section since it did not fit in anywhere else. Here is how Garnier describes this category in the introduction to volume 19 (actually the introduction to *Klim*): "After having taken our readers to the seven planets and having traveled the heavens with them we are now going to take them into the bowels of the earth where they will again be pleasantly surprised to discover a new world, as well as the kinds of beings who live there"(vii–viii). At the beginning of volume 20, Garnier introduces Lamékis as follows:

> Again we are taking the reader to the inside of the earth. But this is not a new world that we are visiting, but only the retreat of the wise, where the faithful devotees of Serapis, in order to celebrate the mysteries of their religion, sought to find a place hidden from prying eyes. Nonetheless extraordinary things happen in this secret part of our globe, and the fertile imagination of the author is given free rein in the various adventures which take place there. (vii–viii)

Once this decision was made, later readers such as Flammarion and Messac simply continued to call it a subterranean work. In this case, however, because the novel has never been reprinted since its appearance in Garnier's anthology (1789), it was not easily accessible, and later critics continued to repeat this description without really knowing what was in the novel.

SELECTIONS

■ Delirium

This incredible scene takes place when Lamékis and his friend Sinouis are carried to the Island of the Sylphs to undergo the first stage of their initiation—the test of the Twelve Tables. Sinouis yields almost immediately to the temptations of the flesh and is transformed into an owl. Lamékis's failure occurs much later, when he hesitates at being skinned alive. This is his punishment.

Try and imagine, if possible, the combination of everything that the human spirit can conceive along with everything that fiction can imagine. . . . I saw above my head, an extraordinary, opaque mass in the shape of a bee with outstretched wings, but a bee larger than the largest whale, whose back seemed to be covered with scales which moved as it breathed. It had a prodigious number of legs, all in perpetual movement, and the rustling of its legs as they rubbed against each other, sounded like the clanking of swords. . . . Its breathing was so violent that its beak opened and closed as it inhaled and exhaled.

Each of the legs of this stupendous bee ended in three claws, and from each claw was hanging the head of a man which seemed to stir with different expressions of despair. Instead of hair, the underside of the bee was covered with crystal plates, like the tiles on a roof, but shining brightly, and each was covered with images of a different star on which one could make out cities and people, and each was unique and different from anything we knew.

I was so astonished by all this, particularly by the atrocious spectacle of these suspended heads, whose expressions of despair continued, that at first I did not pay attention to my own situation. But then sensing that I was plunged into some liquid, I opened my eyes. You can imagine my horror when I realized that I was swimming in a river of blood, and then I was thrust into the air by a pulsing geyser. When I raised my eyes again, the bee's gaping mouth seemed to be trying to suck me in and swallow me. All my philosophical resolve abandoned me at this point and in fear I struggled and raised my arms; like a drowning man, I thrashed about to escape the danger, but my efforts were useless, and the force of the geyser of blood pushed me slowly towards the gaping beak. The monstrous beast then shook its amazing head and moved towards me; it opened wide its mouth, sniffed and then swallowed me whole.

In horror I closed my eyes, when, like a grain of wheat in a mill, I felt myself ground up by rows of teeth as sharp as razors. My soul was quickly separated from my body, but by an astonishing marvel, each part of my hacked-up body still felt the pain which afflicted it. My eyes remained whole and slipped between its teeth. They continued to watch the atrocious dismembering of the body to which they had been attached, and saw my soul which—like a coiled spring—was struggling to escape from the pants pocket in which it had become entangled. . . . In addition to the ability to see, my eyes also seemed to now posses the faculties of my other senses, and were concerned by what had happened to its body. Scanning the immense belly of the bee . . . my eyes were able to find them in the stomach of the beast since my limbs had not yet been so ground up as to make them indistinguishable. But bit by bit the muscles of the bee's stomach were hammering away so furiously that the parts of my body were quickly losing their distinctiveness and were gradually merging into the blood. . . . My eyes first looked for my head in the devouring stomach of the terrible beast, and then found it in the region of the heart. My head was punctured with holes through which could be seen an enflamed red spirit which was slowly consuming the skull, while the brain itself, as black now as ink, was throbbing in agitation. . . . I was astonished and wondered how my eyes could continue to think and feel without a body or soul when I realized that the pupils were attached by a nerve to my soul which was still struggling to free itself.

I was still wondering about these remarkable events when my eyes were assailed by a multitude of insects produced by this decaying flesh; they formed a thick swarm, but were so small that it was difficult to see any individual one. They were round, with stingers which struck at my pupils, now defenseless without their lids which might have been able to defend my eyes against these repeated attacks. Instead my eyes were broken open and the liquid which filled them spilled out. . . . Despite this disintegration, the liquid retained all sensations and feelings, and I realized with horror that I was being licked up and sucked into the creature's stomach where I now lost all feeling, or rather I fell into a lethargic ecstasy.

Meanwhile my soul, which was still thrashing about trying to find its body, suddenly felt itself caught and lifted back into the brain it had so recently left. My eyes opened and I saw that they were again attached to my head, which was in turn again attached to my body which seemed to be awaking from a deep lethargy. In fact, I was myself again, and instead of being inside the bee, I was now on its back, while its ravenous beak was trying to catch and swallow me for a second time!

Fear pushed me to a thousand contortions to escape this second misfortune, but the bee's neck was so flexible that my efforts to avoid becoming its prey were in vain. But then, just as I was about to be swallowed up, a sylph appeared and cried out in a thunderous voice: "Enough, [the high priest] is satisfied." And with that the beast disappeared and I found myself falling through the air. [20:312–318]

■ The Underground World

This episode begins after Motacoa and his mother are lowered into a bottomless pit and left for dead (in a ceremony probably taken from Sinbad's fourth voyage in the Arabian Nights*). The actual descent in a basket takes three days, and they find themselves in a dim cave littered with bones. There they meet another victim of this strange custom who has already spent five years in the caves, living off the various birds and fruits that flourish in this underground world. They live peacefully together for some years when one day, Motacoa —now grown—comes upon a monstrous worm. As the worm pursues him, he is suddenly resuced by a giant blue dog, Falbao.*

I watched the serpent coil up, and then like a spring releasing, it launched itself towards its adversary. Its mouth was wide open and from this frightening gulf emerged a tongue armed with three fangs —whose slightest touch was capable of felling its enemy. . . . The dog, like a skilled fighter, avoided its lunges, jumping to the side each time. . . . Then suddenly, the dog threw himself on his enemy and with his deadly teeth, cut it in two. Furiously the two halves of the serpent tried to rejoin themselves, but the skillful victor picked one up and carried it some distance away. After that precaution dictated to him by his instincts . . . he picked up the monstrous head of his terrible enemy and laid it at my feet. [20:75]

Other encounters with the worm people (hommes-ver) *follow.*

What a terrible sight! A man (shall I call him that?) came towards me. He had the head, arms and chest of a human, but the rest of his body was that of an earth worm, save that he was the same size as the serpent which Falbao had killed. He was enormous, and he moved by using his coils, sometimes pulling himself along with his hands, and sometimes raising up the upper half of his body. His nose was quite large and flat, and ended in a point which hung over his upper lip. His eyes were circled by thick brows, while this frightening face was a blotchy red. His beard and hair, and the hair on his body all grew together. No sooner had I seen him than I started to run, screaming and looking back at every moment. This monster would surely have caught me, for using the palms of his hands, he moved with astonishing bounds, when suddenly Falbao appeared. [20:90]

Later Motacoa is captured by the worm people and taken to their kingdom. There, when one of the worm people realizes that Motacoa is intelligent, he tells him the story of his race. Their religion is based on the promise that "they will pass from this interior world to the world of the surface where there is real light, and that they will see the divine torches which make this light" (20:159). The worm-people have always thought that when someone was lowered into the pit that they were being attacked. But these are not the only underground creatures Motacoa encounters, and his next underground adventure involves an attack of toad-beings riding worms.

I cringed in horror as I saw a horde of monsters, one hundred times worse than the worm monsters from whom we had just escaped. They were about the size of a man, but from afar they looked more like toads, although their faces were vaguely human. They were naked, and yellow with black spots, and they were riding worms with stubby, short legs. The troop moved in unison, and the monster in front was carrying an owl with out-stretched wings perched on a staff. [20:184]

4

The Journey of Niels Klim to the World Underground (1741)

Ludvig Holberg (1684–1754) was probably the most European of Scandinavian writers before Ibsen and certainly the best known; he is often referred to as the father of Danish and Norwegian literature.[1] Although he is usually remembered today as the "Molière of the north" for his satirical plays, he was also, like so many other eighteenth-century figures, the author of historical and political works, of philosophical and legal essays, of "Moral Reflections" and autobiographical "Epistles," and of an important subterranean utopia. First published in Latin in 1741, *The Journey of Niels Klim to the World Underground, with a New Theory of the Earth and the History of the Previously Unknown Fifth Kingdom* [*Nicolai Klimii iter Subterraneum, Novam Telluris Theoriem ac Historiam Quintae Monarchiae adhuc Nobis Incognita Exhibens*] was quickly translated into a number of European languages. The first English edition dates from 1742.

Holberg's utopia recounts the adventures of Niels Klim after his fall through the Earth's crust into the center of the Earth, where a solitary planet moves about a subterranean sun. The first utopian part of his adventures is set in the land of Potu (= "utop"), which is inhabited by a race of intelligent and mobile trees. After several years as the king's messenger, Klim is commissioned to make a tour of the entire planet of Nazar (which is only six hundred miles in circumference). Here the author turns from utopia to satire, as Klim visits twenty-seven different provinces, all inhabited by different species of intelligent trees.

After his return to Potu, a foolish attempt to improve his status leads to his banishment to the underside of the Earth's crust, to which he is carried by a giant bird. His adventures begin in the land of Martinia—a kingdom of intelligent but mercurial apes. Now he is able to enhance his status through his wits, and he makes a fortune by introducing wigs to the Martinians. His success is short-lived, however, and after he rebuffs the advances of the mayor's wife, he is accused of trying to seduce her. In exchange for a guilty plea he is sentenced to the galleys.

From social satire the book now becomes almost entirely fantasy. As a galley slave, Klim is taken on a trading voyage to the Mezandorian islands, which lie across a vast sea and are inhabited by various fabulous creatures, beginning with a country of jackdaws at war with their neighbors the thrushes and including a malodorous land of creatures who speak "a posteriori," as well as a country of string basses who communicate by music. After a shipwreck he finds himself in a remote country inhabited not by intelligent animals or trees, but by "barbarous and uncivilized" humans. Klim's attempt to civilize the human inhabitants is perhaps the most Swiftian part of the book: using his knowledge, he is able to manufacture gunpowder and to conquer all the countries of the firmament. Klim's many conquests lead him to see himself as the "Alexander of the Subterranean world" (204). After his subjects rebel and he is forced into flight; looking for shelter, he falls into the same hole through which he had previously fallen, thus returning to Norway. There he meets an old friend who convinces him that in this time of religious persecution, he would do well to conceal his adventures. Once an emperor, Klim now accepts an appointment as a curate, marries, and has children. After his death, his friend publishes the manuscript.

Published fifteen years after *Gulliver's Travels*, Holberg's utopia has long been overshadowed by Swift's work and is often dismissed as an imitation. It has also been criticized for its mix of genres, in which the utopian is submerged by the fantastic.[2] Sigrid Peters argues, however, that Klim is better understood as a Menippean satire, and the mixture of fantasy and utopian satire are a deliberate strategy and not (as some critics would have it), a confused blend of genres.[3]

Nonetheless, the book's final sections do throw the rest of *Niels Klim* out of balance, as the utopian and satirical directions of the earlier chapters are almost completely abandoned. This unevenness is accentuated by the changes in the character of Klim. In the beginning an amusing and sometimes perceptive observer, he becomes an opportunist and then a vain and superficial tyrant only too willing to participate in slaughter and world conquest.

Nonetheless, in traditional terms, the first Potu section is certainly a utopia, while the many provinces of Nazar offer frequent opportunities for satire. The work is especially important insofar as Holberg has added a third element to the customary two-sided utopian structure: in addition to the conventional juxtaposition of the author's reality and the ideal society, the many provinces of Nazar provide Holberg with the opportunity to satirize various alternatives that have been proposed as utopian solutions. For instance, in the province of Quamso everyone is happy, healthy, and bored; in Lalac, where there is no need to work, everyone is unhappy and sickly; in Kimal the citizens are wealthy and spend all their time worrying about thieves; and in the "land of Liberty" everyone is at war. This philosophy of moderation involves the critique of the expectation that happiness depends on an unlimited supply of something that is lacking: Holberg shows Klim in various unhappy countries with an abundance of doctors, philosophers, health, wealth, or long life. Holberg also addresses the opposite utopian extreme, the belief that the elimination of the source of some present-day evil would bring happiness. Thus Klim visits countries without law, without religion, and without work, where again the inhabitants are dissatisfied and unhappy, in contrast to the citizens of the enlightened monarchy of Potu, which is a utopia because of its calm respect for the Golden Mean. Both in Holberg's utopia of moderation and in his use of satire to ridicule contemporary customs and practices as well as the utopian extremes of other visionaries, *Klim* should be recognized as an important and unjustly neglected utopian work as well as an enjoyable comic fantasy.

From our perspective, *Klim* is the first major representation of the hollow Earth. Although there is little development of the idea beyond the setting, which is little more than a pretext for Klim's adventures, the underground world is clearly delineated, unlike some other fictional settings of this kind.

Where did Holberg get the idea of setting his satirical-utopian fantasy inside the Earth? Nothing in the earlier texts I have examined prepares us for this vision of a hollow Earth with an interior planet revolving around its own sun. As he writes, "I fell to imagining that I was sunk into the subterranean world, and that the conjectures of those men are right who hold the Earth to be hollow, and that within the shell or outward crust there is another lesser globe, and another firmament adorned with lesser sun, stars, and planets" (13). But who are "those men"? The earlier writers do not describe a hollow Earth; Kircher and Halley both mention only hollows, chasms, caves, and subterranean channels running between the Earth. In the most complete study of Holberg's sources, J. Paludan (writing in Danish in 1878) reviews extensively the traditions of the imaginary voyage and Holberg's borrowing from classical authors such as Lucian. His chapters include "Geographical Fictional Voyages" and "Astronomical Fictional Voyages," but as these titles suggest, none of the works mentioned, from the *Odyssey* and Plato's discussion of Atlantis to Godwin and Cyrano's trips to the moon, depicts a subterranean world. This is a question Holberg's later critics are equally unprepared to answer, although, as I mentioned in my discussion of Garnier's influential anthology of imaginary voyages and Messac's review of subterranean fiction, critics often cited earlier works, from Kircher to *Lamékis*, without necessarily knowing much about the contents of the work.[4] But this imagining of a vast inner world is not only the first such example of the hollow Earth—it is the only one of the fictions I have found that includes inhabited worlds on both the Earth's inner crust and on a planet in the center of the Earth. All this is recounted in a humorous and often comic manner.

SELECTIONS

Since my Latin is minimal, I have used the uncredited translation published by Weber in 1812. I assume that this is the original 1742 translation, since it resembles very closely the edition published by James I. Mc Nelis Jr. in 1960. In his introduction, Mc Nelis states that he has made only minimal revisions to the 1742 English translation, which retains what he calls its "characteristic eighteenth century style." I have made some slight corrections based on the French translation in volume 19 of the Garnier anthology, as well as on Thomas De Quincy's translation of the first three chapters. There are complete Danish and Latin versions of the text of Klim *available at the Danish Royal Library Web site: www.kb.dk/elib/lit/dan/old/authors/holberg/klim. Where only one page number or page range is cited, references are to that edition; where there are two, the second set of page numbers refers to Mc Nelis.*

■ Into the Earth

Being now just ready to be let down, I gave my companions to understand . . . that they should continue letting down the rope till they heard me cry out, upon which signal they should stop, and if I persisted to cry out, that then they should immediately draw me up again. In my right hand I held my harpoon, or iron hook, an instrument that might be of use to me to remove whatever might obstruct my passage, and also to keep my body suspended equally between the sides of the cavern. But scarce had I descended about fifteen or twenty feet, when the rope broke. This accident was discovered to me by the sudden outcries of the men I had hired. But their noise soon died away; for with an amazing velocity I was hurried down into the abyss. . . .

For about a quarter of an hour . . . I was in total darkness . . . when at length a thin small light, like twilight, broke in upon me, and I beheld at last a bright serene firmament. I ignorantly thought, therefore, that either by the repercussion or opposite action of the subterranean air, or that by the force of some contrary wind, I had been thrown back, and that the cave had vomited me up again. But neither the sun which I then surveyed, nor the heavens, nor heavenly bodies, were at all known to me, since they were considerably smaller than those of our world. I concluded that either all that whole mass of new heavens existed solely in my imagination, excited by the vertigo my head had undergone, or else that I had arrived at the mansions of the Blessed. But this last opinion I soon rejected with scorn, since I viewed myself armed with a harpoon, and dragging a mighty length of rope after me, knowing full well that a man going to Paradise has no occasion for a rope or a harpoon, and that the celestial inhabitants could not possibly be pleased with a dress which looked as if I intended, after the example of the Titans, to take Heaven by violence, and to expel them from their divine abodes. At last, after the maturest consideration, I fell to imagining that I was sunk into the subterranean world, and that the conjectures of those men are right who hold the Earth to be concave, and that within the shell or outward crust there is another lesser globe, and another firmament adorned with lesser sun, stars, and planets. . . .

That violence with which I was hurried headlong had now continued for some time, when at length I perceived that it was diminishing in proportion to my approach towards a planet . . . which was increasing so sensibly in bulk or magnitude that at last, without much difficulty, I could plainly distinguish mountains, valleys, and seas through that thicker atmosphere with which it was surrounded.

Then I perceived that I did not only swim in a celestial matter or ether, but that my motion—which had hitherto been perpendicular—was now altered into a circular one. At this my hair stood on end, for I was full of apprehension lest I should be transformed into a planet, or into a satellite of the neighbouring planet, and so be whirled about in an everlasting rotation. But when I reflected that by this metamorphosis my dignity would suffer no great diminution, and that a heavenly body, or at least an attendant upon a heavenly body, would surely move with equal solemnity to a famished philosopher, I took courage again, especially when I found, from the benefit of that pure celestial ether that I was no longer pressed by hunger or thirst. Yet upon recollecting that I had in my pocket some of that sort of bread which the people of Bergen call *bolken*, and which is of an oval or oblong figure, I resolved to take it out and make an experiment whether in this situation I had any appetite. But at the first bite perceiving it was quite nauseous, I threw it away as a thing to all intents and purposes useless. The bread thus cast away was not only suspended in air, but (what was very marvelous to behold) it described a little circular motion round my own body. And from thence I learned the true laws of motion, by which it comes to pass that all bodies placed in equilibrium naturally affect a circular motion. Upon this, instead of deploring my wretchedness, as I had done, for being thus the sport of Fortune, I began to plume a little, finding that I was not only a simple planet, but such a planet as would have a perpetual attendant conforming itself to my motions, insomuch that I should have the honour to be reckoned in the number of the greater heavenly bodies or stars of the first magnitude. . . .

For almost three days I remained in this condition. Since I was whirled about the planet, I could easily distinguish day from night; and observing the subterranean sun to rise, and set, and retire gradually out of my sight, I could easily perceive when it was night, though it was not altogether such as it is with us. For at sunset the whole face of the firmament appeared of a bright purple, not unlike the countenance of our moon sometimes. This I took to be occasioned by the inner surface of our Earth, which borrowed that light from the subterranean sun, which was placed in the center of the subterranean world. This hypothesis I framed to myself, being not altogether a stranger to the study of astronomy.

But while I was thus amused with the thoughts of being in the neighbourhood of the gods, and was congratulating myself as a new constellation, together with my satellite that surrounded me, and hoped in a short time to be inserted in the catalogue of stars by the astronomers of the neighbouring planet, behold! an enormous winged monster hovered near me, sometimes on this side, now on that side, and by and by over my head. . . . When the figure approached nearer to me, it appeared to be a grim, huge griffin. So great was my terror that, unmindful of my starry dignity to which I was newly advanced, in that disorder of my soul I drew out my university degree, which I happened to have in my pocket, to signify to this terrible adversary that I had passed my academic examination, that I was a graduate student, and could plead the privilege of my university against anyone that should attack me.

But my disorder beginning to cool, when I came to myself, I could not but condemn my folly. For it was yet a matter of doubt to what purpose this griffin should approach me, whether as an enemy or a friend; or, what is more likely, whether, led by the sole novelty of the thing, he had only a mind to feast his curiosity. For the sight of a human creature whirling about in air, bearing in his right hand a harpoon, and drawing after him a great length of rope like a tail, was really a phenomenon which might excite even a brute creature to behold the spectacle. For the unusual figure I then exhibited gave to the inhabitants of the globe round which I revolved an occasion of divers conjectures and conversations concerning me, as I afterwards learned; for the philosophers and mathematicians would have me to be a comet, being positive that my rope was the tail; and some there were who, from the appearance of so rare a meteor, prognosticated some impending misfortune, a plague, a famine, or some other such extraordinary catastrophe; some also went further, and delineated my figure, such as it appeared to them at that distance, in very accurate drawings; so that I was described, defined, painted, and engraved before ever I touched their globe. . . .

The griffin advanced so near as to incommode me by the flapping of its wings, and even did not scruple to attack my leg with its teeth. . . . Upon this I began to attack this troublesome animal with arms, and grasping my harpoon with both my hands, I soon curbed the insolence of my foe, obliging it to look about for a way to escape; and at last, since it persisted in annoying me, I darted my harpoon with such a force into the back of the animal between its wings, that I could not pull it out again. The wounded griffin, setting up a horrible cry, fell headlong upon the planet. As for myself, quite weary of this starry station, this new dignity, which I saw exposed to infinite hazards and evils, I held to the harpoon and fell with him. And now this circular motion I had described altered once more into a perpendicular one. And being for some time agitated and tossed with great violence by the opposite motions of a thicker air, at length by an easy, gentle descent, I alighted upon the aforesaid planet, together with the griffin, who soon after died of its wound. [118–120; 9–14]

Having thus finished this airy voyage, and being set down upon the planet without the least hurt, I lay for a considerable time without motion, waiting for daybreak. 'Twas then I found the usual infirmities of nature return, and that I stood in great need of sleep as well as food, and I repented I had so rashly discarded my loaf of bread.

My mind thus oppressed with various anxieties, at length I fell into a profound sleep, and had slept (as near as I could guess) two hours, when a horrible bellowing interrupting my sleep, at length entirely dispelled it. . . . and when I saw a bull standing near me, then indeed I concluded my rest had been broken by his bellowing. Presently throwing my eyes around me, the sun now rising, I beheld everywhere green, fertile plains and fields; some trees also appeared, but (what was most amazing) they moved; though such was the silence and stillness of the air at that time that it would not have moved the lightest feather from its place. Immediately the bull came roaring at me, and I in my terror and consternation seeing a tree near me, attempted to climb it. But when I got up into it, it uttered a fine small voice, though something shrill, and not unlike an angry lady's; and presently I received, as it were from the swiftest hand, such a blow as quite stunned me, and laid me prostrate on the ground. I was almost expiring with this thunderbolt of a stroke, when I heard certain confused murmurings round me, like those in a great market, or at the Stock Exchange. Opening my eyes, I beheld all about me a whole grove of trees, all in motion, all animated, and the plain overspread with trees and shrubs, though just before there were not more than six or seven.

It is not to be expressed what disorders this produced in my understanding, and how much my mind was shocked with these delusions. I thought I must certainly be dreaming; or that I was haunted by ghosts and evil spirits; and twenty even more absurd things did I imagine. But I had no time to reflect further, for one of the trees came up to me, let down one of its branches, which had at the extremity of it six large buds in the manner of fingers. With these the tree took me up from the ground and carried me off, attended by a multitude of other trees of various kinds and different sizes, all of which kept muttering certain sounds, articulately indeed, but in a tone too foreign for my ears, so that I could not possibly retain anything of them, except these two words, *pikel emi*, which I heard them very often repeat. By these words (as I afterward understood) was meant "a monkey of an odd shape," because from the make of my body and manner of dress, they conjectured I was a monkey, though of a species different from the monkeys of that country. Others took me for an inhabitant of the firmament, and that some great bird had transported me hither, a thing that had once before happened, as the history or annals of that globe can testify. But all these things I did not understand until some months later, when I had become acquainted with the Subterranean language.

For in my present circumstances, what through fear and what through the disorder of my intellect, I was quite regardless of myself, nor could conceive how there could be any such thing as living and speaking trees, nor to what purpose was this procession, which was very slow and solemn. But yet the voices and murmurs with which all the plains echoed seemed to indicate anger and indignation; and in good truth it was not without ample reason that they had conceived this resentment against me; for that very tree, which I climbed up in my flight from the bull, was the wife of the principal magistrate of the next city; and so the quality of the person injured aggravated the crime; for it looked as if I had a mind to violate not a female of mean and plebeian birth, but a matron of prime rank, which was a most detested spectacle to a people of so venerable a modesty as these were.

At length we arrived at the city to which I was led captive. This city was equally remarkable for its stately edifices, and for the elegant order and proportion of the streets and highways; so lofty were the houses, that they resembled so many towers. The streets too were full of walking trees, which by letting down their branches saluted each other as they met, and the greater number of branches or boughs they dropped, the greater was the compliment. Thus when an oak went out of one of the most eminent houses, the rest of the trees drew back at his approach, and let down every one of their branches; from whence it was easy to infer that that oak was far above the vulgar sort; and indeed I soon understood that it was the chief magistrate himself, and the very person whose wife I was said to have so highly affronted. Forthwith they hurried me to the magistrate's house, upon my entrance into which the doors were immediately locked and bolted upon me, so that I looked upon myself as one condemned to a jail. What greatly contributed to this fear was that there were three guards placed without, like sentinels, each of them armed with six axes, according to the number of their branches; for as many branches as they had, so many arms they had; and as many buds at the extremities, so many fingers. I observed that on the top of the trunks or bodies of the trees their heads were placed, not at all unlike human heads; and instead of roots, I saw two feet, and those very short, by reason of which the pace they used was almost as slow as that of a tortoise; so that had I been at liberty, it had been very easy for me to have escaped their hands, since my Motion was perfect flying compared to theirs.

To be brief, I now plainly perceived that the inhabitants of this globe were trees, and that they were endowed with reason; and I was lost in wonder at that variety which nature uses in the formation of her creatures. These trees do not equal ours in height, since few of them exceed the ordinary stature of a man; some indeed were less; these one would call flowers or shrubs; and such I conjectured were youths and infants.

Words cannot express into what a labyrinth of thought these strange appearances threw me, how many sighs they extorted from me, and how passionately I longed after the dear place of my nativity. For although these trees seemed to me to be sociable creatures, to enjoy the benefit of language, and to be endowed with a certain degree or portion of reason, to such a degree that they had a right to be inserted in the class of rational animals, yet I much doubted whether they could be compared to men; I could not bring myself to think that justice, mercy, and the other moral virtues had any residence among them. [120–121; 16–19]

But it was not without indignation I observed that school disputations do there make a part of shows and theatrical performances. For at set times of the year, wagers being laid, and a reward assigned to the conquerors, the disputants engage like a couple of gladiators, and much upon the same terms that fighting cocks or any such battling animals do among us. Hence it was a custom among the great to maintain a set of disputants, as we do a pack of hounds, and to give them a logical education, that they may be fit for engagement at the stated times of the year. Thus a certain wealthy citizen in three years' time had made prodigious gains . . . from one disputant, whom he maintained for that purpose. This disputant, with an amazing volubility of tongue, by ensnaring syllogisms and every artifice of logic, by distinctions, reservations, and exceptions, eluded every opponent, and silenced whom he would.

I was often present at these entertainments, and that with no small vexation. For it seemed to me a horrid and shameful thing that such noble exercises, which give lustre to our schools, should here be prostituted on the stage. And when I called to mind that I myself, with the highest applause, had disputed in public, and had obtained the laurel, I could scarce withhold my tears. And not only the dispute, but the method of disputing incensed me. For they hired certain stimulators . . . who, when they observed the ardour of the disputants to flag, just pricked their sides with lancets to rekindle it, and to rally their declining spirits. Other things through shame I omit, which in so polished a nation I could not but condemn. . . .

I begged to know of my host how it was possible that so judicious a nation could think of leaving to the theatre those noble exercises whereby a faculty of speaking is acquired, truth is discovered, and the understanding sharpened? He replied that formerly these exercises were in high reputation among their barbarous ancestors; but since they had been convinced by experience that truth was rather stifled by disputes, that their youth were rendered petulant and forward thereby, that disturbances arose from them, and that the more generous studies were so much the more fettered, they turned over these exercises from the university to the playhouse; and the results have showed us that by reading, silence, and meditation the students now make far greater advances in learning. With this reply, though very specious, I was not however altogether satisfied. [124–125; 28–29]

■ The Inner World

The Potuan Empire is of no very great extent. The whole globe is called Nazar, and is about six hundred miles in circumference. A traveller may easily go round it without a guide, for the same language obtains everywhere, though the Potuans differ greatly in their customs and manners from the other states and principalities. And as in our world the Europeans excel the rest of mankind, so the Potuans are distinguished by their superior virtue and wisdom from the rest of the globe. The highroads, at proper distances, are adorned with stones that mark the miles, and abound with directing posts which show the ways and turnings to every city and village. It is indeed a very memorable circumstance, and worthy of admiration, that the same language is spoken everywhere, although the several kingdoms differ so widely in other respects, namely, in their manners, understanding, customs, and condition, that we see here all that variety which nature delights in, and which does not only simply move or affect the traveller, but even throws him into an ecstasy of wonder. . . .

This globe, like ours, has a triple motion, so that the seasons here, namely, those of day and night, winter and summer, spring and autumn, are distinguished like ours; also towards the poles it grows colder. As to light, there is little difference between day and night, for the reasons before assigned. Nay, the night may be thought more grateful than the day, for nothing can be conceived more bright and splendid than that light which the solid firmament receives from the sun and reflects back upon the planet, insomuch that it looks (if I may be allowed the expression) like one universal moon. The inhabitants consist of various species of trees, as oaks, limes, poplars, palms, brambles, etc., from whence the sixteen months, into which the Subterranean year is divided, have their names. . . . Their dates or eras of time are various; these they fix from some memorable circumstance, and particularly from the great comet which appeared three thousand years ago and is said to have caused an universal deluge in which the whole race of trees and other animals perished, except a few which on the tops of mountains escaped the general wreck, and from whom the present inhabitants are descended. [132; 48–49]

■ Fantastic Creatures

After a prosperous voyage which lasted three days, we arrived upon the coast of Crochet Island. . . . Our interpreter carried a sort of musical instrument along with him which is generally called a bass. This ceremony appeared very ridiculous to me, as I could not comprehend for what reason he should load himself with such a useless burden. As the coasts seemed to be deserted and there was no appearance of any living creature, the captain ordered our interpreter to play a march, to give notice of our coming. Upon this about thirty musical instruments, or basses, with one leg came hopping towards us. I thought at first that what I saw was all enchantment, as I never in all my travels met with anything so wonderful.

The make of these basses, whom I afterwards found to be the inhabitants of the country, was as follows: their necks were pretty long with little heads upon them; their bodies were slender and covered with a smooth kind of bark or rind in such a manner as that a pretty large hollow was left between the rind and the body itself. A little above the navel, Nature had placed a sort of bridge with four strings. The whole machine rested upon one foot, so that their motion was like that of hopping, which they performed with wonderful agility. In short, one would have taken them for real basses from their similitude to that instrument, had it not been for their hands and arms, which were in every respect like our own. One of these hands was employed in holding the bow, as the other was in stopping the strings.

Our interpreter began the conference by taking up the instrument he had brought with him and playing a slow strain. An answer was presently returned him in the same strain, and thus they went on warbling their thoughts to one another for a considerable time. Their conversation began with an *adagio* which I cannot but say had a good deal of harmony in it, but it soon slid into discords which were very grating to the ear. The conference ended with a harmonious and delightful *presto*. Upon hearing this last our men were exceedingly pleased, since it was a token, as they told me, that the price of their cargo was agreed upon. I was afterward informed that the slow music in the beginning was only a prelude to the discourse and was employed in mutual compliments on both sides; but that when we heard the discords, they were disputing about the price of our commodities, and that the *presto* in the conclusion signified that the business was happily determined. Accordingly, a little while after we unloaded the ship. The commodity for which there is the greatest demand in this country is rosin, with which the inhabitants rub their bows, which are their instruments of speech. Those that are convicted of any great crime in this country are generally sentenced by the judge to be deprived of their bows, and a perpetual privation of the bow is equal to capital punishment amongst us. As I understood there was to be a final hearing of a lawsuit in a neighbouring court of justice while I stayed there, my curiosity prompted me to hear some of their musical law proceedings. [171–172; 156–158]

■ Pyglossia

Having dispatched our affairs to our satisfaction, we left this place . . . and after a voyage of a few days came in sight of another coast. Our crew guessed it to be Pyglossia from the fetid smell which came from thence. The inhabitants of this country are not unlike human creatures except in one particular, which is the want of mouths. This lays them under a necessity of speaking *a posteriori,* if I may be allowed the phrase. The first person aboard our ship was a wealthy merchant. He very civilly saluted us from behind, according to the custom of the country, and then began to talk with us about the price of our goods. The barber belonging to our ship, to my great misfortune, was at that time sick, for which reason I was obliged to make use of a Pyglossian barber. The people of this profession are more talkative, if possible, in this country than they are in Europe, so that while he was shaving me, he left such a horrid stench behind him in the cabin that we were obliged to burn great quantities of incense to sweeten it again after his departure. I was so accustomed to see strange things and such as were contrary to the usual course of nature that nothing now appeared surprising to me.

As the conversation of the Pyglossians was disagreeable and offensive by reason of this natural imperfection, we were willing to get away from thence as soon as possible, and therefore weighed anchor before the time we had appointed. We hastened our departure the more on account of our being invited to supper by one of the principal inhabitants. We all shrugged up our shoulders at this invitation, and nobody would accept of it but upon condition that a general silence should be observed all suppertime. As we were going out of the harbour, the Pyglossians crowded to the shore to wish us a good voyage, but as the wind blew directly from the land, we made all the signs we could, by nodding our heads and waving our hands, to let them know we would excuse their compliments. I could not help reflecting upon this occasion how very troublesome a man may prove by striving to be over complaisant. The chief trade of the Martinians to this country consists in rose water and divers kinds of spices and perfumes. I have already remarked that this people, in respect to the form of their bodies, resembled much the human being, except in so far that they spoke with that part whereon we always Sit. On our Earth there is no lack of people who, as well in dialect as in shape, perfectly resemble the Pyglossians. [172–173; 158–159]

■ The Author's Banishment to the Firmament

I have hitherto said nothing concerning the strange and very singular punishment the Potuans have, of banishing to the Firmament, wherefore I think myself obliged in this place to give some account of it.

Twice every year certain birds of an enormous magnitude appear upon this globe. They are called Cupac, that is to say, Birds of Post, and at stated seasons they come and go. It has long perplexed the Subterranean naturalists to account for this periodical visit. Some think they descend upon this planet in quest of certain insects, or large flies, of which there are prodigious numbers about this time of the year and of which these birds are exceedingly voracious. This opinion is strengthened by the circumstance that when these flies disappear the birds fly off towards the Firmament. . . . Others think that these birds are trained up and instructed to this very end and purpose by the inhabitants of the Firmament, like our falcons and other birds of prey. This hypothesis receives some countenance from that tenderness, care, and dexterity which these birds use in bringing home their prey and laying it gently down before their masters. Other circumstances also show that these creatures are either thus instructed or else that they have a certain portion of reason to direct them; for at the approach of the season of departure they are so tractable and tame that they suffer certain nets, or small chains, to be thrown over them, under which they lie quiet for many days and are fed out of hand by the inhabitants with the aforesaid flies, of which they take care to provide a great quantity for this very purpose. For it is necessary to keep feeding them till all things are prepared and got ready for those who are to be banished. The apparatus for their departure is as follows: On those nets in which they are entangled a box or cage is fastened with cords. Every cage is capable of containing one person. The time now drawing near and the insects failing which supplied them with food, the birds mount upon wing, and cutting the air, return to the place from whence they came. Such was this wonderful passage by which I and several other exiles were to be translated to a new world. . . .

Being brought to the destined place of departure, I was forthwith thrust into the box or cage with as much provision as would serve me for two or three days. Soon after this, when the birds found no more flies brought them, as if they took the hint they left the place, and flew off with incredible celerity. The distance of the Firmament from the planet Nazar is reputed by the Subterraneans to be about a hundred miles. How long I was in passing from the one to the other I cannot say, but to me this ethereal voyage seemed to be no more than about four and twenty hours.

After a profound silence at last a confused noise seemed to reach my ears, from whence I conjectured I was not far from land. Then it was I perceived that these birds had been carefully exercised and instructed, for with great art and care they landed their burden so as not in the least to injure or hurt it. In a moment I was surrounded with a prodigious number of monkeys, the sight of which put me into a very great fright, remembering what I had suffered from these animals upon the planet Nazar. But my fright redoubled when I heard these monkeys articulately discourse with one another, and when I beheld them clad in diverse coloured vestments. I then conjectured that they were the inhabitants of this country. But as after that heap of wonders I had been accustomed to, nothing now could well seem new or strange, I began to recover my courage, especially as I had observed that these creatures approached me with an air of civility and good nature, taking me gently out of my cage and receiving me with the humanity due to strangers. Even ambassadors in our world are hardly received with more ceremony than I was. They all came one after another and addressed me in these words: *Pulasser.* When they had repeated his salutation pretty often, I repeated the same words. Upon this they set up an immoderate laugh, and by a multitude of comic gestures signified they were highly delighted to hear me pronounce them. This made me conclude these people to be a light, babbling race of creatures, and vast admirers of novelty. When they spoke, you would think so many drums were beating, with so much volubility and so little out of breath they held on their chattering. In a word, as to dress, manners, speech, and form of body, they were the very reverse of the Potuans. At first they were all astonished at my figure, and the chief reason of that astonishment was that I lacked a tail. For as among the whole brute creation none so much resemble the human form as monkeys, so, had I had a tail, they would have taken me for one of their own species, especially as all those who had hitherto been transported from the planet Nazar to this place were of a form extremely unlike their own. About the time of my arrival here the sea ran very high by reason of the near approach of the planet Nazar; for as with us the tides of the ocean correspond with the course of the moon, so the ocean of this Firmament increases and decreases according to the vicinity or remoteness of the aforesaid planet.

Presently I was conducted to a very noble house, all beautifully set off with costly stone, marble, mirrors, vases, and tapestry. At the gate sentinels were posted, which gave me to understand that this could not be the dwelling of a vulgar monkey. And I was soon informed that it was the house of the consul or chief magistrate. He was very desirous of conversing with me, and therefore hired some masters to instruct me in their language. Near three months had been spent upon my instruction, at the expiration of which, as I could now speak the tongue pretty fluently, I hoped to gain the applause and admiration of all upon account of the forwardness of my genius and the strength of my memory. But my tutors thought me slower and duller than ordinary, insomuch that they lost all patience and threatened to leave me off. And as at Potu I was called in derision Skabba, or Quick Parts, so here, by reason of my stupidity and dullness, they gave me the name of Kakidoran, which signifies a clown, or dunce. For those alone are here esteemed who are quick and nimble and cover their meaning in a confused and rapid volley of words. [161–162; 127–131]

■ Machines

I now arrived at a lake, the waters of which were of a yellowish colour. On the bank there was a vessel of three ranks of oars, in which Passengers, for a small consideration, were ferried over into the Land of Reason. Having agreed for my passage, I went aboard and with the highest pleasure imaginable began my voyage, inasmuch as I presently observed that these Subterranean vessels are impelled by secret springs and machines which cleave the waters with an astonishing rapidity, and all without the agency of rowers. [150; 99]

There are also seas and rivers which bear vessels whose oars seem to be moved by a kind of magic impulse, for they are not worked by the labour of the arm, but by machines like our clockwork. The nature of this device I cannot explain, as being not well versed in mechanics; and besides, these trees contrive everything with such subtlety that no mortal, without the eyes of Argus or the power of divination, can arrive at the secret. [132; 49]

The Life and Adventures of Peter Wilkins (1750)

Little is known about Robert Paltock, but his novel *The Life and Adventures of Peter Wilkins* is an important utopia and another instance of a work which is sometimes erroneously called an underground utopia.[1] Described by an early reviewer as "the illegitimate offspring of no very natural conjunction betwixt *Gulliver's Travels* and *Robinson Crusoe*" (Bentley, introduction, ix–x), Robert Paltock's *Peter Wilkins* is described on the cover of a recent edition as "a vivid hybrid of the shipwreck tale, the fantasy, the spiritual autobiography, the sexual idyll, and the Enlightenment Utopia" (Paltock, *Life and Adventures of Peter Wilkins*, 1990). The full title gives a good idea of the book's contents:

> The Life and Adventures of Peter Wilkins, A Cornish Man: Relating particularly, His Shipwreck near the South Pole; his wonderful Passage thro' a subterraneous Cavern into a kind of new World; his there meeting with a Gawry or flying Woman, whose Life he preserv'd, and afterwards married her; his extraordinary Conveyance to the Country of Glums and Gawrys, or Men and Women that fly. Likewise a Description of their strange Country, with the Laws, Customs, and Manners of its Inhabitants, and the Author's remarkable Transactions among them.
>
> Taken from his own Mouth, in his Passage to England, from off Cape Horn in America, in the Ship Hector.
>
> With an INTRODUCTION, giving an Account of the surprizing Manner of his

coming on board that Vessel, and his Death on his landing at Plymouth in the Year 1739.

Illustrated with several CUTS, clearly and distinctly representing the Structure and Mechanism of the Wings of the Glums and Gawrys, and the Manner in which they use them either to swim or fly.

By R. S. a passenger in the Hector.

To expand briefly on this title: the book may be divided into three parts. The first describes Peter Wilkins's early manhood, his education, and the loss of his fortune, followed by his setting out to sea. After several years as a slave in Africa, he escapes and is shipwrecked on a magnetic rock in the South Atlantic. While exploring the exterior of this apparently impenetrable rock, he is sucked into a underground channel, exiting weeks later on a lake in the centre of the island. Here begins the robinsonnade, on an inaccessible island surrounded by unscalable cliffs.

One night, in the middle of a dream about his wife in England, he hears voices, and then something crashes into the roof of his hut. This is his meeting with the flying woman, Youwarkee. After five months of getting to know each other, of mutual liking and chaste behavior, they consummate their marriage "without further Ceremony than mutual solemn Engagements to each other; which are, in truth, the Essence of Marriage, and all that was there and then in our Power" (1990:116). Fourteen years pass in happiness and comfort, and seven children are born of their union. After Youwarkee flies home to visit her father and friends, various Glumms come to visit, eventually convincing Peter to return with them to the kingdom of Doorpt Swangeanti to which he is borne on a chair held aloft by eight flying Glumms (1990:249).

In the final, utopian section of the novel, Wilkins visits the kingdom of Doorpt Swangeanti in the darkness of the polar regions. Here he quickly establishes himself as indispensable, uncovering a plot against the king and then fulfilling an ancient prophecy and returning the people to their true religion, not to mention subduing a rebellious province, establishing trade with their neighbors, and even finding a royal bride for the king.

It is interesting to read *Peter Wilkins* in terms of *Robinson Crusoe*, for Paltock transforms Defoe's classic by recasting Friday as a woman, and a winged woman at that—a transformation which takes us from the realism of Defoe to a charming kind of fantasy. As a natural utopia, the flying Glumms and Gawrys, in their games and physical ability, suggest a world without sexual and social constraints. In fact, Doorpt Swangeanti may be seen more generally as the Land of Cockaigne, as in this fairly explicit allusion to that tradition, when Wilkins discovers that what he believes to be meat and fish are actually fruits: "Well done, says I, this is the first Country I was ever in, where the fish and fowl grew on Trees; 'tis ten to one, but I meet with an Ox growing on some Tree by the Tail, before I leave you" (1990:261).

Yet there are shortcomings in this natural utopia, first and most markedly, because of the existence of slavery. More generally, the Doorpt Swangeanti lack the social and material benefits of technical progress; and to all of these implicit inadequacies, Wilkins will bring solutions and improvements. Years later, musing on the changes he has wrought, he expresses amazement

> that so ingenious and industrious a People, as the *Swangeantines* have since appeared to be; and who till I came amongst them, had nothing more than bare Food, and a Hole to lie in, in a barren rocky Country, and then seemed to desire only what they had; [that they] should in ten Years time, be supplied not only with the Conveniences, but Superfluities of Life; and that they should then become so fond of them, as rather willingly to part with Life itself, than be reduced to the State I found them in. (1990:372)

Even though Wilkins brings reform and technological progress, Doorpt Swangeanti was already a happy society, one that in many ways was better off before the arrival of the civilizing stranger. Wilkins's arrival can be seen as their downfall or, conversely, as the positive transformation of this society into something nearer the European ideal—or, as I would argue, as a contradictory combination of both. Although Wilkins's arrival in Doorpt Swangeanti does not lead to the pillage and destruction that Cortés brought to Mexico, for instance, his adventures do resemble conquest narratives in other ways. Wilkins believes that his paramount obligation is "to insist on the Abolition of [their] Image-Worship, and to introduce true Religion" (1990:269). Moreover, his missionary zeal is tied to the ruthless subjection of the king's rebellious subjects, in a brief military campaign that results in the deaths of thousands of Glumms.

The "primitive" status of the Swangeantines is also marked by the absence of a written language—a common marker of the distinction between so-called advanced and primitive societies. Wilkins's eagerness to teach them to read is connected as well to a familiar missionary enterprise—the translation of the Bible—which has become an important part of their religious services.[2] Moving from the sublime to the ridiculous, I note too that accounts of European missionary expeditions often include attempts to "clothe the savages." Wilkins gives a good deal of attention to the proper attire for various occasions, even though he is living in the midst of a society without clothing. The first example comes when Youwarkee sets out to make some clothes for herself and he carefully explains the relationship of clothing and gender: "If you make such a Jacket as mine [for yourself], there will be no Distinction between Glumm [male] and Gawry [female]; the [Modest Women] in my Country, would not on any Account go dressed like a [Man]" (1990:142). Similarly, we can observe Wilkins's own class ambitions as he frets about his appearance prior to his first meeting with Youwarkee's father, beginning with the decision whether or not to cut off his beard (1990:201); for this decisive encounter he finally decides on "a Cinnamon-coloured Gold-button Coat, Scarlet Waistcoat, Velvet Breeches, white Silk Stockings, the Campaign-wig flowing, a Gold-laced Hat and Feather, Point Cravat, Silver Sword, and over all [a] Cloak (1990:204)."[3]

As can be seen from my description, there are two locales that might lead one to think that this novel is set underground. The first is a "subterraneous voyage" (vol. 1, chapter 10): alone at sea, Wilkins comes upon a remote island with sheer, rocky cliffs. As he makes the circuit of the island "he is sucked under the Rock, and hurried down a Cataract" (1990:72), later emerging in a lake in the center of the island. But this sheltered valley is open to the sky, and it is here that he will be visited by the flying people from Doorpt Swangeanti. This austral land, to which he is carried by the flying men, might also be taken for an underground world, for is almost always dark here, and the capital city is carved out of a single immense stone. However, the stars are clearly visible, and there is no mention that they are underground. This is simply a society set in a southern region.[4]

SELECTIONS

The selections are taken from Weber; the second set of page numbers refers to the Bentley edition.

Most of the time the reader forgets that Youwarkee and her countrymen and women have wings, but those wings are also an evocative sexual symbol. This can be seen on their wedding night as Wilkins struggles to remove her clothing.

[H]aving first disposed of my Lamp, I moved softly towards her, and stepped into Bed too; when, on my nearer approach to her, I imagined she had her clothes on. This struck a thorough damp over me; and asking her the reason of it, not being able to touch the least bit of her flesh, but her face and hands, she burst out a laughing; and running her hand along my naked side, soon perceived the difference she before had made such doubt of between herself and me. [245; 117]

What Wilkins has taken to be Youwarkee's clothing is in fact her "graundee," the covering of her folded wings.

But from an apprehension of her being so wholly incased in it, that though I had so fine a companion, and now a wife, yet I should have no conjugal benefit from her, either to my own gratification, or the increase of our species.

In the height of my impatience, I made divers essays for unfolding this covering, but unsuccessfully. Surely, says I, there must be some way of coming at my wishes. . . . [Suddenly], lest I should grow outrageous . . . she threw down all those seeming ribs flat to her side so imperceptibly to me, that I knew nothing of the matter, though I lay close to her; till putting forth my hand again to her bosom, the softest skin and most delightful body, free from all impediment, presented itself to my wishes, and gave up itself to my embraces. [245; 116–118]

The people of Doorpt Swangeanti wear no clothes, for their "graundee" provides them with a modest covering (except, of course, when they fly—a point that is carefully not mentioned). They are literally a Stone Age people, for they are without metal or writing, money or fire. As Wilkins acknowledges, they were a happy and prosperous people for whom Nature seemed to have amply provided.

And yet, without any embellishments of art, how did this so great a people live under the protection of Providence? Let us first view them at a vast distance from any sort of sustenance, yet from the help of the graundee, that distance was but a step to them. They were forced to inhabit the Rocks, from an utter Incapacity of providing shelter elsewhere, having no tool that would either cut down timber for an habitation, or dig up the earth for a fence, or materials to make one: but they had a liquor that would dissolve the rock itself into habitations. They had neither beast or fish, for food or burden: but they had fruits equivalent to both, of the same relish, and as wholesome without shedding blood. Their fruits were dangerous, till they had fermented in a boiling heat; and they had neither the sun, or any fire, or the knowledge how to propagate or continue it. But they had their hot springs always boiling, without their care or concern. They had neither the skins of beasts, the original clothing, or any other artificial covering from the weather; but they were born with that warm clothing the graundee, which being of considerable density, and full of veins flowing with warm blood, not only defended their flesh from all outward injuries, but was a most soft, comely, and warm dress to the body. They lived mostly in the dark rock, having less difference of light with the change of seasons than other people have; but either by custom or make, more light than what Providence has sent them in the sweecoe is disagreeable: so that where little is to be obtained, Providence by confining the capacity, can give content with that; and where apparent wants are, we may see by these people, how careful Providence is to supply them; for neither the graundee, the sweecoes, or their springs, are to be found where those necessaries can be supplied by other means. [The Sweecoes are glow-worms that the Swangeantines capture and use to light their buildings.] [345; 372–373]

6

A Voyage to the World in the Center of the Earth (1755)

Another version of a hollow Earth with an inner planet is to be found in the anonymous *A Voyage to the World in the Center of the Earth giving an Account of the Manners, Customs, Laws, Government and Religion of the Inhabitants, Their Persons and Habits Described with Several Other Particulars: In which Is Introduced the History of an Inhabitant of the Air, Written by Himself, with Some Account of the Planetary Worlds.* This is a fascinating and almost completely unknown work, not mentioned in any of the overviews of the genre (including the *Dictionary of Literary Utopias* [2000]), although an abridged version of this novel was included in Gregory Claeys's *Utopias of the British Enlightenment* (1994) under the title "Bruce's Voyage to Naples."[1] The work begins with the narrator's fall into the center of the Earth as he is exploring the crater of Mount Vesuvius. In the inner Earth, his fall is first slowed by the gradual diminution of the force of gravity and then cushioned by the lucky fall into a load of hay. The first part of this 275-page novel offers, in familiar utopian fashion, an account of this society in the central world, although unlike the interior world of Klim, it has but a single society.

Among the characteristics of these inhabitants of the inner world is their recognition that all "animals have souls" (49), for, like the inhabitants of the central world, they are guided by the reason which the creator has given them. There are no servants and no nobility, while the king considers himself to be the "principal Servant of the People" (89). This is a fully egalitarian society, based on an "Equality of Fortune":

> In these happy Regions there is no such Thing as Want, the Earth without Labour yields an Abundance of all Necessaries of Life, and the Industry of the People finish their own Families with Clothing; and they are astonished to hear that on Earth, almost the Whole of what God created alike for the Use of every Individual, is in the Hands of few, and *whilst they wallow in Luxury, those, who have as much Right to the Productions of their common Mother, the Earth, are starving for Want*. (61; italics in text)

This is the first hollow Earth (and perhaps the only example well into the twentieth century) where there is an awareness of the existence of the upper Earth, for people from the upper world frequently fall into the underworld, to the extent that the "central inhabitants" have devised and carry around with them an ointment to counteract the magnetic force that binds visitors from the upper world to the ground.[2] Indeed, when the narrator expresses a desire to return home, his host tells him that he will "put you in a Way how to perform it but likewise accompany you myself" to the upper Earth (254). More remarkably, there is even an "earthly quarter" where more than two thousand of these accidental visitors from the upper Earth now reside:

> [Their] Ancestors were formerly part of the Inhabitants of our Globe, but were thrown, by an Earthquake, near an hundred Years ago, upon the Central World; where they and their Posterity, might have enjoyed all the Happiness they could have wished. But their many Crimes, had obliged the central Inhabitants to confine them to a particular District; Even here they might have lived happily; but that mischievous, litigious, and rebellious Disposition, that they had acquired from their Parents, was eternally giving great Uneasiness to the Government: and now the Time was come, that they, and their whole Race, was to be extinguished. (215–216)

The inhabitants of the "earthly quarter" have formed a "dangerous Conspiracy": they have armed themselves and are seeking to "become Masters of all that World" (217).

Like Holberg in his *Niels Klim*, the author seems to lose interest in his utopia, turning instead to more fanciful and fantastic adventures that have little or nothing to do with the utopian society. Here this is constituted by an eighty-page digression, the "History of an Inhabitant of the Air." This narrative begins with a long, complicated story of intrigue that follows Mr. Thompson from planet to planet as he dies and is reborn over and over again until, purified, he has become something like a guardian angel.[3]

> I am, said he, a good Genius, one of those aerial Spirits, that traverse the Regions of unbounded Space, to guard and watch over the Actions of Mankind, and to combat with and for the most part overcome, those Demons, Enemies to them that are eternally endeavouring to bring their Souls and Bodies to Destruction. . . . This has been my employment for several Years. But as I have gone though various Changes, before I arrived at this Degree of Perfection. (118–120)

In terms of the description of the hollow Earth, this is one of the strangest of the works in this collection. While the manner of getting there—falling while exploring a volcanic crater—is one of the preferred modes (along with caves and whirlpools), the description of this inner world seems the furthest from any attempt at a scientific explanation. As with Holberg and Casanova, there is an inner planet, but unlike those two imaginary worlds, there is no inner sun.[4]

Instead, the inner world is illuminated in a doubly fanciful manner, since the inner planet is "enlightened by the concave Part of your World, which is entirely cover'd with Jewels of different Sorts and immense Sizes." These jewels reflect light onto the inner world, but this reflected light comes not from an inner sun, or from light streaming through holes in the earth's crust, but from that inner planet itself! This inner planet is in fact "a luminous Body, which by casting its Rays upon the immense Number of Jewels with which the concave Part of your World is studded, they strike the Surface of our

World with all their Brilliancy" (38). In addition to this bizarre way of illuminating the inner world, this planet is provided with night and day in an equally fantastic way: "There is an opake Body exactly the Size, and Shape of half the concave Part of your World" which circles the planet every twenty-four hours. In this manner it blocks the light, creating "equal Day and Night" (39).

This is also the first example of the argument for life inside the Earth based on an appeal to the perfection of God's design, so that there can be no wasted nor meaningless creation: "GOD CREATES NOTHING IN VAIN" (108). The author, following this logic, introduces two familiar themes of early science fiction: life on other worlds and the microcosm. Humanity is just one small part of a vaster creation, as the narrator affirms his belief "that all the heavenly Bodies were Worlds, and inhabited like ours" (117). At the same time, he is also "convinc'd that no Part of Matter is uninhabited; and this Plumb that I have now in my Hand, is Without a doubt, a World to Millions" (109).[5]

SELECTIONS

■ Theories and Descriptions of the Hollow Earth

The Fall

When I came within a few Yards of the Entrance [of the crater], a dreadful Gust of Smoke issued from it, and the Ground I stood upon sunk under me.

I was instantly surrounded with Fire and Sulphur that almost suffocated me. As I continued falling, I at last came to a Part of the Cavern that was as cold as Ice, and I was almost perished with the excessive Damp that encompassed me; at last I heard such terrible Roarings and Bellowings, occasioned by the pent-up Air, and every now and then saw such Gushes of Flame and Smoke issue from every Part around me, that I expected nothing but instant Death.

The Precipitancy of the Motion with which I continued falling was so great, that I had hardly Power to offer up my Prayers to my Creator, and to accuse myself with the Rashness of the Action I had been guilty of, especially as it was contrary to the Advice of one, to whom I lay under the greatest Obligations. For I must own, that if the Captain had been my own Brother, he could not have behaved in a more affectionate Manner to me than he did, both before and during our whole Voyage.

It is impossible to describe the Variety of Appearances that struck my Eye during my Descent, sometimes I was surrounded with nothing but Fire and Smoke, and the next Minute with a Brilliancy that surpassed any Thing I had ever seen, which I imagine proceeded from the great Quantities of jewels, with which the Sides of this Cavern were stored.

If it was possible (in the Situation I was in) to form a Conjecture how fast I fell, I believe it was about a Mile every Minute. After I had been about an Hour and a half in this Situation, to my great Surprize I discovered Light above me, or below as you please, for my Head was downwards. At that Sight I verily thought that I had fell through the whole Diameter of the Globe, and was arrived at the Antipodes; but it proved otherwise, as will appear in the Sequel.

At last I got to the End of this vast Pit or rather Hole, when I found myself in the open Air, but surrounded with a Lustre, that exceeded any Thing that I had ever seen.

The resplendent Glory was so great, and affected my Eyes so much, that I thought I should have lost the Use of them. However, I perceived that the longer I continued falling, the less was this prodigious Brightness, till at last, and by Degrees, it became an agreeable Light, such as we have on Earth, in the Middle of a fine Summer's Day.

I then perceived a Body at a vast Distance, resembling our Moon at full, but much larger; and I thought I could discover Spots in it, which nearly resembled what we see in the Moon.

At this Sight, I was greatly terrified, for as I still continued falling with an incredible Quickness, I began to imagine myself dead, and that the immortal or spiritual Part of me, was going to that Place to which it was destined, by its good or bad Actions in this World. I still continued falling, and the Body I at first discovered, increased greatly, as I nearer approached it. At last I could discover nothing, but this Globe below me. I then plainly discerned Seas, vast Continents, Mountains and Islands. As at this time, the Rapidity with which I fell was prodigious, I soon perceived that it was neither more nor less than a World like ours, for then I saw Houses, Towns, Trees and Fields. And now I every Moment expected to have my Brains dashed out: But Providence . . . so ordered it that I fell directly upon a Load of Hay. [8–12]

The Central World

[T]his Globe we are now upon, is One Thousand Miles Diameter, consequently Three Thousand, and upwards, of Miles in Circumference. We have no Sun, but every Thing grows spontaneous, and we are enlightened by the concave Part of your World, which is entirely cover'd with Jewels of different Sorts and immense Sizes. The Carbuncles, the Rubies, the vast Quantity of Diamonds, of Saphires, of Emeralds, Topazes and all the various Sorts of precious Stones that are known amongst you, with many others, are there in such Quantities, and all of them of such a prodigious Size, that the Lustre that comes from them, gives Light to our World. But perhaps you'll ask, how these Jewels can shew so great a Lustre, without the Assistance of a light Body to dart its Rays upon them: for that a Diamond cannot be seen in the Dark; and that it is absolutely necessary, to discover its Brilliancy, that it be assisted by the Sun, or some other Body, to dart its Rays upon it. This I will explain to you.

Our World, then, is itself a luminous Body, which by casting its Rays upon the immense Number of Jewels with which the concave Part of your World is studded, they strike the Surface of our World with all their Brilliancy; but even this would only be a partial Light, were it not for our Atmosphere, which is computed at thirty Miles high. Their Rays meeting with it, are refracted, and by that Means occasion an equal and universal Light. For the Sun itself would be but of little Service to you, were it not for your Atmosphere; without that, he would appear as a red hot Piece of Iron, at an immense Distance, and you would only see him (as thro' a smoked Glass) without his being of any Service to you.

Thus our Day is occasion'd, and by this Means we should have had no Night, had not the wise Creator provided otherwise, that we might have a proper Time to rest from the Labours of the Day. In short, there is an opake Body exactly the Size, and Shape of half the concave Part of your World; the Distance of which from the Surface of our Globe, we reckon at Two Thousand Five Hundred and upwards of Miles. This moving round us once in Twenty-four Hours, occasions Day and Night; for by this Means our whole Globe has equal Day and Night, for at Six our Day begins, and at Six the Night takes place. But even our Nights are not entirely dark, for in the Body (before mention'd) are sprinkled by an Omnipotent Hand, Thousands of Precious Stones; of so large a Size, that even at that Distance, they appear as large and bright, as the most brilliant of your Planets: Thus when Day forsakes us, we are comforted by a Sky, as glorious as yours on a starry Night. (And indeed so I found it, for nothing can be more beautiful than their Nights are.) Our World, continues he, is likewise of a warm Nature; and the Particles of Heat, arising from its Surface, diffuse a moderate Warmth over the Whole, and by this Means we have never an Extremity of Heat or Cold, but a constant agreeable Temperature. [37–40]

Magnetic Attraction

The World on which we live is the very Centre of that Globe you call the Earth, and as I shall as far as possible confine my Description to your Ideas, I will call it a vast Magnet or Loadstone; which by its attractive Quality draws every Thing in your World towards it, and the nearer you approach its Surface the greater on Course must be the Power of its Attraction. You may remember that when I first saw you, you seem'd and felt as if you was fixed to the Ground, I reliev'd you by an Ointment which we Central Inhabitants always carry about us, for the Assistance of Strangers like yourself; this proceeded from the vast Power of Attraction that is given to our World, for if it has the Power to attract Bodies, at the Distance of three thousand Miles and upwards, how much more must the Force be, when you are upon its Surface? . . .

I am very sensible that you Earthly Inhabitants think that God has created nothing but your World to be inhabited, and that you are the great Lords thereof; that the Sun, the Moon, Stars and Planets, were made only to enlighten the Grain of Sand that you inhabit. But know, vain Mortals, that there is no End of Creation, and that every Pebble, every Leaf, nay the most minute Thing that can be conceiv'd, is a World to Millions. In a Drop of Water no larger than a Pin's Point, with ordinary Glasses, you may discover Numbers of living Creatures of various Sizes and different Structures. If we see these small Parts of the Creation so plentifully stock'd with Inhabitants, how can we imagine that the vast Bodies that fill the Regions of unlimited Space were only form'd for us to gaze upon, and not full of Beings to glorify the great Author of their Existence! Every Part of Creation is absolutely necessary to keep together the Whole; and like the Wheels in a Clock, if the minutest is remov'd, it puts a Stop to the whole Movement. For this Reason a Fly is of as mush Use in that Part of Creation which it is ordain'd to fill, as a Monarch is in that which he is. Our Central Globe is absolutely requisite for the very Being of your World. If there was no attractive Power, to keep all Things in Order, how could any Thing exist? Your Towns, your Houses, your very selves, instead of adhering to the Surface, would float in the Air, and have no Resting Place. The Accident that brought you here, has made you, in one particular, wiser than your greatest Men; for they, with all their puzzling, could never find out what the Centre was compos'd of; with the Particulars of which you are now made acquainted. [31–34]

Intelligent Animals

Know then that, with us, not only the various feather'd Inhabitants of the Air, but likewise all the different Creatures of our World, are as tame as the most domestic Animals amongst You. And why should they be otherwise? We are, and they know us to be their Friends. Instead of persecuting and destroying them as in your World you do for your Diversion; next after worshipping and adoring our Creator, it is the principal Part of our Religion to protect what he has been pleased to give Life to. For this Reason they are in no Fear of us, and as they fly from and avoid you as their Enemies, they are pleased in being free with us as their Friends. The reason that you never perceiv'd this before, was, that since you have been here, you have wore your earthly Garb, for which Reason they shunn'd you; now as you appear like one of us, they behav'd in the Manner you this Morning saw them. I must further tell you, that we believe every living Creature to be endu'd with a rational Soul . . . and what you are pleased to call Instinct . . . we call Reason. . . .

You allow none but yourselves to have Reason, the more Shame for you, when those (which you unjustly call the Brute Creation) exceed you so far.

Must it not be paying yourselves a bad Compliment, to say you are the only rational Part of Creation, and at the same Time perceive, what you call Brutes behave with infinite more Reason than yourselves? Whilst one of your own Species shall behave in a Manner inconsistent with all Reason? [48–50]

We have a vast Plenty of all Sorts of the Productions of Nature, but to destroy any Creature that has life, to feed our Luxury, is held the greatest Crime, and unknown amongst us; being well assured, that we have no Right to take away that Life, which God has been pleased to give. [41]

Inventions

As soon as we came to the Door, I saw a Vehicle, something resembling one of our one Horse Chairs, but much lighter and neater, for the Back and Sides was only a thin Sort of Lattice. At each Side (instead of Wheels) were two monstrous Bladders, belonging to what Beast I did not then know, but ten Times as large as a Bullock's Bladder. These were fastened (by a Garth) which went under the Bottom of the Chaise, and making two Wing's served to sustain it (whilst in the Air) in a proper Equilibrium. Before the Chaise were two Birds, about twice as large as our largest Swans, but of a different Colour and Make. They resembled the most beautiful green Parrots both in colour and Shape, but far exceeded them in the Beauty of both.

To the Breasts of these were fastened silken Cords, which being introduc'd into the Chaise, serv'd to guide them, as the Reins with us do Horses.

As soon as were seated, and my Conductor had taken hold of the Reins, they spread their Wings, and in an Instant soared to the Height of (at least) a Quarter of a Mile, and my Companion gently moving the Reins, (to direct their Course) they proceeded at a prodigious Rate, and what was very observable, they seldom mov'd their Wings, but after a Flap kept them extended for a considerable Time, as smooth as a Hawk hovering for his Prey: and it is necessary to observe that the Bladders kept the Chaise up in an equal Line with the Birds. [71–73]

Life in the Universe

The Life of a Fly is but a Summer, a Horse is old at Twelve, and if we may believe Historians a Raven lives a thousand Years. And yet this long Term is no more in Comparison to the Raven, than the short one is to *Cicero's* Hypanians.

As we see that the Lives of different Creatures differ so much, on that little Grain of Sand the Earth, no doubt but other Worlds may be peopled by Beings, that are young at a Thousand or ten Thousand; for he that created the one, is able to create the other; and with him there can be no Time: Past, present and to come he comprehends at one View.

For my own Part, continued he, till by meer Accident I was thrown upon this Central World, I had no Idea of there being one, and inhabited, in the Bowels of the Earth, but as I am now convinc'd that there is, I can the readier believe, that no Part of Matter is uninhabited; and this Plumb that I have now in my Hand, is Without a doubt, a World to Millions.

In short, there Things are wonderful to us; yet tho' we cannot comprehend, our Wonder ceases, when we consider that all this is the Work of an omnipotent Being. How vain are we then to attempt to search into his Ways and to pronounce those Things impossible, that we cannot comprehend? This discourse of Mr. *Thompson's* met with universal Approbation, and he was pleased to proceed.

Our Comprehension, says he, is confined to a very narrow Sphere, and beyond that we are no more capable of judging, than the Fly was when perched on the Cupola of St. *Paul's:* Is this, says he, that finely polished Structure, that is the Boast of Mankind? For my Part I can see nothing but a rough, unfinished Piece, full of Inequalities. To his microscopic Eye the most polished Marble or Ivory, would appear full of Rocks and Cavities. So it is with Man, we can comprehend nothing but what we can see; and it is insolent in us to imagine that an omnipotent Hand can form nothing, but what may be taken within the narrow Limits of our Optics.

A Fish sees not Water their Element, neither can we the Air that is ours: but as it is a Liquid as well as the Sea, the same Hand that form'd it so much finer, can make an Eye of such a Structure as to see it, and perhaps therein to discover Myriads of living Creatures, of different Sizes and Species. There is no forming an Idea of Things that are beyond the Limit of our Conceptions: but we must, we cannot refuse to allow, that he who created what we are Eye-Witnesses to, is capable of creating (and undoubtedly has) what we can form no Notions of. As Magnitude, Space, and Time are only comparative, so is Creation. What we see of it, is no more in Comparison to the Whole, than the Time contained in a Second is to Eternity; for as His Power is infinite, so must be his Works.

For this reason, with me it won't admit of a Doubt, but that there are in the Universe, Beings as much superior to us, as we are to the most minute and senseless Reptile.

The Inhabitants of a Leaf or Flower, proudly strut and say, We are the Lords of the Creation, every Thing was made for us; there is no other World than this that we inhabit, and the whole Works of an infinite Creator are limited to that of a Leaf. So it is with silly Man. He has the arrogance to say, that this small Grain of Sand which we possess, is the Whole that God created to be inhabited.

Those stupendous Bodies which are to be seen from the World I came from, and which are well known to the Inhabitants of this, as *Saturn, Jupiter,* two hundred Times larger than the Earth, were only made for its Use, that the Moon was only formed to light it. How ridiculous! when every Requisite necessary for living Beings is discovered in them.

They have their Atmospheres, which can be of no Use to us, nor any in the Universe, unless they be created for the same Use that ours is, *viz.* to be the great Cause of Life; and that they are, is evident from this, GOD CREATES NOTHING IN VAIN.

Jupiter has four Moons, Saturn five and his Belt; these have been discovered lately, were unknown to the Ancients, and are only to be seen by the Help of the best of Glasses. What Use are they therefore of to us? But they are of Use, otherwise they would not have been made, and that must be to the Inhabitants of those vast Orbs; who very probably exceed us in every Perfection, as much as their Worlds do in Magnitude that which we inhabit. [104–109]

I imagine we make no doubt but that the Planets are Worlds and inhabited, especially as they are of so stupendous a Size, and furnished with every Necessary for Life; when we see that the minutest Thing that can be conceived is a World to Thousands. It is said that there are more living Creatures about the *Leviathan*, which are invisible to the naked Eye, than there are visible ones upon the Face of the whole Earth. Nay, a Microscope discovers a Louse to be a very lousy Creature. [113]

Religion

The principal Square (which is in the very Centre of the City), is an Octagon, from each Square of which proceeds a Street of a Mile long, and as broad as the *Hay-Market*. This forms eight principal Streets, and the Intervals between them (which are very considerable) are compos'd of By-streets, and Ground for the Use of the Inhabitants. In the Middle of the Square is the principal Church, much larger than St. *Paul's*, and quite a plain Building, as they say it is impossible they can do Honour to God by outward Show and Grandeur, nothing being so acceptable to him, as Purity and Simplicity of Heart, inclin'd to perform his Commandments, and as far as in us lies, to render Thanks for the inestimable Blessings we every Moment receive. This, say they, may as well be done in a Barn as any other Place, for he delighteth not in Show and Decorations, neither can the Workmanship of Man add to his Glory, which is compleat beyond Comprehension. But as I should be unwilling to prejudice any Set of Men against these worthy good People, I shall give no Account of their Religion, being certain it will disoblige those of a different Way of thinking with them. Therefore let it suffice to say, that they are blessed with all the Morality taught us by the Christian Religion in its Purity, and without Adulteration. [86–87]

Gold

I have often mentioned, that here the Use of Gold is unknown, but it is understood the Use that we put it to. For in this World Gold is as common as common Stones with us, and as such used only in building their Houses, paving their Streets, etc. and precious Stones of all Sorts are so extremely plenty, that they are generally made use of for the same Purposes, being of a prodigious Size. Often have I thought to myself, when I have been walking upon a Pavement of Diamonds, and others the most valuable Jewels, how much I exceeded the greatest or our earthly Monarchs. [227]

Return

The Time being now come for our Departure, after taking the most affectionate Leave of my Friend's Wife and Family, we set out; but our Manner of Travelling differed from the common one, in the Central World.

As soon as we came to the Door, I perceived two monstrous Birds; to the Beak of one of them was fastened a long Ribbon, which my kind Conductor taking in his Hand, he directed me to get upon its Back, and he mounted the other. He kept the Ribbon (that was fastened to mine) in his Hand . . . and upon his giving the Signal, they extended their Wings, and soared up with us at a prodigious Rate. I believe in about six Hours, we had got half way on our Journey; for the World I had left, began to look like a large Moon at Full. . . .

My Conductor now desired me to observe the Glory that surrounded me, (for we were come so near to the concave Part of our World, that the Jewels with which it was studded, almost took away my Eye Sight;) but this did not last long, for presently we were surrounded with a total Darkness. He then told me that we were got into the Crust of our World, and that the passing of it, would be much more difficult than all the former Part of our Journey. And indeed so it was, for the Space was so much confined, that the Birds had hardly Room to move their Wings; but in about an Hour, after we had been in this Darkness, I discovered Light, and presently afterwards, we arrived safe upon my *Mother World*, but in what Part I never knew.

He congratulated me upon our safe Arrival, and told me, that we were within a few Miles of *London*, whither he would accompany me, but that I must submit, for a little while to have my Eyes covered, that I might not know in what Part to find this Entrance to their World. [255–257]

7

L'aventurier françois (1782)

Like Fieux de Mouhy, Robert-Martin Lesuire (1737–1815) was a prolific and now forgotten writer whose works have not been in print for more than a century. His best known work, *L'aventurier françois*, was successful enough to have generated three sequels (or *suites*): the first continues the adventures of the hero, Grégoire Merveil (1783), and the next two, much less interesting, suites contain the memoirs of his son (*Deuxième suite*, 1785–1786) and of his daughter (*Dernière suite*, 1788). The novel and its sequels present a disjointed series of ever more fanciful voyages and adventures, of disguises and mistaken identities, arrests and imprisonments, escapes and bizarre plot-reversals, as Merveil finds and loses again and again his beloved Julie (with numerous sexual dalliances along the way). There are several instances of underground settings although, as with *Lamékis*, they are limited to cellars and caverns, beginning with Merveil's imprisonment in an underground cell from which, after weeks of digging, he escapes. For our purposes, however, the most interesting parts of the novel are those set in the southern or "austral" lands, where the long-suffering hero finds himself shipwrecked on two occasions. Caught in some rapids (in another example of a "subterraneous voyage"), he is hurtled through a rocky tunnel and finds himself in a vast cavern inhabited by the "gnome people"—a society of former convicts sent to mine gold and now trapped by an earthquake in a dark subterranean world where their descendants subsist by trading gold for food and other goods with an outside of which they are only dimly aware. This society is ruled by priests who eventually introduce Merveil to their most important secret: asked to feign death, he is carried in a drugged sleep to "Paradise"—a sunlit garden filled with beautiful young women. Since this is heaven, the unrestricted satisfaction of physical desires is no longer a sin, but a meritorious spiritual pleasure!

> All the pleasures are permitted [a beautiful young woman explains to him]. Passion, which is sinful in the human world, because it is the satisfaction of a physical desire, is here, where there are only spiritual pleasures, a pure union of souls. But since we have the appearance of bodies which give us the impression of touching, as you have realized, we are able to experience feelings which correspond exactly to those physical and sensual pleasures which were forbidden in the other world . . . but which here are now purified and permitted. (*AF*, 2:90–91)

The priests of this land not only reserve this paradise for themselves, they do so by hiding the existence of the sun from the inhabitants of the underground world, in an extreme example of the eighteenth-century confrontation between the role of the church and France and the Enlightenment philosophers as well as a bizarre version of Plato's cave.

Merveil next visits the kingdom of "Austral France," which was established by exiles from France and which deliberately duplicates and is even superior to the original, down to the existence of the capital, Paris Neuf, with many of the same buildings—including Notre-Dame, Les Invalides, the Tuileries, and the Champs-Elysées! The citizens of this "second France" stay in touch by sending officials to spy on France and to report back on buildings and other developments. However bizarre, this is no longer an underground setting. Like the satirical tour of the many different intelligent tree peoples in Holberg's *Niels Klim*, Merveil's journey around the austral lands also provides the opportunity for the author to satirize some utopian schemes, in particular in the reversed sex-roles of the Republic of the Viragos, where men are slaves, serving as beasts of burden and for strictly controlled sexual reproduction: "Fearing that the mixing of sexes might lead to troubles within families, the men were fitted with special belts . . . which could only be unlocked by the female head of the household" (*AF*, 2:233). Rich women are nonetheless able to keep favorites in little country houses—as Merveil reminds us, "just like we keep mistresses in Paris." In his usual heroic fashion, Merveil leads a rebellion, "in order to return his sex to its [masculine] dignity while restricting women to their rightful role" (*AF*, 2:245). Once the men are again in charge, the women revert to their proper station, understanding that "to be happy as women, they must live like women" (*AF*, 2:257). A similar satire of utopian dreams is found in the Land of the Glaciers, where people are periodically frozen and then revived centuries later, in this way prolonging their lives for thousands of years (*AF*, 2:260–273).

Later (in the first *suite*), Merveil is again shipwrecked. He is rescued by the Ondines and taken to the floating city of Océanin—which is linked by a secret tunnel to the land of the Gnomes. This country emerged after the original city was covered by the sea. The inhabitants anchored rafts to their old houses, and now, through an ingenious system of diving suits and underwater air chambers, they live both above and below the water. There is little discussion of their system of government, however, and again the priests keep the population in ignorance (here, of the existence of land) while reserving to themselves the right to sexually initiate the girls (*PS*, 2:138–165). In any case, this is not an underground world.

I can find no allusions to other works dealing with subterranean worlds in Lesuire's text, and as my synopsis has made clear, these marginally subterranean locales are simply stops along the way, as Lesuire (like Mouhy before him) takes his hero from adventure to adventure. What makes the novel interesting in this context—as opposed to societies where people decide to live underground, as in Tyssot de Patot's *La vie, les aventures, et le voyage de Groenland du Révérend Père Cordelier Pierre de Mésange, avec une relation bien circonstanciée de l'origine, de l'histoire, des moeurs et du Paradis des habitans du Pôle Arctique* (1720), or Jules Verne's *Les Indes noires* (1877)—is that here the Gnome people do not know that any other world exists and are deliberately kept in ignorance by the priests.

SELECTIONS

Arrival in the Gnome World

I could see a vast opening in the rock face ahead of me. The current pulled me towards it with an irresistible violence. I saw that the river was plunging into a gulf, and I plunged into it, seeing myself in a great subterranean tunnel. . . . Thrown from my boat, I clung to a branch as I continued through the dark tunnel. I could hear what sounded like the crashing of a hundred thousand hammers, and then I lost consciousness. . . . When I again opened my eyes, I found that I was hanging upside down, and I could hear the sound of voices around me. Waking, I breathed a loud sigh and those around me rushed to let me down. I realized that they had hung me up in order to drain out the water I had swallowed. I looked at them and they looked back at me. I made a gesture of thanks, they replied with gestures of joy.

These men looked strange to me, as I suppose I looked strange to them. Each was holding a torch . . . and I could see above our heads the very high vault. We were on the edge of a river, which was flowing much more peacefully than it had been at the place where I had fallen in. I could hear above us the roar of the falls, but far away. [2:34–35]

The river seemed quite large. It was illuminated on both sides, and lights were strung across it at intervals, providing a steady light. The vault was quite high, indeed immense since in addition to the river, it contained as well the vast fields which spread out on each side. From my side, I could see gardens planted with vegetables and fruit trees, lit by rows of lanterns, and heated by subterranean furnaces which replaced the heat that the sun brings to us. Further on, I could see fields where animals were grazing. . . . Further still, I saw an immense city, built under a soaring vault, with a river through its center, with several attractive bridges. . . . The artificial light of the city was blinding, for the vault was made of a highly polished metal which reflected the lights, giving the impression of a blazing sky over one's head. [2:38–39]

Since it was always light, there were no set hours for meals or sleep. Everyone slept or ate when they felt need to, so that while some were sleeping, others were awake, and there always people about. [2:44]

I could not get over my surprise at seeing that the interior of a mine could be such a pleasant place to live; for this was indeed a mine, although a rather special one. Here my narrative will become a bit gloomy. For I am describing a subterranean people; I am leading my reader into the bowels of the earth. These people had never seen the heavenly vault of the sky; they talked about the sky and the light the way we talk about Heaven and Hell; and indeed, their idea of heaven and the afterlife was to live on the earth's surface, outside, under the light of the sun, without the vault above their heads, and without worrying about where their light would come from. . . . I could see that there were gardens which supplied fruit and vegetables, and cattle which nourished these strange mortals. And I could see that this great river was filled with fish. Still I could not understand where the grain and the feed for the cattle, not to mention the cloth and the wood, and the oil for their lamps, and more generally, most of what they consumed, came from. . . . The Gnome people, like Midas, should have been starving in the midst of all this gold, and yet they had everything. [2:44–46]

[The priests eventually reveal to him that] they considered it their duty to conceal from the people the truth of their world, how they got there and how they were fed. . . . This country was originally a gold mine and one day an earth-quake closed the entrance. Fortunately, when this happened the mine was already quite large, while the miners themselves—who were all criminals who had been sentenced to life imprisonment in the mine—although numerous, had enough provisions to allow them the time to find a way out of the mine. . . . But as they emerged, they came upon Guards who ordered them back into the mine. [2:44–46]

In this way they negotiated an exchange, gold for food and other merchandise, and eventually women, until eventually they became used to this way of life and gradually forgot about the outside world.

■ The Land of the Viragos

Men were considered exactly like animals. The women took the trouble to nurse and raise their daughters; the sons were thrown into a common enclosure with the goats and other animals. These poor infants were nourished haphazardly by various female animals. When they were older, they were taken out and chains attached to their wrists and ankles, and they went to live in the house, like a domestic pet. They were given no education . . . and learned only the coarsest trades. The women knew that they were stronger than them, and the men were given the basest tasks. They served as horses, and they pulled and carried loads, including carriages and plows. They worked as blacksmiths and the like, always under the direction of women, who watched over them with whips. . . . They were always chained, with chains with barbs, so that when pulled, they pierced their flesh . . . while the women carried weapons, and for the slightest mistake the men were cruelly punished and often killed for little or no reason. Since the men were so degraded and oppressed and had never known any other condition, they never thought of trying to shake off this unworthy enslavement.

Nonetheless, the cruel Viragos were obliged to consort with the men in order to reproduce: this was done solemnly, in the temples, where some men were kept and fed to serve as stallions. Fearing that the mixing of the two sexes might produce unseemly desires, the men were fitted with a special belt, which did not otherwise cause any discomfort, and the key was given to the head of each family. In any case, the girls were taught to fear and despise the men so that it took a strong temperament to defy this prejudice. . . . Despite all these obstacles, there was a lot of sexual activity. All the well-to-do women kept young boys in special little houses and whom they worshiped. . . . Indeed some of the richest women had entire harems. [2:253–254]

■ Océanin

I saw beautiful wide canals, well-laid out, with side-walks and porticos in front of the houses. There was water everywhere, in fountains, ponds and canals. . . . And everything around me rocked gently with the movement of the sea, and I realized that I was in a floating city, somewhat like those one finds on the rivers in China, but much larger. I could see that this city was surrounded with high walls, to check the violence of the wind and waves. I walked around the city on the walls: it must have been at least three leagues in circumference, and contained vegetable gardens as well as fields with grazing livestock. The canals were filled with every kind of boat, and there were lots of people in the water who seemed to move without effort. At first I thought that they were somehow different, but looking more closely at their clothing, I realized that they were wearing some kind of skintight diving suit. [2:143–144]

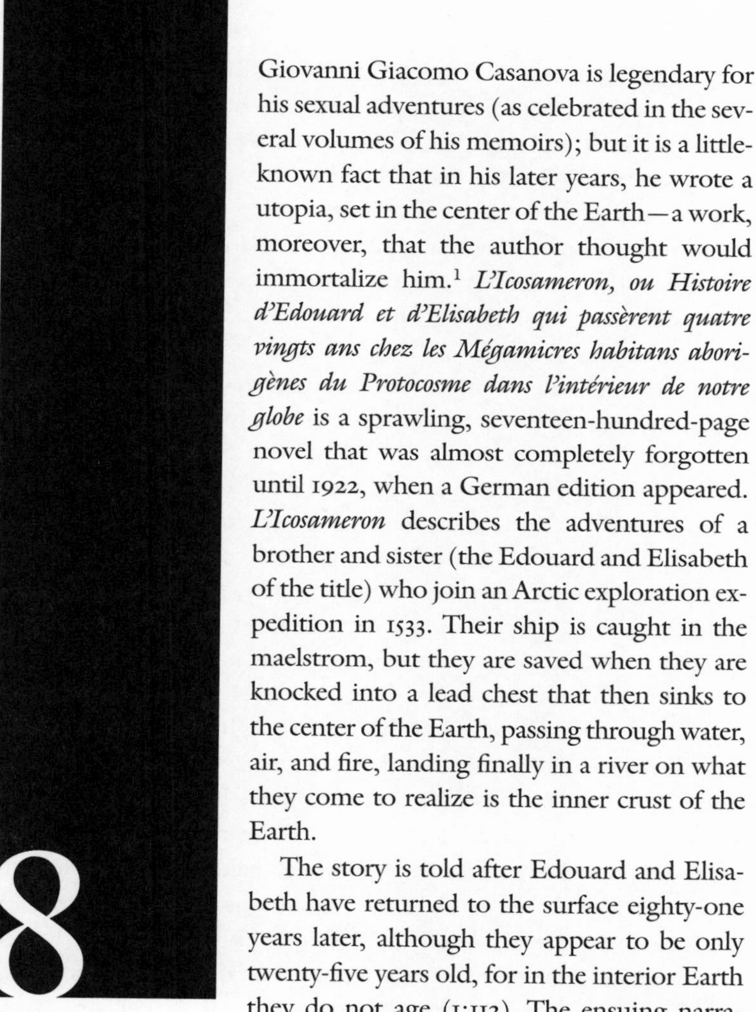

8

The Icosameron (1788)

Giovanni Giacomo Casanova is legendary for his sexual adventures (as celebrated in the several volumes of his memoirs); but it is a little-known fact that in his later years, he wrote a utopia, set in the center of the Earth—a work, moreover, that the author thought would immortalize him.[1] *L'Icosameron, ou Histoire d'Edouard et d'Elisabeth qui passèrent quatre vingts ans chez les Mégamicres habitans aborigènes du Protocosme dans l'intérieur de notre globe* is a sprawling, seventeen-hundred-page novel that was almost completely forgotten until 1922, when a German edition appeared. *L'Icosameron* describes the adventures of a brother and sister (the Edouard and Elisabeth of the title) who join an Arctic exploration expedition in 1533. Their ship is caught in the maelstrom, but they are saved when they are knocked into a lead chest that then sinks to the center of the Earth, passing through water, air, and fire, landing finally in a river on what they come to realize is the inner crust of the Earth.

The story is told after Edouard and Elisabeth have returned to the surface eighty-one years later, although they appear to be only twenty-five years old, for in the interior Earth they do not age (1:112). The ensuing narrative is spread over twenty days (hence the title), and each day's narrative is considerably slowed by pages of dialogue before the actual story begins or is renewed. It takes twenty pages to tell of their descent to the Earth's center and another thirty pages to extract them from the lead chest, for instance; and it takes eighty pages to describe their return climb back to the surface world. The first volume also includes a 33-page preface as well as a 110-page exegesis of the first three chapters of the book of Genesis in which Casanova argues that the inner Earth may well be the Garden of Eden.[2]

As described by Casanova, the inner world (or "Protocosmos") is an immense land on the underside of the Earth's crust with a sun floating in the center of the internal void.[3] It is inhabited by some thirty billion "Megamicres" (big-littles): tiny, androgynous, multicolored humans, peaceful and vegetarian, whose primary nourishment is the milk they drink at their life-partner's breast. They "speak" a musical language that flows into their souls through the skin of their naked bodies;[4] their life is a hymn to nature; their calendar is based on the seasons. In an example of the utopian enthusiasm of the preface, which is not always matched by the text, Casanova writes that the Megamicres "give all their efforts to the cultivation of the arts. . . . They hunt without killing their prey, they fish without depriving fish of their freedom, and they are able to swim in ways which are unknown to us since nature has given them a different structure than us which allows them, like fish, to breathe water" (1:xvii).[5]

This subterranean world is divided into eighty kingdoms and ten republics, all equal squares: each is "11,000 *milles* [= 16,500 kilometers] in length and width, and each has a population of roughly one-hundred and twenty million inhabitants" (2:167). There are in fact two utopias in this immense and verbose work, although neither one is particularly attractive. The first, the eight- or nine-thousand-year-old land of the Megamicres,[6] could hardly be said to be "organized according to a more perfect principle than in the author's community."[7] There are still rich and poor in this land, criminals and social classes (the latter based on skin color), along with various rivalries and intrigues, and even a war (although it is, in truth, triggered by fears about the alarming growth of Edouard's family). In the preface, Edouard explains the word "Megamicre" in flattering terms—small in body, large in intelligence and virtue: "These happy beings . . . are very small, and are called Megamicres—*big-small*—but you will see that they are in reality grander than we are" (1:xxii). This praise notwithstanding, the Megamicres are not very smart, nor do they seem very satisfied with their lives after the Europeans arrive. They are also superstitious and overly dependent on the clergy and theologians, although Edouard's enlightened religion will gradually replace the Megamicres' own sun-worship, putting their priests out of work (in one region "ten to twelve thousand priests have been reduced to begging" [5:45]). Most important, Edouard can be seen as undermining this utopia by introducing a number of inventions that give him increasing power in this very ancient land. As he declares to his interlocutors after his return, "You will learn how we came to sovereignty, and you will see that one could easily suppose that in twenty years, my children will be the masters of the interior world" (1:247). And at another point, he avers that it seems to have been God's will that "he was born to change the laws and religion, the system and nature, and even the tranquility and happiness of that world" (5:238–239). Although he is only fourteen when he arrives, Edouard is able to successfully figure out how to make gunpowder (and later fireworks and poison gas), along with the attendant mining and smelting, and he casts bells as well as making guns.[8] He also improves on the Megamicres' writing system: whereas they have always used five different colors to represent the tones of their musical language, he replaces this with European musical notation, as well as introducing the printing press and establishing paper mills. He even practices healing and performs medical operations, in particular for the cataracts to which the Megamicres are especially prone to given their constant exposure to the sun (he figures out how to do these by practicing on pigs). He becomes a skilled diplomat and a convincing debater, and his theatrical spectacles have no equal. And while there are some positive aesthetic features of this world, particularly the Megamicres' way of communicating through song and dance, little else is very appealing. The food, for instance (other than the milk which partners give each other) is particularly unappetizing.[9] Thus, whatever Casanova may write in the preface about this being the Garden of Eden—that is, a world before sin, and before suffering—the actual narrative shows us a society far from the perfection he attributes to it. For that matter, it could hardly be said to be "more perfect" than Casanova's own society.[10]

The second utopia in the novel is that established by Edouard and

Elizabeth, and by the time they leave the inner world, they have "more than four million descendants . . . all of whom descend from the forty daughters my wife had, along with a twin brother, over forty years. . . . And after all these years, there has not been any crime among my descendants" (1:243–244). As Edouard points out, his children are exempt "from the visible signs of aging, and from illness and the need to sleep" (1:249). Like the society of the Megamicres, however, this is only minimally a utopia. It could hardly be emulated, for it is not so much a model, but a fantasy ideal, a world populated by millions of his descendants, all subject to his paternalistic rule—a world in which he gives "orders to 300,000 men, all my obedient sons, and who all worshiped me" (5:38). In addition to establishing cities, he makes laws as well as developing his own version of Christianity, even going so far as declaring himself the Pantaphilarque or "sovereign head of the religion."[11] As a fantasy, though, the rules Edouard establishes for his children controlling marriage, for instance, and forbidding adultery hardly seem to correspond to the sexual adventurer of the *Memoirs*.

In the selections from the novel, I have focused on the Megamicres, including their peculiar method of giving birth, although Casanova avoids any mention of how the hermaphroditic Megamicres mate or how the eggs are fertilized. Despite these reticences, there is a hint of one theme that was to become popular in science fiction after the 1960s: alien sex. While the mechanics of the Megamicres' sexuality and reproduction are veiled in ambiguous phrases and silences, we do learn that some Megamicres are sexually attracted to the "giant" male humans, but not to the females: "*The male giants appear to have been made to give pleasure rather than to receive it, while the female giants appear to have been made to receive rather than to give pleasure*" (4:29; italics in text). This has some significant consequences, most important among them that human males who become involved with Megamicres become sterile, even though they continue to have sex with their wives. In the final chapters of the novel, Edouard will concentrate on rooting out this evil.

On the other hand, Casanova's interior world includes little in the way of new technology, and it is Edouard who—in familiar fashion—

will introduce a number of Earth technologies to the underworld. At the same time there are, in addition to the Megamicres, a few other subterranean creatures worthy of note, specifically the flying horses.

I have also included some of Casanova's theological arguments for proposing the inner Earth as both plausible and a possible site for the Garden of Eden. This may be the most original part of the book, since by this time (1788) the balance of arguments about the nature of the Earth had moved from attempts to reconcile the Bible with observations about the world (volcanoes and flood, fossils, etc., as in Kircher or Burnet) to attempts to apply scientific reason and deduction to explain these phenomena. Although Casanova abandons earlier biblical datings of the Earth's age (the Megamicres' world is at least seven thousand years old), the Bible remains the final authority. Not only does he argue that it is not reasonable that God in his perfection would waste space (similar to the arguments made by the anonymous author of the *Voyage to the World in the Center of the Earth*), but he uses the book of Genesis to argue for the inner world.

Finally, because of Casanova's verbosity, crucial descriptions are often spread over many pages, interspersed with endless digressions and explanations. I have condensed some of these passages, although in all cases I am quoting directly rather than summarizing. Nonetheless, this is a fascinating version of the hollow Earth, given the author's philological and theological arguments for the likelihood of such a world and for the possibility that this is the location of the Garden of Eden.

SELECTIONS

■ Megamicres

The external structure of their bodies . . . is the same as ours, but with remarkable color variations. The red ones had big blue eyes with a red iris and a green pupil; their lips and tongue were green, and instead of teeth, their jaws were each composed of thirty white balls which were not bone, but hard cartilage. Their nails, like their eye-lids, were green, and their pretty curly, frizzy hair covered their heads. . . . Their chests made us think that they were female, for their breasts began to swell at the base of the neck and ended proportionately in the hollow of the stomach, and had a green nipple in the middle, but looking more closely we thought them male. Later we learned that they were neither male nor female since one can be neither one nor the other in a world where no one realized that the human species needed to be divided into two sexes. We called them "androgynes" to give them a name which in some way described them. . . . But one should not imagine that they resembled the androgynes of Plato . . . for their conformation is different and unique. [1:225–226]

What amazed them the most about us were the [sexual] differences between my sister and me. They saw on me what my sister did not have, and my chest was lacking what should have been there. These two defects made us unimaginable creatures in their eyes. [1:228–29]

Nourishment

[Seeing us trying to drink from our empty bottles] the two leaders danced up to us singing a pretty little aria and then lay down beside us. . . . Embracing us tenderly, they began to kiss our dry mouths with the sweetest kisses, and then, with an exuberant joy, they put their breasts to our mouths. We did not hesitate an instant, although hunger and thirst were perhaps not the most important reason why we accepted this important gesture of friendship. . . . We sucked their milk, being careful not to hurt their delicate skin with our carnivorous teeth. What an exquisite taste . . . what a wonderful food. It filled our senses, taste and smell alike, awakening in us all the pleasurable sensations of which we were capable, all the pleasures we could desire, sensations which no other food had ever given us the least idea. We thought that the stories from mythology were not made up, that we were in the resting place of the immortals, and that this milk that we were sucking was the nectar, the ambrosia which would give us the immortality which seemed to belong to these creatures. [1:233–234]

They were astonished to discover that I did not take from my partner [Elizabeth] the nourishment which they thought belonged to me and whose firm container they could see on her chest, albeit small, for she was only twelve years old; but they were even more astonished to see that I had none whatsoever. They thought that I did not suckle because I was not capable of offering her milk in return. . . .

When the Megamicres saw us for the first time, what struck them immediately was neither our size, nor our color, nor our arrival in a lead chest. . . . The principal cause of their astonishment was the careful observation of how we were made. They saw that I was made just like them, except for my forehead, and my chest, as well as . . . the sign of birth called the navel, which they do not have, apparently because they are not born like us. They could not imagine how nature could have produced an animal lacking the vessels of human nourishment . . . and where did she get her nourishment from? Moreover they observed that she was lacking something which made her essentially different from me, and from them all. They supposed that she was an animal of a different species than me. [2:29]

Birth and Childhood

Note that in the following passages, Casanova uses the expressions "fathers" and "sons" for the Megamicran parents and children, however much this may seem to contradict the statements that they are both male and female.

[The Megamicran couple] spends their first twelve years, which are equal to three of ours, in a sort of cage, where they are denied nothing and where they are raised, separated from one another by metal or bamboo bars. Born at the same time, they spend their time talking with one another. [2:109–110]

At the age of twelve, the two Megamicres are taken from their cages . . . where they have been kept since their birth. They are given instruction in religion, geography, civil and criminal and natural law. [2:145]

These two Megamicres love each other to a degree which it is hard to imagine. Raised side by side, they are aware that they were born to belong to each other until the end of their lives. . . . These two happy beings are led by their fathers to a room where they will seal their perpetual union. [2: 149]

After [about half a year] the new couple asks their fathers to come with them into the bedroom where, sitting facing them, they hold out two eggs, about the size of a chicken egg, which have come out of their mouths at the same time. These eggs emerge through a canal in their throat, from a womb located in their chest . . . The fathers joyfully take the two eggs into the cage room, and place them into two wooden bowls lined with a purple cushion made of the finest hemp (twelve times larger than the eggs). . . . The bowls are then placed in a basin of a naturally warm red liquor which maintains a constant temperature. . . . After [another half year] the fathers go with their sons to uncover the bowls and see that the eggs have grown twelve times larger. They touch the eggs, breaking them open and discover two little Megamicres. [2:151–152]

Death

All of the Megamicres know for certain that they will die when they reach one hundred and ninety two years of age (which is equal to forty-eight of our years). [2:107]

■ Flying Horses

These four-footed birds, which I am calling flying horses, resemble our horses only in that a two-seat saddle is placed on their backs. They have small, pointed heads, with mouths like greyhounds; and the [cartilaginous] bonnet on their foreheads is three inches wider than those of the Megamicres, and higher on the head, allowing them to only see straight ahead. . . . They are thin and very light, and they are covered with feathers; while their long tails . . . are rigid and can be opened or closed. Four wings are attached to the upper part of their short, thick, powerfully muscled legs. . . . The forward wings are about three and a half feet long, the back wings five. . . . They have difficulty walking; and when they fly, they can only fly in a straight line . . . and for about one hundred "milles." When they are flying, they cannot turn or stop. . . . They are launched from a ramp about fifty feet long . . . and the length of the horse's flight is determined by the height of the ramp. [2:82–84]

■ Book of Genesis

[In this] story, you will learn that the interior world is the earthly Paradise, that very garden of Eden whose existence we cannot question, even if its actual location is not known. Some wise men have already said that it might be found on the inside of our globe, but no one has gone there to look for it. . . . Perhaps one was afraid that one would find hell in the center of the earth and not paradise, since many claim that it is there. [1:iv–v]

If God created our world in order that it be populated, is it really logical that he wanted the inhabitable part to be the exterior surface and that he would have preferred it over the interior concavity? Not at all. The hive is not made so that the honey bees could be housed on its exterior; and the mollusk lives inside its shell, while our souls and minds, the seat of the passions and of the virtues, was not placed by God *on* us, but *inside* us. . . . Thus the core of the earth, about which so many philosophers have spoken with hesitation, has a necessary existence, and can be nothing less than the habitable part of the earth, made by God for us to live there in perpetuity: it is the garden of Eden from which we were expelled for having disobeyed him. If it is written [in Scripture] that we were put *out of* the garden, this means that before we were *inside* it. [1:vi–vii]

Adam was the first man that God created on the exterior surface of our world, and after him, he created no others. In saying this I in no way harm the purity of our religion. The other man that God created before Adam was a couple which he did not create on our earth, and although he made him in his image, and although he blessed him, one cannot confuse him with Adam, for God gave him a nature and a form entirely different from ours: he created him in the earthly paradise where his descendants are still today. The globe on which we walk is the outside of a vault which encompasses—with an opposite attraction—an interior space, with a Sun at its center, and which contains air which the descendants of this same first couple can breathe. This inner world could be the earthly paradise. [1:105–106]

9 John Cleves Symmes Jr. and *Symzonia* (1820)

Although it is far from certain that John Cleves Symmes Jr. was the author of the first American subterranean world novel, I will introduce both Symmes and his theories and the novel *Symzonia* here. Symmes was born in 1780 and received what an early biographer called "a common English education." He entered the army in 1802 and served courageously in the war of 1812. Retiring in 1816, he set up a trading post in St. Louis where in 1818, he wrote and distributed copies of his "Circular No. 1," sending copies to "each notable foreign government, reigning prince, legislature, city, college, and philosophical society, quite around the earth" (and he included with this circular a certificate of his sanity!).

> TO ALL THE WORLD!
> I declare the earth is hollow, and habitable within; containing a number of solid concentrick spheres, one within the other, and that it is open at the poles twelve or sixteen degrees; I pledge my life in support of this truth, and am ready to explore the hollow, if the world will support and aid me in the undertaking. . . .
>
> I ask one hundred brave companions, well equipped, to start from Siberia in the fall season, with Reindeer and sleighs, on the ice of the frozen sea; I engage we find a warm and rich land, stocked with thrifty vegetables and animals, if not men, on reaching one degree northward of latitude 82; we will return in the succeeding spring. (Symmes, *Declaration*, ix)

Symmes's most enthusiastic follower was Jeremiah Reynolds, who organized his speaking tours. When Symmes was too sick to continue his touring, Reynolds took over the campaign to outfit a polar expedition. After Symmes's death, however, Reynolds increasingly disassociated himself "from the more extravagant reaches of the theory," focusing instead on the practical advantages of a polar expedition (Stanton, *Great United States Exploring Expedition*, 15).[1] In 1836 the United States Congress passed a bill establishing what would become the first and most famous American naval scientific exploration. The United States Exploring Expedition had begun, according to Stanton, in the "fervent foolishness" of John Cleves Symmes. Inadvertently, this dream also led to the establishment of a national museum of natural history—the Smithsonian Institution—to house the more than 50,000 specimens collected.

Symmes himself wrote only petitions, letters, and short briefs, but his theories have been summarized by some of his followers, most notably James McBride (*Symmes's Theory of Concentric Spheres*, 1826), Jeremiah Reynolds (*Remarks on a Review of Symmes' Theory*, 1827), and P. Clark, based on his notes following some lectures by Symmes at Union College in 1826–1827 ("The Symmes Theory of the Earth"). Later his various circulars and petitions were assembled by his son Americus as *The Symmes Theory of Concentric Spheres, Demonstrating that the Earth Is Hollow, Habitable Within, and Widely Open about the Poles* (1878).[2]

While no direct evidence tells us where Symmes got his idea of the hollow Earth, particularly in the context of his limited education and his army career, there are some references to the astronomer Edmund Halley, for instance, in the first reactions to the work. McBride's semiofficial exposition of Symmes's ideas refers to Halley's article on magnetic variations (McBride cites Euler as well; *Symmes's Theory*, 130–133). The anonymous (and hostile) review of McBride in the *American Quarterly Review* discusses some earlier theories of the Earth, including those of Woodward, Burnet, Whiston, Halley, and Buffon: "But these philosophic fancies have all been far outdone by the theory of our countryman *captain Symmes*" ("Symmes's Theory," 237).[3]

In addition to inspiring disciples and countless jokes in the nineteenth century about "Symmes Hole," his theories were the inspiration for a number of fictional accounts of the subterranean world, the most important of which, *Symzonia*, appeared in 1820 and has often been attributed to him. This novel is the archetypal hollow-Earth fiction, since it contains the three principal elements I have been discussing: that is, more than any other fiction under discussion here, it is an *exposition of a theory of the hollow Earth*; a *proto–science fiction* work, a fantastic imaginary voyage with new technologies and a more advanced civilization; and a description of a society that, in its calm perfection, can be seen as one of the earliest American *utopias*.[4]

This 230-page novel is divided into three by-now familiar parts: the trip to the inner world, the stay in (the land of) Symzonia, and the return, including the author's decision to publish an account of his adventure. Thus, in 1817 Captain Seaborn set out for the South Pole in order to prove "the sublime theory of an internal world, published by Captain John Cleve Symmes" (Seaborn, vi). Fearing the reaction of his crew, however, he does not fully inform them of his intentions, hiring them instead "for a sealing voyage in the South Seas" (19). After leaving some of the crew at a sealing station they continue on, sailing over the edge (or the "verge," as he calls it) onto the concave inner surface of the Earth. Some days later they discover the internal continent, which, in honor of Symmes, he names Symzonia. Their first glimpse of this new world is of a garden paradise:

> Gently rolling hills within an easy sloping shore, covered with verdure, chequered with groves of trees and shrubbery, studded with numerous white buildings, and animated with groups of men and cattle, all standing in relief near the foot of a lofty mountain, which in the distance reared its majestic head above the clouds. (99)

They anchor and Seaborn goes ashore, where (recollecting Captain Ross's description of an encounter with Eskimos[5]) he pulls his nose in greeting and then, "to show him that I had some sense of a Supreme Being, I therefore fell on my knees, with my hands and eyes upraised to heaven" (107–108). He is then granted an audience with the "Best Man" of the "internals" and tries to explain to him the existence of the external world. Already the contrast between the principles and values of the two races is made explicit in the author's decision to avoid any discussion of their motives in seeking out the internal world: "I was already too well acquainted with the sentiments of this people, not to know that it would be extremely imprudent to suffer any expression to escape me which should discover that a desire of wealth, or of the means of sensual gratification, was among the motives which actuate the externals" (143). Similarly, his description of the earthly forms of government is limited to "describing briefly the American constitution, taking care to say nothing about the qualifications for office, nor of the means resorted to to obtain preferment" (148). In describing the habits of his fellow externals, he is careful to "speak only of the most virtuous, enlightened and truly refined people." Nonetheless, "in spite of my caution, he extracted much from me which filled him with disgust and pity" (149). And this is only the beginning. After Seaborn gives his books to be translated and the contents have been digested by the Wise men, he is ordered to leave this paradise inside the Earth. As the Best Man explains:

> That from the evidence before him, it appeared that we were of a race who had either wholly fallen from virtue, or were at least very much under the influence of the worst passions of our nature; that a great proportion of the race were governed by an inveterate selfishness, that canker of the soul, which is wholly incompatible with ingenuous and affectionate good-will towards our fellow-beings; that we were given to the practice of injustice, violence, and oppression. . . . Wherefore he, the Best Man, in council, had come to a resolution, that the safety and happiness of his people would be endangered by permitting any further intercourse with so corrupt and depraved a race. (196–197)

Thus the final part of the book narrates their return after six months in the inner world. They go first to Canton, where they sell their cargo of sealskins at a fair profit. Seaborn then purchases a load of "tea, nankeens, and silks, and as much china ware as was necessary for dunnage" for the return to the United States. There he consigns his cargo to someone who swindles him. Completely destitute, he decides to publish his memoirs as a way of raising money.

■ Utopia

Fully half of the book is a discussion of a utopian people, their economy, their political organization, and their civilization. Throughout this section of the book there are constant comparisons between life in the known world and in Symzonian. . . . These comparisons are moralistic and reformatory—that is, utopian in purpose.
—J. O. Bailey, "An Early American Utopian Fiction"

In the land Seaborn has christened "Symzonia" he is instructed, in familiar utopian fashion, in "the civil polity, customs, manners and habits of this people" (119). While "all power emanated from the people . . . the affairs of the nation were directed" by an elected "Best Man" who holds the position for life, along with a council of (one hundred) "worthies," and a larger deliberative assembly composed of almost "half the men of the nation," which meets once every four years. These Wise men are elected because of their "modest and exemplary merit," and anyone who strives for such a position is automatically excluded (122).

The most essential characteristic of the internals is their modest life style, for they spurn material gain and sensual pleasures. Indeed the latter are considered immoral: "All the real wants of men in society are provided for in the most simple and natural manner. Usefulness is the test of value" (158). They live virtuously, without inordinate desires or the desire for accumulation, while producing only what is socially necessary. Without explicitly having abolished private property this society lives for the collective good, without the "fatal sin of cupidity" (157).

> [For if someone's] labours be blessed with abundance, [he] will not expend the surplus above his wants in things useless and pernicious or in the gratification of his passions, but bestow it upon the meritorious needy, to support the unfortunate, or in useful public works, [while] the vicious man is rendered averse to the performance of his duty, and becomes wasteful of the products of

> the industry of others, without regarding the means, whether just or unjust, by which he may possess himself of them. (150–151)

This moderation extends even to their diet, for they are vegetarians (and do not even cook their food), and the contrast with the externals is sufficient to explain the latter's' "deficiencies":

> Having discovered from my remarks, that we ate the flesh of warm blooded animals . . . and, instead of confining ourselves to the pure fluid provided by nature to quench our thirst, that we indulged in fermented and distilled liquors even to inebriation, [the Best Man] was not at a loss for the cause of disease and misery, and was only surprised that such things were permitted, or, being permitted, that the race did not becomes extinct. (150)

Their virtuousness manifests itself in a number of physical ways, beginning with their intelligence and prodigious memory, their reduced need for sleep (three hours a night[6]), their beauty and white skin, as well as their strength, for they are "able to lift three times as much as any one of the degenerates, or to leap three times as high" (133). Meanwhile Seaborn and his crew's expulsion from this garden paradise reenacts humanity's own expulsion from the Garden of Eden, not only rhetorically, but literally as these biblical overtones are given a new twist when it dawns on Seaborn that humanity has descended from the internal degenerates who were exiled to a remote region of the inner world near the North Pole and who have, over millennia, populated the external world! "The suspicion . . . darted through my mind, that we the externals were indeed descendants of this exiled race; some of whom, penetrating the 'icy hoop' near the continent of Asia or America, might have peopled the external world" (134).

We have already seen this setting of a prelapsarian world in the inside of our globe: Casanova's *Icosameron* (first published in 1788 and virtually forgotten until the twentieth century). Symmes was almost certainly not aware of Casanova's work, although there are parallels. In addition to situating paradise inside the globe, both authors base their view on the argument that God is too economical to waste the interior of the Earth: "It seems neither fitting [*convenable*] nor reasonable [*vraisemblable*] that God would have created an interior for the earth for it to remain empty, and we can without the slightest scruple, believe that it is inhabited." (Casanova, *L'Icosameron*, xiii). Compare to Seaborn:

> I had undertaken this perilous voyage [he explains to the Best Man] only to ascertain whether the body of this huge globe were an useless waste of sand and stones, *contrary to the economy usually displayed in the works of Providence*, or, according to the sublime conceptions of one of our *Wise* men, a series of concentric spheres, like a nest of boxes, inhabitable within and without, on every side, so as to accommodate the greatest possible number of intelligent beings. (143; my italics).[7]

Apart from this weird and wonderful explanation of the origins of life on Earth, the religious beliefs of the internals seem to be a tolerant form of monotheistic deism. When Seaborn is taken to the Auditory, he discovers that the central meeting place of the internals is also "a temple in which they . . . assemble for devotional exercises and expressions of gratitude to the Divine Being" (137); one built, moreover, with the volunteer labor of the entire population, and used for the meetings of council.

Because the "labour necessary to procure all the essential comforts and rational embellishments of life, in this fruitful country, and with the temperate habits of the people, required but a small proportion of the labour which could be performed . . . there was abundant leisure . . . every member of it enjoyed an abundance of the comforts of life, without excessive or constant labour" (126). And yet, given this abundance of leisure, and their prodigious intelligence, it is not at all clear how the internals pass their time—since sensual pursuits and even aesthetic ones are of so little import. More surprisingly, over thousands of years their superior intelligence has not helped them to understand their actual situation inside the Earth:

> During this season, the planets and stars of the southern hemisphere are visible, some directly, and others by reflection. This oc-

casions great mistakes in their astronomical calculations, which they ascribe to the aberrations of the heavenly bodies. *It never occurred to them* that their field of vision was a limited internal concave sphere, and a great part of their firmament nothing but a reflection of the external heavens. (184; my italics)

Interpretations and Authorship

Although relatively little has been written about *Symzonia,* there are two interrelated points of controversy stemming from the identity of the book's author. Although it is signed "by John Seaborn," the book has long been attributed to Symmes himself, based on some early library catalog entries.[8] This continues to be the opinion of the two most recent considerations of the book: David Seed's "Breaking the Bounds" (1995) and Arthur O. Lewis's entry on *Symzonia* in the *Dictionary of Literary Utopias* (2000). Yet there is certainly some reason to doubt that Symmes could have written the novel, particularly given his demonstrated absence of any literary inclination or ability. As William Stanton wrote (in a letter to Dale Mullen): "I am as certain as I can be that Symmes was not Seaborn. Symmes wrote only lectures, communiqués, and letters-to-the-editor. Moreover he was in dead earnest. Seaborn's banter would only have puzzled him" (Mullen, "Authorship," 99).[9]

In 1975 Hans-Joachim Lang and Benjamin Lease put forward the name of Nathaniel Ames as the author of *Symzonia*. Unfortunately, their arguments are inconclusive and based entirely on circumstantial evidence. Ames was the author of a number of humorous and satiric essays as well has having worked as a sailor and visited some of the places described in the novel: "In these circumstances, it is not surprising that a bookish young seaman with literary ambitions and strong antipathies to 'progress' and commerce should draw on Symmes and extensive readings of voyages of discovery (satiric and factual) to produce a satiric fantasy (permeated with factual detail) titled *Symzonia: A Voyage of Discovery*" (Lang and Lease, "Authorship," 248). There is no mention in their article of why Ames should have settled on Symmes's ideas for such a satiric fantasy, nor do the authors discuss the utopian society which is juxtaposed to these "antipathies to progress and commerce," and which takes up almost half of the novel. Considering *Symzonia* purely as satiric fantasy and burlesque suits their argument better, although it runs counter to the views of most of the critics who tend to read it instead as an exposition of Symmes's theory. Readers who consider the novel as a defense or illustration of Symmes's theory include one of the novel's first reviewers (in the *North American Review*) who mocked the theory and the book equally, while J. O. Bailey, Arthur Lewis, Joel Nydhal, and David Seed all discuss *Symzonia* in terms of Symmes's theories, as well as its utopianism; and more generally, they discuss as well the continuation of these ideas in other writers, most especially in the work of Edgar Allen Poe. Similarly, the Dutch critic A. N. J. den Hollander also situates the novel in the context of Symmes's ideas and its influence on Poe, while the identity of the book's author, he says, remains a "mystery" (Hollander, *De verbeeldingswereld van Edgar Allan Poe*, 99).

Although I too doubt that Symmes wrote the novel, the question of the authorship of *Symzonia* is finally not very important to reading the novel; and until some more evidence is uncovered, this issue cannot be resolved. On the other hand, the question of whether it is primarily "a satiric fantasy" or an early utopian novel that attempts to flesh out Symmes's theory does seem essential. Lang and Lease flatly reject Bailey's assessment that "the evident intention of the book is to 'prove' Symmes's theory in a matter-of-fact-discovery of the internal world." (Bailey, introduction, [x]).[10] Yet, as Dale Mullen wrote,

> This American continuation of the 18th-century tradition of the imaginary voyage is perhaps most interesting for its exposition of the "science" supporting the theory of a warm Antarctic and an inner world, but it is also interesting as utopian fiction, as commentary on the state of the world as seen during the American age of reason, and even as an often humorous account of the troubles of the harassed narrator. (Mullen, "Arno Reprints," 181–182)

In the same vein, Joel Nydahl calls *Symzonia* "a hybrid work":

> part pure imaginary voyage, part satire, and part eutopia. . . . Our

> discussion of it could just as easily have fallen under the heading . . . of *progressive eutopias*. Yet the author's obvious interest in casting Seaborn in the mode of Gulliver and his use of the fantastic voyage to show us a mirror image of ourselves seem to beg us to consider this work as a satiric utopia. (Nydahl, "Early Fictional Futures," 261)

And finally, David Seed writes, "*Symzonia* combines two genres: the imaginary voyage and the utopia" (Seed, "Breaking the Bounds," 77).

As most discussions of the genre have pointed out, the literary utopia usually contains both satirical and expository modes, an argument which is central to Robert Elliot's *The Shape of Utopia,* for instance, and which is summed up by Darko Suvin as "Utopia explicates what satire implicates, and vice versa" (Suvin, *Metamorphoses,* 54). Rather than burlesque, the sections describing the voyage to the internal world take up the first ninety pages of the book and are filled with factual details (dates, nautical readings, etc.), a literary strategy seemingly designed to make the subsequent fantastic elements more believable by using the style of actual travel narratives—like Ross's own account of an Arctic journey. This matter-of-fact record of discovery of the internal world resembles the various expositions of Symmes's theory which detail at great length anomalous observations about the polar regions (the warm weather and open sea, the abundant flora and fauna, the aurora borealis, etc.) which Symmes then explained by insisting that there were holes at the poles from which warm air and wildlife escaped.

Rather than consider the work a satire of Symmes's theory or even of the internals' utopian society, the actual target of the satirical passages is precisely that society which stands in opposition to Symzonia, the United States and its representative in the inner world, Captain Seaborn: "Here utopia is used directly to criticize the values of contemporary America, and to destroy Seaborn's self-image in the process" (Seed, "Breaking the Bounds," 78):

> Read superficially *Symzonia* could appear to be a "voyage of discovery" undertaken with the confidence that God has underwritten commercial expansion by providing empty lands for the dis-

> posal of American merchant adventurers. But the new land is peopled by citizens whose rational meritocracy highlights the failings of America and the final part of the book appropriately narrates the remorseless diminution of Seaborn from explorer-hero to bankrupt. (Seed, "Breaking the Bounds," 79)

Finally, there is perhaps another reason for doubting Symmes's authorship: the fact that the internal world of the novel does not really present the theory of concentric circles, apart from one general reference; when Seaborn writes that

> I had undertaken this perilous voyage only to ascertain whether the body of this huge globe were an useless waste of sand and stones, contrary to the economy usually displayed in the works of Providence, or, according to the sublime conceptions of one of our *Wise* men, a series of concentric spheres, like a nest of boxes, inhabitable within and without, on every side, so as to accommodate the greatest possible numbers of intelligent beings. (143)

In terms of Symmes's ideas, however, it is important to point out that Symmes himself (perhaps under the influence of Reynolds) seems to have gradually discarded the "concentric spheres" part of his theory. In his account of Symmes's lectures at Union College in 1826–1827, Clark explicitly states that Symmes had abandoned the notion of concentric spheres: "In [McBride's] little book it is also stated that Captain Symmes held that our earth had at least *five concentric spheres*. Such may have been his views as early as 1823 and 1824, at and prior to the time when this work was published, but such were not the views expressed in his lectures at Union College in 1827" (Clark, "The Symmes Theory," 480).

While the illustration of "A Sectional View of the Earth" (which serves as a frontispiece to the novel shows a second globe within the first, in the course of the novel itself there is no mention of any other globes. It is the underside (or concave hollow) of the Earth which is inhabited (as the illustration shows as well), and there is no discussion of what else is to be found in the center of the Earth. The novel focuses instead on the surprising warmth at the poles and the likelihood of polar openings. In conclusion, to doubt Symmes's authorship does not mean subscribing to the Lang and Lease argument for Nathaniel Ames—there is simply not enough evidence. More importantly, in contrast to their view of *Symzonia* as a satire of Symmes's theories, I read this novel—as have most of my colleagues in the fields of science fiction and utopia—as a satirical utopia which includes a defense of Symmes's theory.

SELECTIONS

These selections are divided into two parts, the first dealing with Symmes's theories and the second with the novel Smyzonia.

■ Symmes's Theory

Since Symmes himself wrote only petitions, letters, and short briefs, I have included excerpts from accounts of his theories prepared by some of his followers, most notably James McBride, Symmes's Theory of Concentric Spheres *(1826). There was a hostile review of McBride published the following year in the* American Quarterly Review *(March 1827), which Jeremiah Reynolds then replied to in his* Remarks on a Review of Symmes' Theory. *Symmes' various circulars and petitions were assembled by his son Americus as* The Symmes Theory of Concentric Spheres, Demonstrating That the Earth Is Hollow, Habitable Within, and Widely Open about the Poles *(1878). McBride's account can be considered the "official" one. The New York Public Library catalog notes that McBride's book was written "under the direction and with the revision of Captain Symmes" (New York Public Library catalog, "James McBride"). In the "Apology to Captain Symmes," with which McBride's book begins, he concludes by writing that "I hope that you will permit [this book] to pass as the Pioneer to a more completer demonstration of your Theory of Concentric Spheres" (McBride,* Symmes's Theory, *ix). The table of contents gives a good idea of the book's arguments.*

James McBride. *Symmes's Theory of Concentric Spheres, Demonstrating that the Earth Is Hollow, Habitable Within and Widely Open about the Poles*

CONTENTS

Concentric Spheres, with a few suggestions to the Congress of the United States, to authorize and fit out an Expedition for the discovery of the Interior Regions; or at least, to explore the northern parts of the continent of America.

CHAPTER IX. A few brief suggestions, relative to the description, tonnage, and number of vessels, necessary to be equipped for a voyage of discovery to the interior regions of the earth; the number of men necessary to be employed on board, articles necessary for the outfit, and probable expense attending the same; also, as to the route most proper to be pursued to accomplish the object of the expedition.

CHAPTER X. A short biographical sketch of Captain Symmes; with some observations on the treatment which he has met with in the advancement of his theory. [x–xi]

ACCORDING to Symmes's Theory, the earth, as well as all the celestial orbicular bodies existing in the universe, visible and invisible, which partake in any degree, of a planetary nature, from the greatest to the smallest, from the sun, down to the most minute blazing meteor or falling star, are all constituted in a greater or lesser degree, of a collection of Spheres, more or less solid, concentric with each other, and more or less open at their poles; each sphere being separated from its adjoining compeers by space replete with aerial fluids; that every portion of infinite space, except what is occupied by spheres, is filled with an aerial elastic fluid, more subtile than common atmospheric air; and constituted of innumerable small concentric spheres, too minute to be visible to the organ of sight assisted by the most perfect microscope, and so elastic that they continually press on each other, and, change their relative situations as often as the position of any piece of matter in space may change its positions. [25–26]

According to him, the planet which has been designated the Earth, is composed of at least five hollow concentric spheres, with spaces between each, an atmosphere surrounding each; and habitable as well upon the concave as the convex surface. Each of these spheres are widely open at their poles. The north polar opening of the sphere we inhabit, is believed to be about four thousand miles in diameter, and the southern above six thousand. [28]

Each of the spheres composing the earth, as well as those constituting the other planets throughout the universe, is believed to be habitable both on the inner and outer surface; and lighted and warmed according to those general laws which communicate light and heat to every part of the universe. The light may not, indeed, be so bright, nor the heat so intense, as is indicated in high northern latitudes (about where the verge is supposed to commence) by the paleness of the sun, and darkness of the sky; facts, which various navigators who have visited, those regions confirm; yet, they are no doubt sufficiently lighted and warmed to promote the propagation and support of animal and vegetable life. [35–36]

The principal aims of the great author of all things, appear to have been animation, diversity, and usefulness; and the air we breathe, the water we drink, the vegetables on which we feed; indeed every leaf and plant of the forest and field—all teem with animal life. Why then should we believe, or even presume to think, that the Almighty Fiat, which spoke matter into existence, for the support and maintenance of living creatures, innumerable and endless in the variety of their organization, their colours, their passions, and their pursuits—why I say, should we then presume, that the omnific word would create even the smallest particle of any of the immense, the innumerable orbs in the universe, of inert or useless matter, devoid of activity and design? This earth, when compared with the magnitude and number of other planets we know, is but as a point; yet we can hardly conceive, small as she appears by comparison, that she was only designed to have animate life on her surface, and all the rest to remain useless! Such an idea seems unworthy of the Divine Being, whose essence is all perfection. Can we for a moment suppose, that the interior parts of the earth, have received less attention from the Creator, than the objects which are under our immediate inspection? On the contrary, may it not be more rationally inferred, that for the object of more widely disseminating animation, spheres are formed within spheres, concentric with each other, each revolving on its own axis, and thus multiplying the habitable superficies? [125–127]

Of the many various and conflicting theories which have been advanced, relative to the form, structure, and motion of the earth, the theory of Concentric Spheres deserves to rank as one of the most important: for should it hereafter be found correct, the advantages resulting to the civilized and leaned world, must cause it to stand pre-eminent among the improvements in philosophy. The habitable superficies of our sphere would not only be nearly doubled; but the different spheres of which our earth is probably constituted, might increase the habitable surface ten-fold.

That such may be the construction of the earth, every law of matter with which I am acquainted, seems to admit, at least of the possibility; the different appearances of the other planets render it probable; and the various concurring terrestrial facts existing in the artic regions, to my mind, render such a conclusion almost certain. And further, that matter and space are never uselessly wasted, is an axiom, not only of sound philosophy, but of natural religion, and of common sense. [129–130]

Review of McBride, *American Quarterly Review*

In this critical appraisal the anonymous reviewer begins with a quick survey of the theories of the Earth up until 1827.

The earth is nearly eight thousand miles in diameter, and the deepest excavations that have been made in it, by human art, do not extend to half a mile below its surface. We are, therefore, utterly ignorant of the nature and constitution of the interior of this immense mass, and must, perhaps, for ever remain so. The subject is of too much interest, however, not to have excited the particular attention of philosophers, and, in the absence of facts, many of them have not hesitated to resort to speculation and conjecture.

Dr. Burnet, the earliest cosmogonist whose system is worthy of notice, supposed that the earth was originally a fluid, chaotic mass, composed of various substances differing in form and density. In the course of time, the heaviest portions subsided, and formed about the centre a dense and solid nucleus. The waters took their station around this body; on the surface floated an ocean of oil and unctuous matters; and the whole was surrounded by the air and other ethereal fluids. This atmosphere was at first full of impurities, being charged with particles of the earth with which it had been previously blended. By degrees however, it purified itself, by depositing these particles upon the stratum of oil; and there was thus formed a thick and solid crust of mould, which was the first habitable part of the glove. After many centuries, this crust, having been gradually dried by the heat of the sun, cracked and split asunder, so as to fall into the abyss of waters beneath it; and this great event was the universal deluge. Our present earth is composed of the remains of the first; our continents and islands being portions of the primordial crust, from which the waters have retired.

Dr. Woodward, who immediately followed Burnet in this career of speculation, supposed that the bodies which compose the earth, were all dissolved or suspended in the waters of the general deluge; and that, on the gradual retiring of the waters, these substances subsided, successively, in the order of their specific gravities; so that the earth is now formed of distinct strata, arranged in concentric layers, "like the coats of an onion."

Whiston supposed the original earth to be a comet, having, like other comets, a very eccentric orbit; and, therefore, subject to such extremes of heat and cold, as to be uninhabitable. At the period of creation described by Moses, the earth was placed in its present orbit, which is nearly circular, and was in consequence subjected to a great variety of important changes. The heavier parts of the chaotic atmosphere, by which the comet was surrounded, fell gradually upon the nucleus, and formed a great liquid abyss, on which the crust of the earth was finally deposited, and now floats. This crust, and the subterraneous fluid, are each fifty or one hundred miles in thickness; and within them lies the solid nucleus or original comet, which contains another rarer fluid, and a central load-stone. . . .

It will be observed, that all these theories agree in supposing the earth to be composed of successive shells, placed one within the other. The great astronomer Halley, also adopted the hypothesis of a sphere revolving with the earth, in order to account for the variation of the magnetic needle, and in this opinion he was followed by Euler; so that the theory of "concentric spheres," has been one of the oldest and most prevalent in geology.

The theory of the celebrated Buffon is very generally known. He supposed that the earth was struck off from the sun by a comet, and was, therefore, at first no more than an irregular mass of melted and inflamed matter. This mass, by the mutual attraction of its parts, assumed a globular figure, which in its rotary motion, caused by the obliquity of the first impulse, changed into a spheroid. The interior of the globe is, according to this theory, a vitrified mass, which the author maintains to be homogeneous, and not, as is generally thought, disposed in layers following the order of density.

These are the most remarkable theories that have been presented, on the subject of the structure of the earth. It is proper to remark, that they were the productions of men of genius and learning; that they were maintained by arguments full of plausibility, and, even now, difficult of refutation; and that they attracted great attention, and made many proselytes. Yet, such is the just destiny reserved for all extravagant and romantic speculations, that, at the present day, they have not a single advocate or believer, and are mentioned only to be condemned.

But these philosophic fancies have all been far outdone by the theory of our countryman *captain Symmes*, who, for the last nine or ten years, has been using every exertion to convince the world of its past errors, and to inculcate his own new and true theory. The newspapers have teemed with essays; circulars have been addressed to all the learned societies of Europe and America; addresses and petitions have been presented to our national and state legislatures; certificates of conviction and "adhesion" have been procured from men in high literary and political stations; the master and his disciples have traversed the whole country, from south to north, and from west to east, so that all men, in all places, might be enlightened in the truth; and, finally, the whole subject has been reduced to a regular body of doctrine, in the work now under review. [235–237]

■ *Symzonia*

Theories of the Hollow Earth

I concurred in the opinion published by Capt. Symmes, that seals, whales, and mackerel, come from the internal world through the openings at the poles; and was aware of the fact, that the nearer we approach those openings, the more abundant do we find seals and whales. I felt perfectly satisfied that I had only to find an opening in the "icy hoop," through which I could dash with my vessel, to discover a region where seals could be taken as fast as they could be stripped and cured. I therefore employed myself chiefly in procuring comforts for my people, and in studying the habits and propensities of those amphibious animals which might be supposed to have communication with the internal world, whither I was ambitious to find my way. [29–30]

When the sun has great southern declination, it is seen directly through the opening at the south pole, a little above the horizon—this gives an interval of bright light; and as the rays of heat are more refrangible than those of light, a sufficient degree of heat is experienced to ripen the most delicate fruits.

At this season, during night, the rays of the sun are reflected from the opposite rim of the polar opening, and afford so much light as to render the stars invisible. The full moon is never seen at this period; for while the sun is in south declination, the moon fulls to the north of the equator, to give light to the north polar region, and the northern internal hemisphere.

March and September are the darkest months. Both the sun and full moon are then in the equator, and shine very obliquely by refraction, into both polar openings. Yet, by reflection from side to side, they afford a faint light quite to the internal equator, where two reflected suns and moons are dimly seen at the same time. This circumstance had led the internals to suppose that there were actually duplicates of those luminaries. Their situation, it should be considered, did not admit of such observations of the celestial bodies, as were necessary to correct that error.

During this season, the planets and stars of the southern hemisphere are visible, some directly, and others by reflection. This occasions great mistakes in their astronomical calculations, which they ascribe to the aberrations of the heavenly bodies. It never occurred to them that their field of vision was a limited internal concave sphere, and a great part of their firmament noticing but a reflection of the external heavens.

When the sun is in north declination, it is not seen at all to the south; but as it then shines into the north polar opening, its influence is felt at Symzonia by a repeated reflection, and being aided both by the powerful light of the moon (which always fulls in high south declination, when the sun is near the northern tropic, and shines directly into the southern opening) and by the direct and reflected light of the planets and stars of the southern hemisphere, gives light enough for all necessary purposes. [182–184]

In the first place, [Seaborn explains to one of his crew,] we have no account of any navigator having sailed to a higher southern latitude than 71°, and 82° appears, from the most authentic accounts, to be the highest northern latitude that has been visited. Navigators to these high latitudes have always found ice between the parallels of 70° and 80°, which space that profound philosopher, John Cleve Symmes, denominates the "icy hoop." It is true he has not taken the trouble to explain to the world, in a satisfactory manner, why and wherefore this narrow strip of ice should exist in that region; which omission, I judge, must have arisen from the circumstance of its being obvious to his capacious mind, that such a "hoop" must necessarily exist, "according to the laws of matter and motion." The causes of it appearing to him perfectly simple, he could not suppose it necessary to state them to "the most enlightened people on the face of the globe." Now, sir, I will explain the matter to you. At the pole, that is, ninety degrees from the equator, there is seven months summer, without any interval of night . . . and when the sun has twenty-three and a half degrees of south declination, its rays must strike the pole, allowing but three degrees for the effect of refraction, on an angle of 26½° with the plane of the horizon, and must appear nearly as high as in Scotland in the months of March and September. It is true it does not continue at this extreme declination for any great length of time. On the other hand, it does not recede so far as to withdraw its rays from the pole for a single hour during seven months of the year. This we know; and you can imagine, from the effect of a March sun, which in your country, Mr. Slim, loosens the icy fetters of winter, although withdrawn one half of the time, what must be its effect when exerting its influence for months without any interruption? Now in latitude 70°, with the exception of a few days, there is an interval of night the year round. In the winter months the climate cannot differ much from that of the pole. The cold is then no doubt severe, and forms ice in both those positions. In the early part of summer, that is, September, October, and November, there is at the pole a steady blaze of heat and light, which must melt the ice accumulated in winter, by causing a constant thaw. This sunshine continues at the pole till the 1st of April, and prevents the forming of ice until that time. But at 70°, there is, through most of these months, a short period of night, sufficient for the atmosphere to cool. This will be more obvious, if we consider the powerful influence of the ice, during this absence of the sun's rays, and remember the great change of temperature which occurs in our climate immediately after sunset at the close of a sunny day in February or March. This interval of night in latitude 70°, counteracts most of the effects of the sun's heat in the day time. Nearly as much ice forms in the night as is thawed during the day. This accounts for the "icy hoop." There is not summer enough to dissipate the ice of winter; while at the pole there is summer enough to dissolve a globe of ice." [42–44]

The discoveries I had already made were so far from satisfying my ambition that my desire to push on and explore the internal world was more intense than ever. I was now convinced of the correctness of Capt. Symmes's theory, and of the practicability of sailing into the globe at the south pole, and of returning home by way of the north pole, if no land intervened to obstruct the passage. My first thought was to enter the river I had seen, and ascend to its source, which must necessarily be in the internal world; for if the poles were open, there was not room enough for a sufficient body of land to the south of 84 degrees, to maintain so mighty a river. But I abandoned this idea, on reflecting that by confining myself to this river, I should at best enter the internal world but a few hundred miles, while by entering on the open ocean, I should be able to visit every accessible part of it. [66]

I told [my crew] that I should proceed to the S.E. along the coast, to ascertain where was the best sealing ground to remove to when these Islands should be cleared of seals, and to discover whether the land extended a sufficient distance on the other side of the pole to open a passage for us to sail over the pole, and thus proceed to Canton by steering due north, which would save a great deal of time. This was all according to their notions of things; but I was well aware that when they would suppose we were sailing northward on the other side of the globe, we should in fact be sailing directly into it through the opening. No objections were made to this plan, as it all seemed feasible enough. [71]

First Contact

Being determined to open an immediate communication with this people, who from the comforts with which they were surrounded could not be savages, I took off my sword, and gave it to Whiffle, and ordered him to lay off with the boat a half pistol shot from the shore, and not to fire a shot, nor to show his arms, unless he saw me run, or heard me fire a pistol; in which cases be must pull into the most convenient place to take me off, and to defend me.

I then walked slowly up the jettee. When I reached the head of it, I took off my hat and made a low bow towards the building, to show the Internals that I had some sense of politeness. No one appeared. I walked slowly up the sloping lawn, stopped, looked about me, and bowed, but still no one appeared to return my civilities. I walked on, and had arrived within one hundred yards of the portico, when I recollected, that when Captain Ross was impeded in his progress northward by the northern "icy hoop," he met with some men on the ice who told him they came from the north, where there was land and an open sea. These men were swarthy, which Capt. Symmes attributes to their being inhabitants of the hot regions within the internal polar circle; in which opinion he was no doubt correct. I had frequently reflected on this circumstance, and had settled the matter in my mind that they were stragglers from the extreme north part of the internal regions; and could not but consider Capt. Ross as a very unfit person for an exploring expedition, or he would not have returned without ascertaining where those men came from, or how a great sea could exist to the northward of the "icy hoop," through fear of wintering in a climate where he saw men in existence who had passed all their lives there.

I remembered that these men so seen by Capt. Ross, saluted him by pulling their noses; and surely it is not surprising that men, inhabiting such different positions on this earth as the inside and outside of it, should differ so much as to consider that a compliment in the one place, which is deemed an insult in the other. Indeed it seemed to me a small thing, when I considered how widely the most enlightened of the externals differ in opinion upon the most simple propositions of religion, politics, and political economy.

I was full in the faith that those men of Ross had been internals, and that their mode of salutation was much more likely to be in accordance with the manners of the Symzonians, than the rude fashion of us externals. I therefore pulled my nose very gracefully, without uncovering my head.

This was a happy thought. It arose from my having read much, seen a great deal of the world, and observed with tolerable accuracy, for a shipmaster, the important ceremonies and sublime rules of etiquette, by which the distinguished and the noble, the enlightened and the great, are implicitly governed; they being considered matters of more consequence than religious forms, or mere regulations of convenience.

I remembered that, on being honored with an audience of a sublime sovereign of the Mussulman empire, it was particularly enjoined upon me by the vizier, not to take my hat off, nor to sit cross-legged, the etiquette of the court forbidding any one to do so in the presence of the sovereign; and showing the top of the head or bottom of the feet being considered an insult to that exalted personage. Happily I recalled to my mind all those weighty matters; and now, that I might not be guilty of insult to this new found people, I stood bolt upright, kept my hat on, and pulled my nose stoutly.

This had the desired effect. Several persons from within the building assembled on the platform of the portico. They stared much at me, which convinced me they were people of high fashion; conversed eagerly with one another, and seemed undetermined how to act. More than one hundred men collected, before any one showed any disposition to advance even to the front of the portico; and on the other hand, I dared not advance towards them, lest I should again put them all to flight, being already sensible that it was my dark and hideous appearance that created so much distrust amongst these beautiful natives. I therefore kept my position, occasionally pulling my nose out of politeness.

Full twenty minutes passed in this suspense; when one of the group, a man near five feet high, came to the threshold of the platform, and, raising his hand to his forehead, he brought it down to the point of his nose, and waved it gracefully in salutation, with a slight inclination of the body, but without actually pulling the nose as I had done. At the same time he spoke to me, in a soft, shrill, musical voice. His language was as unintelligible to me as the notes of a singing bird; but his mode of salutation was not. I caught it with the aptness of a monkey, returned his courtesy after his own fashion, and answered him in English, with as soft a whine as I could affect, that my rude voice might not offend his ears.

Seeing him still in doubt whether it was a mortal or a goblin that stood before him, I bethought me to show him that I had some sense of a Supreme Being. I therefore fell on my knees, with my hands and eyes upraised to heaven, in the attitude of prayer. This was distinctly understood. It produced a shout of joy, which was followed by the immediate prostration of the whole party, who seemed absorbed in devotion for a few minutes. They then rose, and the one who had first advanced came towards me. I stood still to receive him, and as he walked close up to me, I extended my hand to ascertain if a thing so fair were tangible. He put out his hand, and seized mine with a grip that made me start; but instantly let it go again, and gazed upon me.

We spoke to each other in vain: he walked round, and surveyed my person with eager curiosity. I did the like by him, and had abundant cause; for the sootiest African does not differ more from us in daintiness of skin and grossness of features, than this man did from me in fairness of complexion and delicacy of form. His arms were bare; his body was covered with a white garment, fitted to his shape, and hanging down to his knees. Upon his head he wore a tuft of feathers, curiously woven with his hair, which afforded shade to his forehead, and was a guard for his head against the rain. There was no appearance of any weapon about either him or any of the others.

Having both satisfied our eyes, I again endeavored to make myself intelligible to him; and, by the aid of signs, succeeded so far as to convince him that I came in peace, and meant no harm to any one. He pointed to the building, which I took as an invitation to go in, and walked towards the portico, with the Internal by my side.

The fair skinned people by whom I was now surrounded, kept at a respectful distance from me. They formed a circle, and sat down upon their feet, with their bodies perfectly upright, and invited me to do the same. I admired the firmness of knee and strength of muscle which enabled them to make such a posture easy and pleasant, but took my seat on the floor cross-legged, like a Turk. Several of the principal men of the party seated them-selves near me, and moved nearer and further off, as occasion required, with great facility, and without changing their sitting posture. [103–109]

Proto–Science Fiction

FLYING MACHINE

I had not been long at my study of language, when Mr. Albicore sent me word that a bird as big as the ship was coming towards us. I went on deck, and immediately saw that Albicore's bird was no other than an aerial vessel, with a number of men on board. It came directly over the ship, and descended so low that the people in it spoke with the internals who were with me; but I was not yet qualified to understand a word of what passed. I observed its appearance to be that of a ship's barge, with an inflated wind sail, in the form of a cylinder, suspended longitudinally over it, leaving a space in which were the people. It had a rudder like a fishes tail, and fins or oars, which appeared to be moved by the people within. On the whole, it was not a matter of great surprise to me. I only inferred from it, that the internals understood aerostatics much better than the externals.

I afterwards learned, that the air vessel over the boat was charged with an elastic gas, which was readily made by putting a small quantity of a very dense substance into some fluid, which disengaged a vast quantity of this light gas. By this means, the specific gravity of the vessel was diminished, in the same manner as that of a fish is by its sound. I also learned that this vessel had been despatched by the government of the country to make observations upon the stranger who had entered their waters. [113–114]

WEAPONS

This man, named Fultria, [who] invented the air vessels . . . also invented the engine of defence, the description of which was prohibited. The knowledge of its construction, and the manner of using it, was confined to a few select Good men, who were bound to secrecy by the most solemn obligations. I could obtain no other idea of it, than that it was a vast machine moved upon wheels, and rendered of but little specific gravity, by means of the apparatus employed in their air vessels, by the help of which it could, on an emergency, be raised into the air for a short time, to cross rivers or broken ground.

It was propelled by means of a great number of tubes, projecting very obliquely through the bottom near the ground, through which air was forced with such prodigious violence, that the resistance of the earth and atmosphere impelled the machine forwards: in this way it was moved with astonishing velocity. From all sides of this engine a great number of double tubes projected, through which two kinds of gas were caused to issue. These gases uniting at the extremities, produced a flame of intense heat, like that of our compound blowpipe on a large scale, which flame, according to tradition, was ejected with such force, as to consume every thing for half a mile in every direction. The interior of the machine was sufficiently capacious to admit men enough to direct its motions and prepare the gases, and also the materials and apparatus necessary to their production. [168–169]

SPEED BOAT

Here it may be well to explain the cause of the astonishing velocity of the Symzonian vessels, which enabled the one we had seen on approaching the coast to avoid us so easily. It appears that the Symzonians, in ancient times . . . devised a plan for accelerating their motion, by means of a number of tubes which perforated the after part of the vessel under water, through which air was forced with extreme violence by the agency of a curious engine, of which I could not obtain a particular description. This rush of air against the water forces the vessel forward with amazing rapidity. Every vessel going far from the coast must be furnished with one of these engines, but they are used only on emergencies. [210–211]

FABRIC

Their cloth is a beautiful substance, manufactured in a peculiar manner, by a process resembling that employed by the natives of the South Sea Islands, and not unlike our mode of making paper.

The material is found in caves and amongst the rocks of the mountains, where a species of insects, larger than our spider, produce it in great abundance. They form webs somewhat like those of spiders, but of a firmer texture, and more compactly woven. These webs have the properties of asbestos, owing probably to the insects subsisting upon that or some similar substance. The inhabitants collect them with great care, and lay them in a mould of the dimensions of the piece of cloth to be made, placing so many of them one upon another as the intended thickness of the cloth requires. This done, a fluid preparation which hardens by the influence of fire, without losing its elasticity, is poured over it. It is then pressed firmly together, and passed over a heated cylinder, which completes the operation.

This cloth is extremely convenient. Being incombustible, like asbestos, it is only necessary to pass a garment through the fire to purify it perfectly. It is also very durable; and being exquisitely white, it corresponds admirably with the delicate complexions of the people, and the mild light of the region they inhabit. [159–160]

Internals

At the end of the first week, I was astonished and delighted to find my instructors addressing me in very good English. I could not help arguing, from their wonderful quickness of intellect, and faithfulness of memory, that I should find them intelligent and refined, beyond the conception of external mortals. In this I was not disappointed. My greatest misfortune was a want of capacity to comprehend intelligence so far beyond my powers of mind. They never forgot any thing, and it was only necessary to name a thing once to fix it on their memories. The alphabet once read, and sounds pronounced, they had it perfectly, and expressed the greatest astonishment that I should require them to repeat the same names of things over five or six times, to fix them in my mind. [115]

I had indeed observed, that notwithstanding their inferiority in size, they were much stronger, and more active than the Externals. The tallest men were about five feet high, but they leaped twenty or thirty feet in a bound without much apparent exertion, and easily lifted burthens which three of our men would find it difficult to move. [136]

Utopia

To me, who had been accustomed to see a great proportion of mankind constantly devoted to hard labour, or incessantly applying to business, to obtain a precarious subsistence; to see them, not content with the efforts which might be made by day, wearing out their health and lives in toil by the midnight lamp, and scarcely obtaining what are considered the necessaries of life,—it was difficult to comprehend how a great proportion of this people [the Internals] could leave their business and their homes, to pass months in a nonproductive state, without oppressing the remainder of the people with intolerable burdens. But I was told that the Worthies [councilors] received nothing for their services, and were able to provide without difficulty for themselves: all the revenue of the country was devoted to the maintenance of the Efficients (who were paid for the time actually devoted to public affairs) and to works of public utility.

This state of things appeared to me at first to be beyond the limits of possibility in the external world. My mind was for some time occupied by reflecting upon the extraordinary difference in the *natural* condition of the internals and externals; and I commenced a comparison of the varieties and objects of industry in the two worlds, and of those necessities and habits which demanded the products of labour. This brought me to a clear view of the matter. I perceived that the greater part of the labour of the externals was devoted to the production of things useless or pernicious; and that of the things produced or acquired, the distribution, through defects in our social organization, was so unequal, that some few destroyed, without any increase of happiness to themselves, the products of the toil of multitudes. Instead of devoting our time to useful purposes, and living temperately on the wholesome gifts of Providence, like the blest internals, so as to preserve our health and strengthen our minds, thousands of us are employed in producing inebriating liquors, by the destruction of wholesome articles of food, to poison the bodies, enervate the minds, and corrupt the hearts, of our fellow beings. Other thousands waste their strength to procure stimulating weeds and narcotic substances from the extreme parts of the earth, for the purpose of exciting diseased appetites, whereby, in the case of those who possess good things, the ability to enjoy them is destroyed. Still greater numbers give their industry and their lives to the acquisition of mere matters of ornament, for the gratification of pride, an insatiable passion, which is only stimulated to increase its demands by every new indulgence. I saw that the internals owed their happiness to their rationality, to a conformity with the laws of nature and religion; and that the externals were miserable, from the indulgence of inordinate passions, and subjection to vicious propensities. [128–130]

No crowded cities, the haunts of vice and misery, hung like wens upon the lovely face of nature. An appearance of equality in the condition and enjoyments of the people pervaded the country. The buildings were all of them large enough for comfort and convenience, but none of them so large, or so charged with ornament, as to appear to have been erected as monuments of the pride and folly of the proprietor. . . .

As we passed on through this enchanting country, Surui, the eldest of my conductors, instructed me in the civil polity, customs, manners, and habits of his people. From him I learned that in Symzonia all power emanated from the people; that the affairs of the nation were directed by

1. A chief, who was honored with the title of *Best Man*, and who held his situation for life, unless impeached of crime; but whose issue was considered ineligible to the same office for one generation after his decease.
2. An ordinary council of one hundred worthies, who assembled twice in each year and oftener when circumstances made it necessary, to give advice to the Best Man.
3. A grand council of worthies, who assembled once in four years, to admit members to their body, collect the sense of the nation on all public affairs, and aid the Best Man with their judgment in the appointment of Efficients to discharge the executive duties of the state.

The Best Man could only be elected by an unanimous vote of the grand council.

The Worthies are of three orders—the GOOD, the WISE, and the USEFUL. [118–120]

That the fatal sin *cupidity*, which drove our first parents out of Paradise, is almost wholly unknown to the pure and uncontaminated Internals. They view the gifts of a bountiful Providence as an abundant supply of good things for the benefit of all, and sufficient to gratify all the rational wants of all the creatures for whom they are provided. They admire and adore the beneficence which could find pleasure in creating intelligent beings, and in providing for all their wants; and are emulous to approximate towards the spirit of love and goodness to which they are indebted for all their blessings. They are continually striving to improve themselves in this respect, by unceasing efforts to render one another, and all creatures within the sphere of their influence, happier and better; instead of exerting all their faculties, like the Externals, to gain advantages over their fellow men, to acquire the means of gratifying the worst passions of their nature, or to advance their own pleasures by rendering others miserable.

All the real wants of men in society are provided for in the most simple and natural manner. Usefulness is the test of value. That artificial wealth which exists amongst the Externals, and depends for its support upon their capricious passions, has no place with the Symzonians; our whole list of fancy articles, all our ornaments, every description of things which are only calculated to gratify pride or vanity, are considered by them as worse than useless. They wear garments because they defend the body, and are necessary to decency; but it never occurred to their simple minds, that the fairest work of an Infinite Being could be improved by trinkets and fripperies of man's device. Their judgments are not so much perverted, nor their tastes so much depraved. Therefore, having ascertained a mode of providing necessary raiment in the most convenient manner, they one and all adopted it and, by dressing alike, they maintain a perfect equality in their wants in that respect. . . .

All the divisions of labour necessary to the convenience and welfare of society, are here perfectly understood. The community is not bewildered by a voluminous and complex system of political economy, consisting of abstract principles, buried in abstract and unintelligible words, and, rendered too intricate to be understood by those who have common sense, or too inapplicable to civilized society to be adopted by those who have any sort of sense—invented by the *Wise* men of one country to mislead the politicians of another, and to depress the Good and the Useful.

Their circulating medium consists of tokens for every variety of things, and every description of services. These tokens are originally issued by the government, for services performed and articles supplied for the national benefit. One description represents one day's labour; a second, a standard measure of grain; a third, a small measure of pulse; a fourth, a given quantity of a particular fruit; a fifth, a measure of cloth, and so forth. There being a sufficient variety to represent all the articles which are in common use, they have all the advantages of exchange, without the trouble of delivery when the things are not wanted for actual consumption.

When, by any circumstances, the supply of any particular article in any district falls short of the demand to such a degree, that the tokens will not command what they represent, it is the business of the government to draw from the more fruitful districts a sufficiency to equalize the value, either by direct purchase, or by requiring the contributions of the fruitful districts in kind, and sending the articles to the place of scarcity, or by receiving the contributions of the district in which scarcity prevails, in tokens, and thus raising their value, or by both these operations in extreme cases.

Commerce is practised only for the common convenience of society. The accumulation of wealth, and indulgence in luxury, being disreputable, and a bar to admission to the distinguished orders, an overreaching and avaricious spirit is not generated by traffic, as in the external world, but every operation of trade and transfer is performed on the most reasonable terms, which will enable him who performs it to live upon an equality with his fellow-men.

All contributions are required directly from the people, that every one may know the full extent of his proportion of the expense of government. Every man under the age of one hundred years, is rated at the same amount, unless he have young children; in which case the tax is reduced in proportion to the number of such children, according to a graduated scale. This tax is so light that nothing but a criminal want of industry or frugality can hinder any one from paying it.

The whole revenue of government requires no more than one or two days labour of each man per annum; and as the government exists for the sole purpose of preserving the freedom of the citizens, in the pursuit of happiness, and the enjoyment of all those privileges and immunities which are compatible with the well-being of society, all are equally indebted for its benefits. Property being altogether a matter of secondary consideration, is not considered a proper object of taxation. In case of an accumulation of good things in the hands of an individual, beyond his wants, the surplus is in general voluntarily devoted by him to the use and benefit of his fellow-beings, in some shape or other, for the promotion of his own happiness. Doing good is here considered as the highest of earthly gratifications. When a man is more than one hundred years of age, he is considered to have performed his full share of public service, and to be entitled to exemption for the remainder of his days. [157–164]

Origins of Life on Earth

Most of the people, seeing the happy condition of the Worthies, and being extremely desirous to partake of the refined enjoyments of the grand assemblage, strove earnestly to become deserving of a place among them; but some, giving way to their carnal appetites and passions, fell into intemperate indulgences, whereby they produced disease to their bodies, and a necessity for much labour to supply their unreasonable consumption, and at the same time an aversion to the performance of the labour which is necessary to the preservation of health; that the constant exhortations and efforts of the Worthy were found insufficient to restrain some of the youth from forming such pernicious habits, so that before they were sufficiently taught by experience and the examples before them, that to be good is to be happy, they degenerated into vice. This too often led to crime. To support their wastefulness, they infringed the rights of others. When such men became, in the opinions of the select worthies, incorrigible and dangerous to society, they were transported to a land far distant to the north, the extreme limit of the world, where a part of the year the heat is intense. There they continue in their vicious course, pursuing the gratification of their sensual appetites, and are punished with diseases of body which enervate their faculties, inordinate passions which torture their minds, and fierce desires which are incapable of being satisfied.—The influence of their gross appetites and of the climate, causes them to lose their fairness of complexion and beauty of form and feature. They become dark coloured, ill favoured, and mis-shapen men, not much superior to the brute creation. They retain, indeed, said Surui, some of the customs and manners of Symzonia; and the ceremony of pulling the nose in salutation by those who had strayed to the "icy hoop," and were seen by Captain Ross, of whom I had spoken, was no doubt a corruption of the graceful mode of salutation practised where I then was. On my first appearance, they had apprehended that I was of that outcast race; for it had been observed by those who had conveyed delinquents to the place of exile, that the descendants of the outcasts were enlarged in stature and size, owing to the grossness of their habits, and at the same time that they had lost their strength and activity. One of the pure race, it was believed, was able to lift three times as much as any one of the degenerates, or to leap three times as high. Their suspicions of my being of the outcast tribe, were allayed by the testimony of reverence to the Supreme Being which I had given, by falling on my knees, and imploring the aid of heaven in my embarrassed situation; whereby they knew that I could not be unworthy of their regard.

I felt not a little humbled by this account of the origin of the northern internal people, and cautiously avoided any observation that might discover, to my intelligent conductor, the suspicion which darted through my mind, that we the externals were indeed descendants of this exiled race; some of whom, penetrating the "icy hoop" near the continent of Asia or America, might have peopled the external world. The gross sensuality, intemperate passions, and beastly habits of the externals, all testified against us.

I inquired of Surui where this place of exile was situated. He said it was at the extreme northern part of the earth, as near the fountain of light and heat as mortals could go, without danger of perishing by fire: that they could only visit it in the temperate season, because during the rest of the year, the sun was seen directly over head, when the heat was so great as to render existence extremely painful. By this account I knew that the place of exile must be situated somewhere on the verge of the rim of the north polar opening, as there and there only, could the sun be seen directly over head, without going to the external tropic. [131–134]

Gender

The women of Symzonia are not regarded as inferior in intellectual capacity, or in moral worth, to the other sex. The female character is there respected, for the qualities of the female mind are developed and employed. Their personal beauty exceeds my powers of description, I can liken their complexion to nothing but alabaster slightly tinged with rose. . . .

The domestic duties of the Symzonian women are very simple, pleasing, and easily performed. To prepare the frugal family meal requires no roasting heat, nor black array of pots, kettles, spits, and gridirons. The little culinary preparation which vegetables and fruits require, is neatly and conveniently done in silver vessels; for silver is abundant, and well adapted for utensils for household use. To arrange their basins of milk and honey, and set out their baskets of fruit for a family united in esteem and love, is a pleasurable exercise.

The preparation of clothing for a people of such simple habits requires comparatively little labour. The garden occupies a portion of their time, but the greater part is devoted to the instruction of their children, the improvement of their own minds, religion, and social intercourse. [184–186]

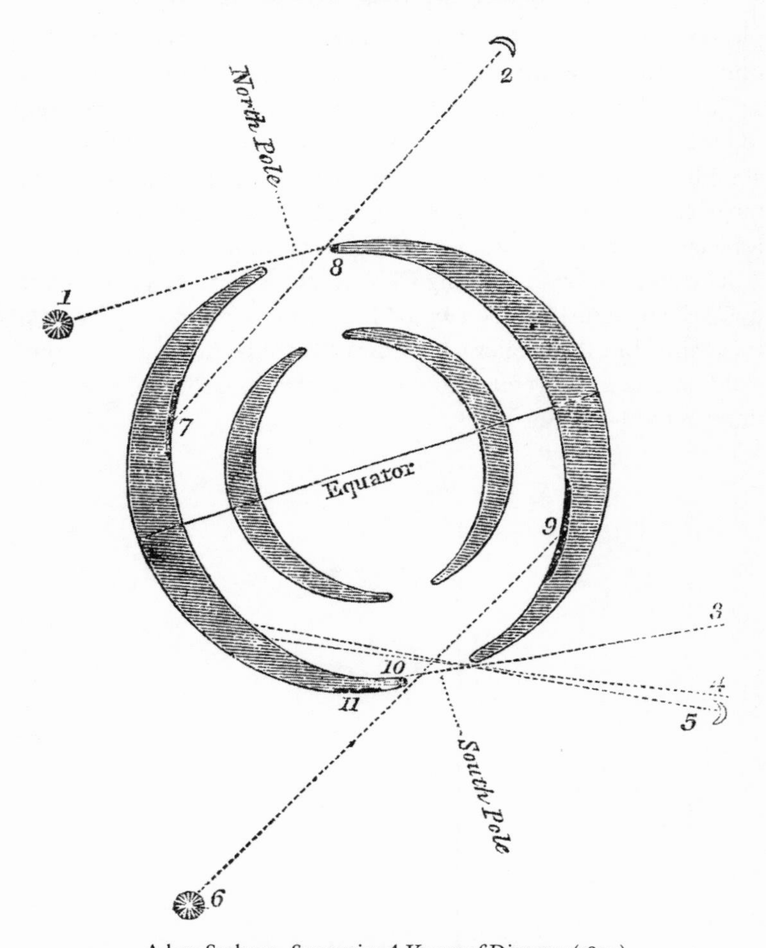

Adam Seaborn, *Symzonia: A Voyage of Discovery* (1820)
"I declare the earth is hollow, and habitable within; containing a number of solid concentrick spheres, one within the other, and that it is open at the poles twelve or sixteen degrees; I pledge my life in support of this truth, and am ready to explore the hollow, if the world will support and aid me in the undertaking" (Symmes, *Declaration*, ix). Note that this drawing of the subterranean world of Symzonia does not correspond to Symmes's original theory: the inner world contains only a single "concentrick sphere."

Collin de Plancy *Voyage au centre de la terre* (1821)

Jacques Collin de Plancy (1794–1881) was a prolific author, compiler and translator, whose 179 published works are today completely forgotten, with one singular exception, the *Infernal Dictionary* (1818).[1] His life is usually divided into two parts, marked by his very public conversion to Christianity in 1841. Before that he was known as an "anti-clerical, anti-monastic, anti-feudal writer" (Roudaut, *Fonds*, 12).

The *Voyage au centre de la terre* is almost completely forgotten today, but, along with *Symzonia*, it is the most complete attempt to explain and defend the existence of an interior world. It begins with an explicit reference to Symmes and includes apparent borrowings from Holberg's *Niels Klim* and from the theories of Halley and Mather.[2] The novel begins when a fishing boat catches fire off Greenland. The story is told by one of the survivors, as some of the crew fight off marauding polar bears and then land on the island of Spitzberg. After they set up camp on the frozen island, a party of six strikes off in search of game. Pushing ever further north, the countryside grows warmer and greener, until they eventually reach the polar mountains, where they are violently sucked into the underworld by a whirlwind. Unable to move, they are fixed to the ground: the globe on which they have landed is magnetized. They free themselves by removing all traces of metal, including the nails in their shoes. (This magnetism will become significant later.)[3]

Once inside the Earth, they meet a number of different peoples who vary in color and size, from the Alburians, who are about two feet tall, to the people of Sanor, who are closer to three and a half feet tall; skin colors range from olive-green through white and dark brown. Although the origins of these subterranean peoples (not to mention their physical differences) are never explained, they can trace their history back at least seven thousand years, and they have had the printing press for fifteen hundred years.

The travels of the European visitors take them to four of the forty-six countries of the underworld, where, in each case, they might be said to wear out their welcome. These countries offer a number of utopian features, but like Klim's adventures in Potu, the Europeans' habits and ways of doing things (as well as their restlessness) lead them into trouble. As a utopian work, the novel lacks consistency, particularly in terms of the contradictions to be found in the various societies. It is not so much that each society is a mixture of good and bad qualities, but that the utopian features of each are often contradicted by some other aspect of that society. As in Holberg's novel (but here even more so), utopia and social satire are gradually overwhelmed by the fantastic adventure story.

The European visitors first encounter a tribe of forest-dwelling nomadic "little green men"[4] who believe that the Earthmen are demons sent to torment them. Moving closer to civilization—both in terms of beliefs and in terms of agriculture—as they approach the center,[5] the Europeans encounter a first utopian society, that of Albur with its farms and cities, inhabited by white-skinned humans only slightly taller than the first tribe. This kingdom is the largest of the interior world: 120 leagues (360 miles) long and 75 leagues (225 miles) wide. There are 415 cities, with many towns, hamlets, and farms, and almost 45 million inhabitants (2:67).[6] The city of Silone impresses them with its architectural harmony and grace, for the streets have been laid out symmetrically, while the houses are "tasteful and elegant" and well maintained: "each is four stories high and about twenty feet wide," with light-yellow walls and green roofs (2:53). At the center of each city is a pyramid inscribed with the precepts of the Alburians' religion: "Such a pure and simple morality astonished us. We had been told so often that a natural religion could not exist, and here it was, at the core of a wise, well-regulated society whose customs were simpler and better observed that in any country we had ever seen!" (2:108).[7]

The modest citizens of this peaceful, hereditary monarchy are vegetarians (much to the chagrin of the six Europeans), for the Alburians believe it wrong to "take away life which God as given the animals as well as to animals" (2:100).[8] The Alburians dress modestly and uniformly, in colors and styles according to their occupations. There are scant laws or courts and no prisons, and the only duty of the few priests is to "preach clemency and forgiveness, love of country, social virtues and obedience to the law" (2:110). This is indeed a utopia, but the six travelers become bored with its uniformity of life. Told that they will be taken to the capital in a month's time to meet the king, they resolve to make a brief visit to the neighboring island empire of Sanor, whose inhabitants do eat meat.

The Sanorliens are taller, about three and a half feet tall—and the women are taller and more attractive than the men. As the narrator observes: "This is the most beautiful of the countries of the little globe. There are many feasts, and wealth and pleasure are allowed, as in every despotic country where there must be pleasures for the oppressed people to make up for the loss of liberty" (2:143). Here the city displays little of the planned uniformity of Silone, and the streets contain palaces and ostentatious public buildings. Morals and customs are also much looser, and everyone but the narrator becomes involved with and soon marries a Sanorlian woman. But this leads to various complications, and they are forced to flee for their lives.

They return to Silone and are then taken to the capital of Albur for the scheduled meeting with its monarch. But after a few months, their restlessness—as well as their craving for meat—has returned: when they secretly kill and eat some wild boars, they are expelled from the country. The next country they visit is the land of the Banois, who sing rather than talk (like Casanova's Megamicres). One day, listening to an account of the Banois religion, they realize that the report of the prophet Burma's miraculous ascent into the heavens suggests a way to return to the upper world: every few years, some of the prophet's followers climb to the top of a sacred mountain in the quest to attain heaven. At the mountaintop, after the priests have fitted them with special helmets, the faithful are lifted into the sky. The European visitors suppose that these helmets are magnetic and are thus attracted to the iron mountains of the polar regions of the upper Earth. Accordingly, they have helmets made for themselves and, rising into the sky, find themselves at the South Pole after seven years in the underworld.

The remarkable features of this novel include the attempt to represent literally Halley's hypothesis that magnetic variations in compass readings can be explained if the Earth is considered as a hollow globe with a second, inner globe. (Cotton Mather argued for Halley's ideas in *The Christian Philosopher*; see chapter 1). In fact, Collin de Plancy's descriptions of the inner world seem much closer to Halley's theories than do, for instance, the descriptions of the inner world in *Symzonia*, especially when compared to the "theory of concentric spheres" as explicated in John Symmes's writings. (And yet this novel is far less "realistic" than *Symzonia*.) At the same time, while Halley suggests that the inner Earth may be inhabited, he does not go into any details; as Cotton Mather put it, "We have dug as far as 'tis fit any *Conjecture* should carry us!" Here is Halley's conjecture:

> It must be allowed indeed, that these included Globes can be of very little service to the Inhabitants of this outward World; nor can the Sun be serviceable to them, either with his Light or Heat: But since we see all the parts of the Creation abound with animate Beings, why should we think it strange that the prodigious Mass of Matter, whereof this Globe does consist, should be capable of some other Improvements, than barely to serve to support its Surface?

SELECTIONS

If America was thought to be a fable and a heresy, until the moment when Columbus's three ships had landed on this foreign land, one can assume that the existence of a planet at the center of our earth will only be acknowledged when we will have established colonies there. . . . There were numerous derisive comments a few years ago when an American announced that he wanted to go to the North pole to find a great opening through which he hoped to reach the center of the globe in search of habitable lands. This project was in no way ridiculous, and the success of the voyage that we are publishing here proves it. And one day this American will return from his expedition to explain to sceptical Europeans that one should not judge too lightly matters that they know little about.

In 1818, a German scientist (Steinhauser) announced in the *Halle Literary Gazette* that he had made a discovery which seemed to confirm the ideas of the American. To explain the "magnetic variations" in [compass directions], Steinhauser claims that inside our globe, at a depth of about one-hundred and seventy miles, there is a smaller globe, which revolves around the center of the globe, from west to east, every four-hundred and forty years. It is the magnetism of this smaller globe which is responsible for the variations in the [north-south poles of the compass]. [1:vi–viii]

■ How They Get There

Our hair stood on end as we realized that we stood on the edge of a bottomless chasm . . . but before we could react, we were carried off by a whirlwind; and although we were still conscious, it was only to realize that we were being plunged into the depths of the earth. . . . From the moment that an overpowering force began to pull us into the bowels of the earth, we thought that we were falling into a dark, bottomless pit. We were surprised then to perceive a faint, seemingly endless light, although at first our terror did not permit us to observe the path that we were following . . . when suddenly we crashed sideways into some rocks. [183–185]

■ The Nature of the Inner World

Here is what I think [says Clairancy, one of the six survivors]. The earth, whose surface is inhabited by humans, has a circumference of nine-thousand leagues and is only 50 or one-hundred leagues thick.[9] Its interior is hollow . . . and in its center, there is another, smaller planet whose core is a magnet. . . . The masses of iron at the two poles attract equally the magnetic vapours from this interior planet, holding it in equilibrium. . . . As for the light, it is also the result of these magnetic vapours which ascend through the openings at the pole and reflect the light of the sun [into the inner Earth]. [1:196–198]

To avoid keeping the reader in doubt any longer, I will explain now what we learned later: that Clairancy's theories were fairly accurate. This planet inside the earth has a diameter of 800 leagues.[10] It is covered in top-soil, except at the poles which are of solid lodestone. . . . Its sky is the reflection of the light which shines through the polar openings and is reflected off the underside of our earth. [1:199–200]

■ Inside the Earth

[The underground world] is divided into forty-six different states: fifteen kingdoms, six empires, eleven republics, all for the most part under a single ruler, and fourteen countries still in a barbarian phase with no real government. This globe is traversed by seas and rivers, strewn with lakes and ponds, and covered with forests, just like our own. [3:137]

[The Alburians] were about twenty-two inches tall and a man who is two feet tall is thought handsome. The women are proportionate to the men . . . about eighteen inches tall. They have regular and attractive features, and the women in particular have skin with a dazzling brightness. The men have beards and moustaches, and let their grow long. They are mostly blonds, although a few have light brown hair, but there is rarely anyone with darker hair than that, and there are no red-heads. They dress somewhat like the ancient Greeks, in tunics with high boots and bare legs and without hats. . . . The women dress more or less the same, although their tunics cover their legs to the ankles. . . . [Since] the children were only about a foot high, they appeared to us as living puppets. [2:49–51]

[The Sanorliens] were about three and a half feet tall. Their features were regular but less attractive than those of the Alburians. . . . [T]heir clothing was quite rich, and their hair was perfumed. [2:139]

Each people has customs which accord with their ways of thinking and feeling . . . Thus the Alburians say hello with their hand on their hearts because they give primacy to feelings, while the Banois say hello by taking off their hats, because they give primacy to the head. [2:111]

■ Their Return

The Felinois have been ascending into the sky for four thousand years. We hear of pygmies who lived in the days of Ancient Greece and who were only one and a half feet tall. Perhaps some of the Felinois appeared in some of the countries of our world. . . . More recently, we have heard of little men hiding in the forests . . . and of little men living near the poles . . . while the cabbalists have written of gnomes. Saint Anthony supposedly met one in the desert . . . while Leloyer writes somewhere of meeting two little men in the north . . . who claimed to be from the polar regions. . . . It is thus reasonable to suppose that these pygmies, as well as demons of the mines and the gnomes of the Cabbala are in fact some Felinois who arrived thinking that they were going to Heaven. [3:168–170]

The [specially made] headgear fit us perfectly. The helmets were wide and round, and flat on top, while the inside was well-cushioned. In addition to a strong copper chin-strap, lined with cloth. . . . [S]trong cords ran from this magnetic helmet and could be attached under the arms and legs, and beneath our feet, to support equally the weight of our bodies. [3:186]

As soon as [I came out of the cave] the magnetic vapours took over. . . . I barely had time to see the crowds on their knees and to hear the sound of the musical instruments when an overwhelming force took hold of me like a flash of lightning. But I was so completely attached to the magnetic helmet and my weight was so evenly distributed that I felt no discomfort. I don't know how long I rose in this fashion, but I lost sight of the globe less than a minute after leaving it, and I moved gently upward as if I were in a boat, despite the speed with which I was being drawn to the pole.

I would have given myself over to the wonder and pleasure at this gentle ascent, but those feelings were mixed with fear of crashing into the polar mountains. . . . I cannot describe the relief and joy I felt when I saw in front of me, like a high barricade, the walls of the polar opening. This was followed by some violent shocks and then I was beyond the polar mountain. A mortal fear gripped me that I was rising beyond the surface of the earth. "Good God!" I thought, "where am I going? Could I really be on the way to the paradise of the prophet Burma?" But this fear quickly receded. The power of the magnetic vapours, having lifted me above the iron mountain, now brought me back, head first! And I found myself stopped with a jolt, in a very uncomfortable position. The flat part of my helmet was attached to the iron rocks, and as a result, I was upside down, my feet and body in the air. [3:189–192]

Edgar Allan Poe and "The Narrative of Arthur Gordon Pym" (1838)

Edgar Allan Poe refers to the hollow Earth, and especially to the possibility of polar openings in several of his stories, while also making reference to *Peter Wilkins*, *Klim*, and Athanasius Kircher.[1] But perhaps the most important reason for including Poe's writing in this collection is the link—via Jeremiah Reynolds—between Symmes and Poe. As Kafton-Minkel reminds us, not only did Poe keep calling for "Reynolds" in his delirium as he lay dying, but in the same issue of the *Southern Literary Messenger* in which the first installment of "The Narrative of A. Gordon Pym" was published, there was an article by Poe "praising Reynolds's speech promoting Antarctic exploration before the House of representatives in 1836" (Kafton-Minkel, *Subterranean Worlds,* 250). In "The Narrative of A. Gordon Pym," the narrator commends Reynolds for his "great exertions and perseverance [which] have at length succeeded in getting set on foot a national expedition, partly for the purpose of exploring these regions" (*Tales and Poems*, 3:157).[2]

"The Narrative of A. Gordon Pym," set in the year 1828, recounts a series of misadventures (shipwrecks, mutiny) Pym experiences on various sailing ships until finally he and another sailor are rescued and taken on board the *Jane Guy*, whose captain is trying to penetrate "to a high southern latitude" if weather and seas permit. Beyond the Kerguelen Islands, they discover an island populated by black "savages." Amplifying the familiar racism of this association of dark skin with treachery and ignorance, the islanders are terrified of anything white: "It was quite evident that they had never before seen any of the white race—from whose complexion, indeed, they appeared to recoil" (chapter 18). The sight of a white handkerchief or the carcass of a strange white animal sends them into a panic, and in fact there is nothing white anywhere on their island.

Pretending to befriend Captain Guy and his crew, the islanders lure the expeditionary force inland and then trigger an avalanche, which buries everyone but Pym and his friend Peters. Pym and Peters take refuge in a cave, where they discover some hieroglyphs that provide the reader clues regarding the fear of whiteness observed in the islanders. Although Pym dismisses these marks as only "the work of nature" rather than as writing (chapter 23), the note at the end of the novella, explaining that Pym's narrative is unfinished, also includes a discussion of these "singular figures," which bear some resemblance to ancient human writing—a combination here of Ethiopian, Egyptian, and Arabic. As the note observes, "the chain of connection" is not complete, but it suggests a connection between whiteness—in the birds and the strange animal that so frightens the "savages"—and the "shrouded human figure" that appears at the end. Pym's account breaks off on the "verge" of Symmes's hole, as their small boat rushes toward the abyss in the final sentences of this unfinished narrative:

> And now we rushed into the embraces of the cataract, where a chasm threw itself open to receive us. But there arose in our pathway a shrouded human figure, very far larger in its proportions than any dweller among men. And the hue of the skin of the figure was of the perfect whiteness of the snow.

While there are is no explicit naming of the inner Earth nor any explanation of the shrouded giant, there are indications of some other race. The islanders' canoe, for instance, was constructed from "the bark of a tree unknown":

> [It differed] vastly in shape from those of any other inhabitants of the Southern Ocean with whom civilized nations are acquainted. We never did believe them the workmanship of the ignorant islanders who owned them; and some days after this period discov-

ered, by questioning our captive, that they were in fact made by the natives of a group to the southwest of the country where we found them, having fallen accidentally into the hands of our barbarians. (*Tales and Poems*, 3:220)

Another story that calls attention, however obliquely, to Symmes can be found in "The Unparalleled Adventure of one Hans Pfall." When the hero passes over the North Pole in a balloon, he seems to detect a hole:

> [The sheet of unbroken ice] is very sensibly flattened, farther on depressed into a plane, and finally, becoming *not a little concave*, it terminates, at the Pole itself, in a circular centre, sharply defined, whose apparent diameter subtended at the balloon an angle of about sixty-five seconds, and whose dusky hue, varying in intensity, was, at all times, darker than any other spot upon the visible blackness. Farther than this, little could be ascertained. (*Tales and Poems*, 2:48; italics in text)

This particular version of the polar opening is visually represented in archaic maps, as Poe indicates in a note at the end of another of his stories:

> The "Ms. found in a Bottle," was originally published in 1831, and it was not until many years afterward that I became acquainted with the maps of Mercator, in which the ocean is represented as rushing, by four mouths into the (northern) Polar Gulf, to be absorbed into the bowels of the earth; the pole itself being represented by a black rock, towering to a prodigious height. (*Tales and Poems*, 1:215)[3]

Finally, in the "Descent into the Maelstrom," the narrator speculates on previous attempts to explain the "phenomenon" of the whirlpool. In reviewing the different theories, he mentions that "Kircher and others imagine that in the centre of the channel of maelstrom is an abyss penetrating the globe, and issuing in some very remote part" (1:222–223). While Poe did not write a hollow-Earth fiction per se, these references reveal both an awareness of the theme and, in the case of "Pym," a story whose ending has prompted endless speculation about what lies beyond the abyss.[4]

SELECTIONS

■ Reynolds

In the November following [1773, Captain Cook] renewed his search in the Antarctic. . . . In latitude 71 degrees 10', longitude 106 degrees 54' W., the navigators were stopped, as before, by an immense frozen expanse, which filled the whole area of the southern horizon. The northern edge of this expanse was ragged and broken, so firmly wedged together as to be utterly impassable, and extending about a mile to the southward. Behind it the frozen surface was comparatively smooth for some distance, until terminated in the extreme background by gigantic ranges of ice mountains, the one towering above the other. Captain Cook concluded that this vast field reached the southern pole or was joined to a continent. Mr. J. N. Reynolds, whose great exertions and perseverance have at length succeeded in getting set on foot a national expedition, partly for the purpose of exploring these regions, thus speaks of the attempt of the *Resolution*. "We are not surprised that Captain Cook was unable to go beyond 71 degrees 10', but we are astonished that he did attain that point on the meridian of 106 degrees 54' west longitude. Palmer's Land lies south of the Shetland, latitude sixty-four degrees, and tends to the southward and westward farther than any navigator has yet penetrated. Cook was standing for this land when his progress was arrested by the ice; which, we apprehend, must always be the case in that point, and so early in the season as the sixth of January—and we should not be surprised if a portion of the icy mountains described was attached to the main body of Palmer's Land, or to some other portions of land lying farther to the southward and westward." [3:156–157]

Warmer at the Pole

We had now advanced to the southward more than eight degrees farther than any previous navigators, and the sea still lay perfectly open before us. We found, too, that the variation uniformly decreased as we proceeded, and, what was still more surprising, that the temperature of the air, and latterly of the water, became milder. The weather might even be called pleasant, and we had a steady but very gentle breeze always from some northern point of the compass. The sky was usually clear, with now and then a slight appearance of thin vapour in the southern horizon—this, however, was invariably of brief duration. . . . So tempting an opportunity of solving the great problem in regard to an Antarctic continent had never yet been afforded to man, and I confess that I felt myself bursting with indignation at the timid and ill-timed suggestions of our commander. I believe, indeed, that what I could not refrain from saying to him on this head had the effect of inducing him to push on. While, therefore, I cannot but lament the most unfortunate and bloody events which immediately arose from my advice, I must still be allowed to feel some degree of gratification at having been instrumental, however remotely, in opening to the eye of science one of the most intensely exciting secrets which has ever engrossed its attention. [3:166–167]

[Later they find the carcass of "a singular-looking land-animal"] three feet in length, and but six inches in height, with four very short legs, the feet armed with long claws of a brilliant scarlet, and resembling coral in substance. The body was covered with a straight silky hair, perfectly white. The tail was peaked like that of a rat, and about a foot and a half long. The head resembled a cat's, with the exception of the ears—these were flapped like the ears of a dog. The *teeth* were of the same brilliant scarlet as the claws. [3:168–169]

■ Approaching the Verge

March 1st. Many unusual phenomena now indicated that we were entering upon a region of novelty and wonder. A high range of light grey vapor appeared constantly in the southern horizon, flaring up occasionally in lofty streaks, now darting from east to west, now from west to east, and again presenting a level and uniform summit—in short, having all the wild variations of the Aurora Borealis. The average height of this vapor, as apparent from our station, was about twenty-five degrees. The temperature of the sea seemed to be increasing momentarily, and there was a very perceptible alteration in its colour. [3:221]

March 21st. A sullen darkness now hovered above us—but from out the milky depths of the ocean a luminous glare arose, and stole up along the bulwarks of the boat. We were nearly overwhelmed by the white ashy shower which settled upon us and upon the canoe, but melted into the water as it fell. The summit of the cataract was utterly lost in the dimness and the distance. Yet we were evidently approaching it with a hideous velocity. At intervals there were visible in it wide, yawning, but momentary rents, and from out these rents, within which was a chaos of flitting and indistinct images, there came rushing and mighty, but soundless winds, tearing up the enkindled ocean in their course.

March 22d. The darkness had materially increased, relieved only by the glare of the water thrown back from the white curtain before us. Many gigantic and pallidly white birds flew continuously now from beyond the veil, and their scream was the eternal *Tekeli-li!* as they retreated from our vision. Hereupon Nu-Nu stirred in the bottom of the boat, but upon touching him we found his spirit departed. And now we rushed into the embraces of the cataract, where a chasm threw itself open to receive us. But there arose in our pathway a shrouded human figure, very far larger in its proportions than any dweller among men. And the hue of the skin of the figure was of the perfect whiteness of the snow. [3:224–225]

12

Jules Verne *Voyage au centre de la terre* (1864)

Jules Verne's *Voyage au centre de la terre* (1864) is the best-known fiction set inside the Earth and one that, thanks to Verne's penchant for some scientific basis for his "voyages," follows the familiar pattern of scientific exposition and plausibility. Moreover, as has often been pointed out, Professor Liedenbrock, along with his nephew Axel—the narrator—and their Icelandic guide, Hans, are following in the tracks of a sixteenth-century savant and explorer, Arne Saknussemm (who was persecuted for heresy, and whose books were burned). Liedenbrock discovers a strange manuscript with an encrypted message that sets them off on their voyage of discovery: "Descend, bold traveler, into the crater of the jokul of Sneffels, which the shadow of Scartaris touches before the kalends of July, and you will attain the centre of the earth; which I have done, Arne Saknussemm" (chapter 4).[1]

Following these indications they travel to Iceland and then descend into the crater of the extinct Sneffel volcano. Their diagonal descent takes over a month and brings them to a depth of 30 leagues (90 miles); 45 days after they entering the crater, they find themselves in an immense cavern, at the edge of vast subterranean sea, which is illuminated by some unknown electrical phenomenon (Axel compares it to the aurora borealis). Crossing the sea on a raft, they witness a battle between two prehistoric sea monsters, an ichthyosaurus and a plesiosaurus (chapter 33). After more than a week at sea (and some 270 leagues = 800 miles), they are caught in a storm; days later, they find themselves on a beach with most of their provisions and supplies. There, on the shores of the of what the professor has named the Liedenbrock sea, they come across "a vast plain of bleached bones":

> It seemed like an immense cemetery, where the remains of twenty ages mingled their dust together. Huge mounds of bony fragments rose stage after stage in the distance. They undulated away to the limits of the horizon, and melted in the distance in a faint haze. There within three square miles were accumulated the materials for a complete history of the animal life of ages, a history scarcely outlined in the too recent strata of the inhabited world. (chapter 37)

And then, on the outskirts of a vast forest, they see a herd of mastodons followed by a giant shepherd.

> In stature he was at least twelve feet high. His head, huge and unshapely as a buffalo's, was half hidden in the thick and tangled growth of his unkempt hair. It most resembled the mane of the primitive elephant. In his hand he wielded with ease an enormous bough, a staff worthy of this shepherd of the geologic period. (chapter 39)

But this is only a glimpse, for they flee in fear; and afterward Axel doubts what he has seen.[2] Finally, at the shores of the sea, they find traces of Arne Saknussemm's passage—at the entrance to a tunnel that leads down further into the Earth. But the tunnel is blocked by an enormous boulder, which they try to blast out of the way. They waited at a safe distance on their raft, but the explosion "caused a kind of earthquake in this fissured and abysmal region," opening a great gulf into which the sea now rushes (chapter 41). Sucked down a tunnel, they suddenly reverse direction, and they are shot out of the Stromboli volcano near Sicily.

Arthur Evans has examined the question of Verne's influences and sources and, in this context, his penchant for citing contemporary scientists, as seen in Axel and Liedenbrock's ongoing argument about the theories of Sir Humphry Davy and the composition of the Earth.[3] Moreover, at one point the narrator "remembered the theory of an English captain, who likened the earth to a vast hollow sphere, in the interior of which the air became luminous because of the vast pressure that weighed upon it" (chapter 29). This could be a reference to Symmes; Arthur Evans traces it to Alexandre Dumas.[4] In fact, as Evans points out, it is an explicit reference to Symmes in the *Voyages et aventures du capitaine Hatteras*, where

> Verne's scientist Dr. Clawbonny explains to the crew of the British ship *Forward* during their voyage toward the north pole: "Finally, it has recently been claimed that, at the poles, there was an immense opening, which was the source of the lights of the aurora borealis, and by which one could penetrate into the interior of the world. Then, inside this hollow sphere, it was imagined that there existed two planets, Pluto and Proserpine, and that the air was luminous because of the strong pressure exerted on it."
>
> "They said all that?" asked Altamont.
>
> "And wrote about it, and very seriously. Captain Synness [*sic*], one of our countrymen, even proposed to Humphry Davy, Humboldt, and Arago that they attempt an expedition. But these scientists refused." (Evans, "Literary Intertexts," 172–173)

On the question of influence, Pierre Citron first dismisses three often-cited subterranean novels that are not really set inside the earth: the *Relation*, *Lamékis*, and Tyssot de Patot's *La vie, les aventures et le voyage de Groenland du Réverend Père Cordelier Pierre de Mésange*. He then examines the likelihood that Verne knew three other subterranean fictions: *Klim*, *L'Icosameron*, and Collin de Plancy's *Voyage au centre de la terre*, deciding that Verne did not know any of these works. Although these works are traditional utopias, "Verne was a *scientific* writer, not a *utopian* one" ("Sur quelques voyages," 69). Moreover, as utopias, these three works describe inner worlds populated with intelligent beings, while in Verne's novel there is only a fleeting glimpse of a prehistoric shepherd with his flock of mammoths. Furthermore, "Unlike the other works, there is no contact between the explorers and the inhabitants." Indeed, as Citron reminds us, this episode was added later. In the same vein, these works are set inside the Earth, whereas Verne, following his scientific approach, limits his explorers to the Earth's crust. I suggest that it is precisely the difference in approaches that might allow one to argue the contrary—that those differences demonstrate that Verne could have known them but wanted to avoid their unscientific excesses. As for Collin de Plancy's work, Citron also argues that if Verne had know of it, he would not have used the same title.[5]

Following Verne's concern for plausibility, the manner of getting into and out of the Earth's center seems fairly familiar: they enter through an extinct volcano and are shot out through an active one. Within the Earth, they seem to be inside a vast cavern within the earth's crust, although the maximum depth they reach is almost thirty-five leagues (105 miles), while, as Axel points out, the Earth's crust is about sixteen leagues (or 25 miles) thick.[6]

The most interesting speculation in the novel lies in the descriptions of the flora and fauna of the underworld, along with speculations that they date from an earlier period in the Earth's past and have somehow been preserved without change and without responding to their environs (in opposition to Darwin's accounts of diversity in the Galapagos, for instance, in *Origin of the Species* [1859]). Liedenbrock speculates that they had fallen into the underworld in some cataclysmic event in the distant past:

> If you ask me how he came there, how those strata on which he lay slipped down into this enormous hollow in the globe, I confess I cannot answer that question. No doubt in the post-tertiary period considerable commotions were still disturbing the crust of the earth. The long-continued cooling of the globe produced chasms, fissures, clefts, and faults, into which, very probably, portions of the upper earth may have fallen. (chapter 38)

But, as the title of Edgar Rice Burroughs's novel about a land of prehistoric creatures puts it, this is "the land that time forgot"—somehow these creatures have been exempted from the changes that have affected the inhabitants of the upper Earth, although, at twelve feet tall, these hominids certainly seem to have grown.

SELECTIONS

■ The Inner World

A vast sheet of water, the commencement of a lake or an ocean, spread far away beyond the range of the eye, reminding me forcibly of that open sea which drew from Xenophon's ten thousand Greeks, after their long retreat, the simultaneous cry, "*Thalatta! thalatta!*" the sea! the sea! The deeply indented shore was lined with a breadth of fine shining sand, softly lapped by the waves, and strewn with the small shells which had been inhabited by the first of created beings. The waves broke on this shore with the hollow echoing murmur peculiar to vast enclosed spaces. A light foam flew over the waves before the breath of a moderate breeze, and some of the spray fell upon my face. On this slightly inclining shore, about a hundred fathoms from the limit of the waves, came down the foot of a huge wall of vast cliffs, which rose majestically to an enormous height. Some of these, dividing the beach with their sharp spurs, formed capes and promontories, worn away by the ceaseless action of the surf. Farther on the eye discerned their massive outline sharply defined against the hazy distant horizon. It was truly an ocean, with the irregular shores of earth, but deserted and frightfully wild in appearance. If my eyes were able to range afar over this great sea, it was because a peculiar light brought to view every detail of it. It was not the light of the sun, with its dazzling shafts of brightness and the splendor of its rays; nor was it the pale and uncertain shimmer of the moonbeams, the dim reflection of a nobler body of light. No. The illuminating power of this light, its trembling diffusiveness, its bright, clear whiteness, and its low temperature, showed that it must be of electric origin. It was like an aurora borealis, a continuous cosmical phenomenon, filling a cavern of sufficient extent to contain an ocean.

The vault that spanned the space above, the sky, if it could be called so, seemed composed of vast plains of cloud, shifting and variable vapors, which by their condensation must at certain times fall in torrents of rain. I should have thought that under so powerful a pressure of the atmosphere there could be no evaporation; and yet, under a law unknown to me, there were broad tracts of vapor suspended in the air. . . . The play of the electric light produced singular effects upon the upper strata of cloud. Deep shadows reposed upon their lower wreaths; and often, between two separated fields of cloud, there glided down a ray of unspeakable lustre. But it was not solar light, and there was no heat. The general effect was sad, supremely melancholy. Instead of the shining firmament, spangled with its innumerable stars, shining singly or in clusters, I felt that all these subdued and shaded lights were ribbed in by vast walls of granite, which seemed to overpower me with their weight, and that all this space, great as it was, would not be enough for the march of the humblest of satellites.

Then I remembered the theory of an English captain, who likened the earth to a vast hollow sphere, in the interior of which the air became luminous because of the vast pressure that weighed upon it; while two stars, Pluto and Proserpine, rolled within upon the circuit of their mysterious orbits.

We were in reality shut up inside an immeasurable excavation. Its width could not be estimated, since the shore ran widening as far as eye could reach, nor could its length, for the dim horizon bounded the new. As for its height, it must have been several leagues. Where this vault rested upon its granite base no eye could tell; but there was a cloud hanging far above, the height of which we estimated at 12,000 feet, a greater height than that of any terrestrial vapor, and no doubt due to the great density of the air.

The word cavern does not convey any idea of this immense space; words of human tongue are inadequate to describe the discoveries of him who ventures into the deep abysses of earth.

Besides I could not tell upon what geological theory to account for the existence of such an excavation. Had the cooling of the globe produced it? I knew of celebrated caverns from the descriptions of travelers, but had never heard of any of such dimensions as this. [chapter 30]

■ The Bone Yard

"Yes," he pursued with animation, "this is a fossil man, the contemporary of the mastodons whose remains fill this amphitheatre. But if you ask me how he came there, how those strata on which he lay slipped down into this enormous hollow in the globe, I confess I cannot answer that question. No doubt in the post-tertiary period considerable commotions were still disturbing the crust of the earth. The long-continued cooling of the globe produced chasms, fissures, clefts, and faults, into which, very probably, portions of the upper earth may have fallen. I make no rash assertions; but there is the man surrounded by his own works, by hatchets, by flint arrow-heads, which are the characteristics of the stone age. And unless he came here, like myself, as a tourist on a visit and as a pioneer of science, I can entertain no doubt of the authenticity of his remote origin." [chapter 38]

In fact it was a wonderful spectacle, that of these generations of men and animals commingled in a common cemetery. Then one very serious question arose presently which we scarcely dared to suggest. Had all those creatures slid through a great fissure in the crust of the earth, down to the shores of the Liedenbrock sea, when they were dead and turning to dust, or had they lived and grown and died here in this subterranean world under a false sky, just like inhabitants of the upper earth? Until the present time we had seen alive only marine monsters and fishes. Might not some living man, some native of the abyss, be yet a wanderer below on this desert strand? [chapter 38]

■ Flora and Fauna

Here was the vegetation of the tertiary period in its fullest blaze of magnificence. Tall palms, belonging to species no longer living, splendid palmacites, firs, yews, cypress trees, thujas, representatives of the conifers were linked together by a tangled network of long climbing plants. A soft carpet of moss and hepaticas luxuriously clothed the soil. A few sparkling streams ran almost in silence under what would have been the shade of the trees, but that there was no shadow. On their banks grew tree-ferns similar to those we grow in hothouses. But a remarkable feature was the total absence of color in all those trees, shrubs, and plants, growing without the life-giving heat and light of the sun. Everything seemed mixed-up and confounded in one uniform silver grey or light brown tint like that of fading and faded leaves. Not a green leaf anywhere, and the flowers—which were abundant enough in the tertiary period, which first gave birth to flowers—looked like brown-paper flowers, without color or scent. [chapter 39]

I am trying to recall the peculiar instincts of the monsters of the preadamite world, who, coming next in succession after the mollusks, the crustaceans and le fishes, preceded the animals of mammalian race upon the earth. The world then belonged to reptiles. Those monsters held the mastery in the seas of the secondary period. They possessed a perfect organization, gigantic proportions, prodigious strength. The saurians of our day, the alligators and the crocodiles, are but feeble reproductions of their forefathers of primitive ages.

I shudder as I recall these monsters to my remembrance. No human eye has ever beheld them living. They burdened this earth a thousand ages before man appeared, but their fossil remains, found in the argillaceous limestone called by the English the lias, have enabled their colossal structure to be perfectly built up again and anatomically ascertained.

I saw at the Hamburg museum the skeleton of one of these creatures thirty feet in length. Am I then fated—I, a denizen of earth—to be placed face to face with these representatives of long extinct families? No; surely it cannot be! Yet the deep marks of conical teeth upon the iron pick are certainly those of the crocodile.

My eyes are fearfully bent upon the sea. I dread to see one of these monsters darting forth from its submarine caverns. I suppose Professor Liedenbrock was of my opinion too, and even shared my fears, for after having examined the pick, his eyes traversed the ocean from side to side. What a very bad notion that was of his, I thought to myself, to take soundings just here! He has disturbed some monstrous beast in its remote den, and if we are not attacked on our voyage. . . . "There's a whale, a whale!" cried the Professor. "I can see its great fins. See how he is throwing out air and water through his blowers."

And in fact two liquid columns were rising to a considerable height above the sea. We stood amazed, thunderstruck, at the presence of such a herd of marine monsters. They were of supernatural dimensions; the smallest of them would have crunched our raft, crew and all, at one snap of its huge jaws.

Hans wants to tack to get away from this dangerous neighborhood; but he sees on the other hand enemies not less terrible; a tortoise forty feet long, and a serpent of thirty, lifting its fearful head and gleaming eyes above the flood.

Flight was out of the question now. The reptiles rose; they wheeled around our little raft with a rapidity greater than that of express trains. They described around us gradually narrowing circles. I took up my rifle. But what could a ball do against the scaly armor with which these enormous beasts were clad?

We stood dumb with fear. They approach us close: on one side the crocodile, on the other the serpent. The remainder of the sea monsters have disappeared. I prepare to fire. Hans stops me by a gesture. The two monsters pass within a hundred and fifty yards of the raft, and hurl themselves the one upon the other, with a fury which prevents them from seeing us.

At three hundred yards from us the battle was fought. We could distinctly observe the two monsters engaged in deadly conflict. But it now seems to me as if the other animals were taking part in the fray—the porpoise, the whale, the lizard, the tortoise. Every moment I seem to see one or other of them. . . . "The first of those monsters has a porpoise's snout, a lizard's head, a crocodile's teeth; and hence our mistake [his uncle exclaims]. It is the ichthyosaurus (the fish lizard), the most terrible of the ancient monsters of the deep. . . . The other is a plesiosaurus (almost lizard), a serpent, armored with the carapace and the paddles of a turtle; he is the dreadful enemy of the other."

Two monsters only were creating all this commotion; and before my eyes are two reptiles of the primitive world. I can distinguish the eye of the ichthyosaurus glowing like a red-hot coal, and as large as a man's head. Nature has endowed it with an optical apparatus of extreme power, and capable of resisting the pressure of the great volume of water in the depths it inhabits. It has been appropriately called the saurian whale, for it has both the swiftness and the rapid movements of this monster of our own day. This one is not less than a hundred feet long, and I can judge of its size when it sweeps over the waters the vertical coils of its tail. Its jaw is enormous, and according to naturalists it is armed with no less than one hundred and eighty-two teeth.

The plesiosaurus, a serpent with a cylindrical body and a short tail, has four flappers or paddles to act like oars. Its body is entirely covered with a thick armor of scales, and its neck, as flexible as a swan's, rises thirty feet above the waves.

Those huge creatures attacked each other with the greatest animosity. They heaved around them liquid mountains, which rolled even to our raft and rocked it perilously. Twenty times we were near capsizing. Hissings of prodigious force are heard. The two beasts are fast locked together; I cannot distinguish the one from the other. The probable rage of the conqueror inspires us with intense fear.

One hour, two hours, pass away. The struggle continues with unabated ferocity. The combatants alternately approach and recede from our raft. We remain motionless, ready to fire. Suddenly the ichthyosaurus and the plesiosaurus disappear below, leaving a whirlpool eddying in the water. Several minutes pass by while the fight goes on under water.

All at once an enormous head is darted up, the head of the plesiosaurus. The monster is wounded to death. I no longer see his scaly armor. Only his long neck shoots up, drops again, coils and uncoils, droops, lashes the waters like a gigantic whip, and writhes like a worm that you tread on. The water is splashed for a long way around. The spray almost blinds us. But soon the reptile's agony draws to an end; its movements become fainter, its contortions cease to be so violent, and the long serpentine form lies a lifeless log on the laboring deep.

As for the ichthyosaurus—has he returned to his submarine cavern? or will he reappear on the surface of the sea? [chapter 33]

The diffused light revealed the smallest object in the dense and distant thickets. I had thought I saw—no! I did see, with my own eyes, vast colossal forms moving amongst the trees. They were gigantic animals; it was a herd of mastodons—not fossil remains, but living and resembling those the bones of which were found in the marshes of Ohio in 1801. I saw those huge elephants whose long, flexible trunks were grouting and turning up the soil under the trees like a legion of serpents. I could hear the crashing noise of their long ivory tusks boring into the old decaying trunks. The boughs cracked, and the leaves torn away by cartloads went down the cavernous throats of the vast brutes. [chapter 39]

At a distance of a quarter of a mile, leaning against the trunk of a gigantic kauri, stood a human being, the Proteus of those subterranean regions, a new son of Neptune, watching this countless herd of mastodons. . . . Yes, truly, huger still himself. It was no longer a fossil being like him whose dried remains we had easily lifted up in the field of bones; it was a giant, able to control those monsters. In stature he was at least twelve feet high. His head, huge and unshapely as a buffalo's, was half hidden in the thick and tangled growth of his unkempt hair. It most resembled the mane of the primitive elephant. In his hand he wielded with ease an enormous bough, a staff worthy of this shepherd of the geologic period.

We stood petrified and speechless with amazement. But he might see us! We must fly! "Come, do come!" I said to my uncle, who for once allowed himself to be persuaded. In another quarter of an hour our nimble heels had carried us beyond the reach of this horrible monster. And yet, now that I can reflect quietly, now that my spirit has grown calm again, now that months have slipped by since this strange and supernatural meeting, what am I to think? what am I to believe? I must conclude that it was impossible that our senses had been deceived, that our eyes did not see what we supposed they saw. No human being lives in this subterranean world; no generation of men dwells in those inferior caverns of the globe, unknown to and unconnected with the inhabitants of its surface. It is absurd to believe it!

I had rather admit that it may have been some animal whose structure resembled the human, some ape or baboon of the early geological ages, some protopitheca, or some mesopitheca, some early or middle ape like that discovered by Mr. Lartet in the bone cave of Sansau. But this creature surpassed in stature all the measurements known in modern paleontology. But that a man, a living man, and therefore whole generations doubtless besides, should be buried there in the bowels of the earth, is impossible.

However, we had left behind us the luminous forest, dumb with astonishment, overwhelmed and struck down with a terror which amounted to stupefaction. We kept running on for fear the horrible monster might be on our track. It was a flight, a fall, like that fearful pulling and dragging which is peculiar to nightmare. Instinctively we got back to the Liedenbrock sea, and I cannot say into what vagaries my mind would not have carried me but for a circumstance which brought me back to practical matters. [chapter 39]

13 After Verne: Later Developments

Jules Verne's account of a descent into the Earth gained for this motif a much wider audience among the general public, as well as a certain legitimacy, particularly since his explorers restricted themselves to the Earth's crust. Still, the scientific focus of this narrative certainly did not mean that later uses of this setting would respect Verne's own concern for plausibility or scientific fact. In this final chapter, I want to review four of the best-known novels published over the following fifty years that used a subterranean setting, partly to show the continuity of many of the themes and concerns that have emerged in earlier works, but also to see how little plausibility and scientific fact actually count for when it comes to choosing a setting, as these works move further and further from plausibility and scientific fact. They are: a utopia set in the Earth's crust, Edward Bulwer-Lytton's *The Coming Race* (1871); another utopia set inside the hollow Earth, Mary Lane's *Mizora* (1890); an adventure story with utopian overtones that reprises and defends many of Symmes's ideas without ever mentioning him, Willis George Emerson's *The Smoky God* (1908); and finally, the first of what would be a series of five novels set inside the Earth, Edgar Rice Burroughs's *At the Earth's Core* (1914).

The Coming Race

Edward George Bulwer-Lytton was a British novelist and poet (1803–1873) known for his historical novels, particularly *The Last*

Days of Pompeii (1834) and *Rienzi* (1835), and for the utopian novel *The Coming Race* (1871).[1]

In *The Coming Race*, the hero and a friend are descending into a deep chasm when their rope breaks, trapping him and killing his friend (whose body is devoured by a "monstrous reptile"). In the underworld, he discovers "a vast valley, which presented to my astonished eye the unmistakable evidences of art and culture." This land is the home to an ancient race of advanced beings—the Vril-ya—who fled the upper Earth millennia before and who are almost certainly descended from frogs (although now they resemble humans). This race has by now achieved an egalitarian society of social harmony, which is the result of "the intensity of their earlier struggles against obstacles in nature" (chapter 15).

What is memorable about this novel is not so much the utopian society itself, but the author's application of some of Darwin's ideas about evolution and the struggle for survival to the question of the emergence of human intelligence and the better society, and the focusing of this long evolutionary process of racial improvement in the figure of the vril force, a power through which, by actions "akin to those ascribed to mesmerism, electro-biology, odic force, &c., but applied scientifically, through vril conductors, [this race] can exercise influence over minds, and bodies, animal and vegetable" (chapter 7). The vril force also gives the Vril-ya the ability to fly using artificial wings, and it makes a formidable weapon, through which the Vril-ya have maintained their supremacy over the millions of "primeval savages who dwell in the most desolate and remote recesses of uncultivated nature, unacquainted with other light than that they obtain from volcanic fires, and contented to grope their way in the dark, as do many creeping, crawling and flying things" (chapter 7). Their superiority is marked not only by their physical strength and longevity, but also by their vegetarianism: "'For many generations,' said my host, with a sort of contempt and horror, 'these primitive forefathers are said to have degraded their rank and shortened their lives by eating the flesh of animals'" (chapter 9).[2]

The superiority of the Vril-ya and especially their awareness of this superiority, as well as their disdain for the other, less advanced races of the underworld, make for a very ambiguous utopia. The author's attitudes toward the Vril-ya seem contradictory, for he both admires and fears this advanced underground race, which, as the title suggests, will eventually supplant our own:

> [O]ur race, therefore, even before the discovery of vril . . . [was] driven from . . . the world you come from, in order to perfect our condition and attain to the purest elimination of our species by the severity of the struggles our forefathers underwent; and . . . *when our education shall become finally completed, we are destined to return to the upper world, and supplant all the inferior races now existing therein.* (chapter 15; my italics)

The other races—including our own—are doomed to extinction.

Interestingly enough, this attitude is repeated in the depiction of gender and the role of women, presenting a very ambiguous resolution of the issue of what the narrator calls "the Rights of Women": instead of gender equality, or the role reversal of Lesuire's Viragos, or the all-women society of Mizora, here the women retain most of the so-called feminine virtues, particularly the emotions, "a more loving disposition," and the like. Yet, at the same time, women are stronger then men, and they take the lead in courtship.

> Among this people there can be no doubt about the rights of women, because . . . the Gy [female], physically speaking, is bigger and stronger than the An [male]; and her will being also more resolute than his, and will being essential to the direction of the vril force, she can bring to bear upon him, more potently than he on herself, the mystical agency which art can extract from the occult properties of nature. (chapter 26)[3]

When one of the Vril-ya women falls in love with the narrator, a love that means his certain death, she offers to help him escape, carrying him in her arms up "through the terrible chasm" and back to the mine.

Although this world is seemingly boundless, for there are more than a million Vril-ya communities and untold millions of "savages," it is somehow contained in the Earth's crust. Yet, as with the much smaller caverns of the Gnome people in *L'aventurier françois,* for instance, the lighting is completely artificial. Indeed the Vril-ya are superior to other subterranean races precisely because those others are "unacquainted with other light than that they obtain from volcanic fires" (chapter 7). Vril-ya society includes a "Light-preserving Council," while the husband of the host family is the "chief Administrator of the Lighting Department."

Their advanced civilization includes—in addition to the awesome power of the vril—the illumination of the vast farms, the parks, and the more than one million communities of the Vril-ya. They have also developed a number of advanced technologies and mechanical devices, most notably the "air boats" and the ever-present robots ("automata") that carry out many domestic tasks: "Machinery is employed to an inconceivable extent in all the operations of labour within and without doors, and it is the unceasing object of the department charged with its administration to extend its efficiency" (chapter 9).

In addition to the evolutionary speculation and the vril force, the improbabilities of this inner world lie in the vision of millions and millions of people living inside the Earth's crust in caverns so vast that contact between the many Vril-ya communities is maintained by airboats, while this enormous underground world is fully illuminated twenty-four hours a day! "They have a great horror of perfect darkness, and their lights are never wholly extinguished" (chapter 17). Finally, like so many of his predecessors, Bulwer-Lytton also makes the argument that the inner world is inhabited since God is not wasteful: "Wherever the All-Good builds . . . there, be sure, He places inhabitants. He loves not empty dwellings" (chapter 11).

Mizora

I have been thus explicit in detailing the circumstances of my entrance into the land of Mizora, or, in other words, the interior of the earth. . . . It does seem a little astonishing that a woman should have fallen by accident, and without intention or desire, upon a discovery that explorers and scientists had for years searched for in vain.

—Mary Lane, *Mizora*

It is sometimes forgotten that the utopian society of women Mary Lane depicts in her 1890 novel *Mizora* is set in the "inner world." As with so many of the works we have seen, the novel begins with a shipwreck in the "Northern Seas," from which the heroine is rescued by "Esquimaux." She sets off alone to sail south but is caught in a whirlpool, and after hours in a "semi-stupor, born of exhaustion and terror," she finds herself in a beautiful, "enchanted country" in the interior of the Earth. Although the author explicitly refers to the society as set inside a "hollow sphere, bounded North and South by impassable oceans" (25), the setting is of little importance, and there is little description of the subterranean world as a whole.[4]

There are, however, some rather vague descriptions of the illumination of the inner world. Six months of the year, the primary source of daylight is the reflection and amplification of the rays of our sun, while, during the winter months, light is provided by the aurora borealis, which is caused by the meeting of the "two great electric currents of the Earth, the one on its surface, and the one known to the inhabitants of Mizora" (25).

Mizora is a world now inhabited only by "lovely blond women," their female ancestors having long ago learned the "secret of life" and thereupon having decided to "let the race [of men] die out" (103). Moreover, the racism implicit in *Symzonia*, for instance, is in Lane's utopia explicit: "We believe that the highest excellence of moral and mental character is alone attainable by a fair race. The elements of evil belong to the dark race" (92).

When the heroine desires to return to her own country, she is accompanied by one of the Mizoran women, who takes her in a motorized boat against the current and out to the upper world. As this return suggests, the novel is not very concerned with the essentials of the interior world, and I shall cite only the description of their light.

The Smoky God

As opposed to writers who use the inner Earth as the setting for an adventure or a utopia, Willis George Emerson's *The Smoky God or A Voyage to the Inner World* (1908) is a book written by someone who believes in the hollow Earth. It begins with a preface in which the author wonders "whether it is possible that the world's geography is incomplete, and that the startling narrative of Olaf Jansen is predicated upon demonstrable facts." Indeed, the novel is larded with footnotes to accounts of polar explorers and sailors, as well as to books of mythology and anthropology—but there is no reference to Symmes nor to any other book dealing with the hollow Earth.

Olaf Jansen is the author's ninety-five-year-old Norwegian neighbor, who, after some hesitation, tells him of his incredible adventure seventy-five years earlier. Before beginning Olaf's story, the author "indulges in one or two reflections" about some recent geographical speculation that there might be "a land inside the earth." He informs the reader that he is but the "humble instrument" for Olaf Jansen's "startling announcement" that "the world was created by the Great Architect of the Universe, so that man might dwell upon its *inside* surface, which has ever since been the habitation of the *chosen*" (1).[5]

Olaf's narrative begins with a fishing trip he made in 1829 along the coast of Franz Josef Land in the Arctic, when his father tells him of a legend "that still farther northward was a land more beautiful than any that mortal man had ever known, and that it was inhabited by the *Chosen*." They set out to find this land and, after a terrible storm, find themselves on a calm sea under a smoky red sun. In fact, they have sailed over the verge into the inner world, where they encounter a "Pleasure Excursion" ship filled with singing giants:

> [A] huge ship [was] gliding down the river directly toward us. Those aboard were singing in one mighty chorus that, echoing from bank to bank, sounded like a thousand voices, filling the whole universe with quivering melody. The accompaniment was played on stringed instruments not unlike our harps. It was a larger ship than any we had ever seen, and was differently constructed. (chapter 3)

This electric boat is filled with happy twelve-foot-tall men who take them to the city of Jehu, and later they are taken on an electric monorail to the capital city, Eden. There is only a brief description of the giants' society: this is not a utopia, but the description of paradise. Olaf and his father spend several years visiting the country, but the descriptions focus almost entirely on the interior flora and fauna, all of which are many times larger than our own—from giant trees and plants to colossal tortoises and elephants. After two and a half years, they decide to return, "to cast our fortunes once more upon the sea, and endeavor to regain the *outside* surface of the earth" (chapter 4).

Buffeted by contrary winds, his father decides that they will have to sail out at the South Pole. Later, "among the ice-packs," his father is killed by a falling iceberg. After Olaf is rescued and returns home, his story leads to his confinement in a mental institution, where he remained for twenty-eight "long, tedious, frightful years of suffering!" (1).

There is little description of the society or of the structure of the inner world. Since they did sail there, they must be on the inner surface of the Earth's crust; and they do refer to the sun—the "smoky god" of the title—as a "planet." It is also interesting to find again the notion of the inner Earth as the original site of the Garden of Eden, a point emphasized here by the discovery that "the language of the people of the Inner World is much like the Sanskrit" (chapter 3).

At the Earth's Core

The first of Edgar Rice Burroughs's novels set inside the Earth opens when the narrator comes across David Innes in the midst of the Sahara Desert. Innes and an inventor friend have built a "mechanical subterranean prospector" with which they set out to explore the depths of the Earth. They lose control of their machine, and it plunges out of control into the depths. After passing through hot and cold layers and reaching a depth of five hundred miles, they break through into open air. At first they think that their machine has turned and taken them back to the Earth's surface, but they soon discover that they are at the Earth's core.[6]

Now begins a series of adventures with prehistoric dinosaurs and "manlike creatures" with tails and prehensile feet. These "ape-things" are at war with the gorillalike Sagoths, who in turn have enslaved a race of wild, primitive humans; and we soon meet the cruel and most powerful race of Pellucidar, the winged, reptilian Mahars. Burroughs continues with the sort of improbable and all too familiar tale of love and adventure for which he is famous. Like the fantastic and impossible world of Mars in his Barsoom novels, the descent into subterranean world of Pellucidar is a descent into complete fantasy, the twentieth-century equivalent of the Chevalier de Mouhy's *Lamékis*. Still, it is fascinating to see just how this motif or setting has evolved over two hundred years, and the novel does herald a new method of exploring and penetrating the underworld—one that has resurfaced in some popular films (for example, *Deep Core*, directed by Rodney McDonald [2000]).

SELECTIONS FROM *The Coming Race*

■ The Arrival

When I recovered my senses I saw my companion an inanimate mass beside me, life utterly extinct. While I was bending over his corpse in grief and horror, I heard close at hand a strange sound between a snort and a hiss; and turning instinctively to the quarter from which it came, I saw emerging from a dark fissure in the rock a vast and terrible head, with open jaws and dull, ghastly, hungry eyes—the head of a monstrous reptile resembling that of the crocodile or alligator, but infinitely larger than the largest creature of that kind I had ever beheld in my travels. I started to my feet and fled down the valley at my utmost speed. I stopped at last, ashamed of my panic and my flight, and returned to the spot on which I had left the body of my friend. It was gone; doubtless the monster had already drawn it into its den and devoured it. The rope and the grappling-hooks still lay where they had fallen, but they afforded me no chance of return; it was impossible to re-attach them to the rock above, and the sides of the rock were too sheer and smooth for human steps to clamber. I was alone in this strange world, amidst the bowels of the earth. [chapter 2]

Slowly and cautiously I went my solitary way down the lamplit road and towards the large building I have described. The road itself seemed like a great Alpine pass, skirting rocky mountains of which the one through whose chasm I had descended formed a link. Deep below to the left lay a vast valley, which presented to my astonished eye the unmistakable evidences of art and culture. There were fields covered with a strange vegetation, similar to none I have seen above the earth; the colour of it not green, but rather of a dull and leaden hue or of a golden red. There were lakes and rivulets which seemed to have been curved into artificial banks; some of pure water, others that shone like pools of naphtha. At my right hand, ravines and defiles opened amidst the rocks, with passes between, evidently constructed by art, and bordered by trees resembling, for the most part, gigantic ferns, with exquisite varieties of feathery foliage, and stems like those of the palm-tree. Others were more like the cane-plant, but taller, bearing large clusters of flowers. Others, again, had the form of enormous fungi, with short thick stems supporting a wide dome-like roof, from which either rose or drooped long slender branches. The whole scene behind, before, and beside me far as the eye could reach, was brilliant with innumerable lamps. The world without a sun was bright and warm as an Italian landscape at noon, but the air less oppressive, the heat softer. Nor was the scene before me void of signs of habitation. I could distinguish at a distance, whether on the banks of the lake or rivulet, or half-way upon eminences, embedded amidst the vegetation, buildings that must surely be the homes of men. I could even discover, though far off, forms that appeared to me human moving amidst the landscape. As I paused to gaze, I saw to the right, gliding quickly through the air, what appeared a small boat, impelled by sails shaped like wings. It soon passed out of sight, descending amidst the shades of a forest. Right above me there was no sky, but only a cavernous roof. This roof grew higher and higher at the distance of the landscapes beyond, till it became imperceptible, as an atmosphere of haze formed itself beneath. [chapter 3]

■ The Vril-ya

My eyes opened upon a group of silent forms, seated around me in the gravity and quietude of Orientals—all more or less like the first stranger; the same mantling wings, the same fashion of garment, the same sphinx-like faces, with the deep dark eyes and red man's colour; above all, the same type of race—a race akin to man's, but infinitely stronger of form and grandeur of aspect—and inspiring the same unutterable feeling of dread. Yet each countenance was mild and tranquil, and even kindly in expression. And, strangely enough, it seemed to me that in this very calm and benignity consisted the secret of the dread which the countenances inspired. They seemed as void of the lines and shadows which care and sorrow, and passion and sin, leave upon the faces of men, as are the faces of sculptured gods, or as, in the eyes of Christian mourners, seem the peaceful brows of the dead. [chapter 5]

I learned from Zee, who had more lore in all matters than any male with whom I was brought into familiar converse, that the superiority of the Vril-ya was supposed to have originated in the intensity of their earlier struggles against obstacles in nature amidst the localities in which they had first settled. "Wherever . . . goes on that early process in the history of civilisation, by which life is made a struggle, in which the individual has to put forth all his powers to compete with his fellow, we invariably find this result—viz., since in the competition a vast number must perish, nature selects for preservation only the strongest specimens. With our race, therefore, even before the discovery of vril, only the highest organisations were preserved; and there is among our ancient books a legend, once popularly believed, that we were driven from a region that seems to denote the world you come from, in order to perfect our condition and attain to the purest elimination of our species by the severity of the struggles our forefathers underwent; and that, when our education shall become finally completed, we are destined to return to the upper world, and supplant all the inferior races now existing therein." [chapter 15]

■ Robots

There were several curious-looking pieces of mechanism scattered about, apparently models, such as might be seen in the study of any professional mechanician. Four automata (mechanical contrivances which, with these people, answer the ordinary purposes of domestic service) stood phantom-like at each angle in the wall. [chapter 5]

In all service, whether in or out of doors, they make great use of automaton figures, which are so ingenious, and so pliant to the operations of vril, that they actually seem gifted with reason. It was scarcely possible to distinguish the figures I beheld, apparently guiding or superintending the rapid movements of vast engines, from human forms endowed with thought. [chapter 18]

A figure in a simpler garb than that of my guide, but of similar fashion, was standing motionless near the threshold. My guide touched it twice with his staff, and it put itself into a rapid and gliding movement, skimming noiselessly over the floor. Gazing on it, I then saw that it was no living form, but a mechanical automaton. [chapter 4]

■ Flying

But my attention was soon diverted from these nether landscapes. Suddenly there arose, as from the streets below, a burst of joyous music; then a winged form soared into the space; another as if in chase of the first, another and another; others after others, till the crowd grew thick and the number countless. But how to describe the fantastic grace of these forms in their undulating movements! . . .

I turned my gaze on my host in a feverish wonder. I ventured to place my hand on the large wings that lay folded on his breast, and in doing so a slight shock as of electricity passed through me. I recoiled in fear; my host smiled, and as if courteously to gratify my curiosity, slowly expanded his pinions. I observed that his garment beneath them became dilated as a bladder that fills with air. The arms seemed to slide into the wings, and in another moment he had launched himself into the luminous atmosphere, and hovered there, still, and with outspread wings, as an eagle that basks in the sun. Then, rapidly as an eagle swoops, he rushed downwards into the midst of one of the groups, skimming through the midst, and as suddenly again soaring aloft. Thereon, three forms, in one of which I thought to recognise my host's daughter, detached themselves from the rest, and followed him as a bird sportively follows a bird. My eyes, dazzled with the lights and bewildered by the throngs, ceased to distinguish the gyrations and evolutions of these winged playmates, till presently my host re-emerged from the crowd and alighted at my side. [chapter 5]

These wings, as I before said, are very large, reaching to the knee, and in repose thrown back so as to form a very graceful mantle. They are composed from the feathers of a gigantic bird that abounds in the rocky heights of the country—the colour mostly white, but sometimes with reddish streaks. They are fastened round the shoulders with light but strong springs of steel; and, when expanded, the arms slide through loops for that purpose, forming, as it were, a stout central membrane. As the arms are raised, a tubular lining beneath the vest or tunic becomes, by mechanical contrivance inflated with air, increased or diminished at will by the movement of the arms, and serving to buoy the whole form as on bladders. The wings and the balloon-like apparatus are highly charged with vril; and when the body is thus wafted upward, it seems to become singularly lightened of its weight. I found it easy enough to soar from the ground; indeed, when the wings were spread it was scarcely possible not to soar, but then came the difficulty and the danger. I utterly failed in the power to use and direct the pinions, though I am considered among my own race unusually alert and ready in bodily exercises, and am a very practiced swimmer. I could only make the most confused and blundering efforts at flight. I was the servant of the wings; the wings were not my servants—they were beyond my control; and when by a violent strain of muscle, and, I must fairly own, in that abnormal strength which is given by excessive fright, I curbed their gyrations and brought them near to the body, it seemed as if I lost the sustaining power stored in them and the connecting bladders, as when the air is let out of a balloon, and found myself precipitated again to the earth; saved, indeed, by some spasmodic flutterings, from being dashed to pieces, but not saved from the bruises and the stun of a heavy fall. I would, however, have persevered in my attempts, but for the advice or the commands of the scientific Zee, who had benevolently accompanied my flutterings, and, indeed, on the last occasion, flying just under me, received my form as it fell on her own expanded wings, and preserved me from breaking my head on the roof of the pyramid from which we had ascended. [chapter 20]

■ Vril

I should call it electricity, except that it comprehends in its manifold branches other forces of nature, to which, in our scientific nomenclature, differing names are assigned, such as magnetism, galvanism, &c. These people consider that in vril they have arrived at the unity in natural energetic agencies, which has been conjectured by many philosophers above ground, and which Faraday thus intimates under the more cautious term of correlation. . . . These subterranean philosophers assert that by one operation of vril, which Faraday would perhaps call "atmospheric magnetism," they can influence the variations of temperature—in plain words, the weather; that by operations, akin to those ascribed to mesmerism, electro-biology, odic force, &c., but applied scientifically, through vril conductors, they can exercise influence over minds, and bodies animal and vegetable, to an extent not surpassed in the romances of our mystics. [chapter 7]

[Vril] is capable of being raised and disciplined into the mightiest agency over all forms of matter, animate or inanimate. It can destroy like the flash of lightning; yet, differently applied, it can replenish or invigorate life, heal, and preserve, and on it they chiefly rely for the cure of disease, or rather for enabling the physical organisation to reestablish the due equilibrium of its natural powers, and thereby to cure itself. By this agency they rend way through the most solid substances, and open valleys for culture through the rocks of their subterranean wilderness. From it they extract the light which supplies their lamps, finding it steadier, softer, and healthier than the other inflammable materials they had formerly used.

But the effects of the alleged discovery of the means to direct the more terrible force of vril were chiefly remarkable in their influence upon social polity. As these effects became familiarly known and skillfully administered, war between the vril-discoverers ceased, for they brought the art of destruction to such perfection as to annul all superiority in numbers, discipline, or military skill. The fire lodged in the hollow of a rod directed by the hand of a child could shatter the strongest fortress, or cleave its burning way from the van to the rear of an embattled host. If army met army, and both had command of this agency, it could be but to the annihilation of each. The age of war was therefore gone, but with the cessation of war other effects bearing upon the social state soon became apparent. Man was so completely at the mercy of man, each whom he encountered being able, if so willing, to slay him on the instant, that all notions of government by force gradually vanished from political systems and forms of law. It is only by force that vast communities, dispersed through great distances of space, can be kept together; but now there was no longer either the necessity of self-preservation or the pride of aggrandisement to make one state desire to preponderate in population over another. [chapter 9]

I have spoken so much of the Vril Staff that my reader may expect me to describe it. This I cannot do accurately, for I was never allowed to handle it for fear of some terrible accident occasioned by my ignorance of its use; and I have no doubt that it requires much skill and practice in the exercise of its various powers. It is hollow, and has in the handle several stops, keys, or springs by which its force can be altered, modified, or directed—so that by one process it destroys, by another it heals—by one it can rend the rock, by another disperse the vapour—by one it affects bodies, by another it can exercise a certain influence over minds. It is usually carried in the convenient size of a walking-staff, but it has slides by which it can be lengthened or shortened at will. When used for special purposes, the upper part rests in the hollow of the palm with the fore and middle fingers protruded. I was assured, however, that its power was not equal in all, but proportioned to the amount of certain vril properties in the wearer in affinity, or 'rapport' with the purposes to be effected. Some were more potent to destroy, others to heal, &c.; much also depended on the calm and steadiness of volition in the manipulator. They assert that the full exercise of vril power can only be acquired by the constitutional temperament—i.e., by hereditarily transmitted organisation—and that a female infant of four years old belonging to the Vril-ya races can accomplish feats which a life spent in its practice would not enable the strongest and most skilled mechanician, born out of the pale of the Vril-ya to achieve. All these wands are not equally complicated; those intrusted to children are much simpler than those borne by sages of either sex, and constructed with a view to the special object on which the children are employed; which as I have before said, is among the youngest children the most destructive. In the wands of wives and mothers the correlative destroying force is usually abstracted, the healing power fully charged. I wish I could say more in detail of this singular conductor of the vril fluid, but its machinery is as exquisite as its effects are marvellous. [chapter 16]

■ Other Subterranean Races

[Said my host,] "There are societies in remote regions, but we do not admit them within the pale of civilised communities; we scarcely even give them the name of Ana, and certainly not that of Vril-ya. They are savages, living chiefly in that low stage of being, Koom-Posh, tending necessarily to its own hideous dissolution in Glek-Nas. Their wretched existence is passed in perpetual contest and perpetual change. When they do not fight with their neighbours, they fight among themselves. They are divided into sections, which abuse, plunder, and sometimes murder each other, and on the most frivolous points of difference that would be unintelligible to us if we had not read history, and seen that we too have passed through the same early state of ignorance and barbarism. Any trifle is sufficient to set them together by the ears. They pretend to be all equals, and the more they have struggled to be so, by removing old distinctions, and starting afresh, the more glaring and intolerable the disparity becomes, because nothing in hereditary affections and associations is left to soften the one naked distinction between the many who have nothing and the few who have much. Of course the many hate the few, but without the few they could not live. The many are always assailing the few; sometimes they exterminate the few; but as soon as they have done so, a new few starts out of the many, and is harder to deal with than the old few. For where societies are large, and competition to have something is the predominant fever, there must be always many losers and few gainers. In short, they are savages groping their way in the dark towards some gleam of light, and would demand our commiseration for their infirmities, if, like all savages, they did not provoke their own destruction by their arrogance and cruelty.

"Can you imagine that creatures of this kind, armed only with such miserable weapons as you may see in our museum of antiquities, clumsy iron tubes charged with saltpetre, have more than once threatened with destruction a tribe of the Vril-ya, which dwells nearest to them, because they say they have thirty millions of population—and that tribe may have fifty thousand—if the latter do not accept their notions of Soc-Sec (money getting) on some trading principles which they have the impudence to call 'a law of civilisation'?"

"But thirty millions of population are formidable odds against fifty thousand!"

My host stared at me astonished. "Stranger," said he, "you could not have heard me say that this threatened tribe belongs to the Vril-ya; and it only waits for these savages to declare war, in order to commission some half-a-dozen small children to sweep away their whole population."

At these words I felt a thrill of horror, recognising much more affinity with "the savages" than I did with the Vril-ya, and remembering all I had said in praise of the glorious American institutions, which Aph-Lin stigmatised as Koom-Posh. [chapter 17]

Of course, [my host explained,] we cannot settle in lands already occupied by the Vril-ya; and if we take the cultivated lands of the other races of Ana, we must utterly destroy the previous inhabitants. Sometimes, as it is, we take waste spots, and find that a troublesome, quarrelsome race of Ana, especially if under the administration of Koom-Posh or Glek-Nas, resents our vicinity, and picks a quarrel with us; then, of course, as menacing our welfare, we destroy it: there is no coming to terms of peace with a race so idiotic that it is always changing the form of government which represents it. [chapter 18]

■ Origins

According to the earliest traditions, the remote progenitors of the race had once tenanted a world above the surface of that in which their descendants dwelt. . . . According to these traditions the earth itself, at the date to which the traditions ascend, was not indeed in its infancy, but in the throes and travail of transition from one form of development to another, and subject to many violent revolutions of nature. By one of such revolutions, that portion of the upper world inhabited by the ancestors of this race had been subjected to inundations, not rapid, but gradual and uncontrollable, in which all, save a scanty remnant, were submerged and perished. Whether this be a record of our historical and sacred Deluge, or of some earlier one contended for by geologists, I do not pretend to conjecture; though, according to the chronology of this people as compared with that of Newton, it must have been many thousands of years before the time of Noah. On the other hand, the account of these writers does not harmonise with the opinions most in vogue among geological authorities, inasmuch as it places the existence of a human race upon earth at dates long anterior to that assigned to the terrestrial formation adapted to the introduction of mammalia. A band of the ill-fated race, thus invaded by the Flood, had, during the march of the waters, taken refuge in caverns amidst the loftier rocks, and, wandering through these hollows, they lost sight of the upper world forever. Indeed, the whole face of the earth had been changed by this great revulsion; land had been turned into sea—sea into land. In the bowels of the inner earth, even now, I was informed as a positive fact, might be discovered the remains of human habitation—habitation not in huts and caverns, but in vast cities whose ruins attest the civilisation of races which flourished before the age of Noah, and are not to be classified with those genera to which philosophy ascribes the use of flint and the ignorance of iron.

The fugitives had carried with them the knowledge of the arts they had practised above ground—arts of culture and civilisation. Their earliest want must have been that of supplying below the earth the light they had lost above it; and at no time, even in the traditional period, do the races, of which the one I now sojourned with formed a tribe, seem to have been unacquainted with the art of extracting light from gases, or manganese, or petroleum. They had been accustomed in their former state to contend with the rude forces of nature; and indeed the lengthened battle they had fought with their conqueror Ocean, which had taken centuries in its spread, had quickened their skill in curbing waters into dikes and channels. To this skill they owed their preservation in their new abode. . . .

When what we should term the historical age emerged from the twilight of tradition, the Ana were already established in different communities, and had attained to a degree of civilisation very analogous to that which the more advanced nations above the earth now enjoy. They were familiar with most of our mechanical inventions, including the application of steam as well as gas. The communities were in fierce competition with each other. They had their rich and their poor; they had orators and conquerors; they made war either for a domain or an idea. Though the various states acknowledged various forms of government, free institutions were beginning to preponderate; popular assemblies increased in power; republics soon became general; the democracy to which the most enlightened European politicians look forward as the extreme goal of political advancement, and which still prevailed among other subterranean races, whom they despised as barbarians, the loftier family of Ana, to which belonged the tribe I was visiting, looked back to as one of the crude and ignorant experiments which belong to the infancy of political science. It was the age of envy and hate, of fierce passions, of constant social changes more or less violent, of strife between classes, of war between state and state. This phase of society lasted, however, for some ages, and was finally brought to a close, at least among the nobler and more intellectual populations, by the gradual discovery of the latent powers stored in the all-permeating fluid which they denominate Vril. [chapter 9]

■ Evolution

But the greatest curiosity in the collection was that of three portraits belonging to the pre-historical age, and, according to mythical tradition, taken by the orders of a philosopher, whose origin and attributes were as much mixed up with symbolical fable as those of an Indian Buddha or a Greek Prometheus. From this mysterious personage, at once a sage and a hero, all the principal sections of the Vril-ya race pretend to trace a common origin.

The portraits are of the philosopher himself, of his grandfather, and great-grandfather. They are all at full length. The philosopher is attired in a long tunic which seems to form a loose suit of scaly armour, borrowed, perhaps, from some fish or reptile, but the feet and hands are exposed: the digits in both are wonderfully long, and webbed. He has little or no perceptible throat, and a low receding forehead, not at all the ideal of a sage's. He has bright brown prominent eyes, a very wide mouth and high cheekbones, and a muddy complexion. According to tradition, this philosopher had lived to a patriarchal age, extending over many centuries, and he remembered distinctly in middle life his grandfather as surviving, and in childhood his great-grandfather; the portrait of the first he had taken, or caused to be taken, while yet alive—that of the latter was taken from his effigies in mummy. The portrait of his grandfather had the features and aspect of the philosopher, only much more exaggerated: he was not dressed, and the colour of his body was singular; the breast and stomach yellow, the shoulders and legs of a dull bronze hue: the great-grandfather was a magnificent specimen of the Batrachian genus, a Giant Frog, "*pur et simple.*" . . .

[Shocked, I wondered that] "though these horrible daubs may be of great antiquity, and were intended, perhaps, for some rude caricature, I presume that none of your race even in the less enlightened ages, ever believed that the great-grandson of a Frog became a sententious philosopher; or that any section, I will not say of the lofty Vril-ya, but of the meanest varieties of the human race, had its origin in a Tadpole."

"Pardon me," answered Aph-Lin: "in what we call the Wrangling or Philosophical Period of History, which was at its height about seven thousand years ago, there was a very distinguished naturalist, who proved to the satisfaction of numerous disciples such analogical and anatomical agreements in structure between an An and a Frog, as to show that out of the one must have developed the other. . . .

"In the Wrangling Period of History, whatever one sage asserted another sage was sure to contradict. . . . In short, these two schools raged against each other; one asserting the An to be the perfected type of the Frog; the other that the Frog was the highest development of the An. The moralists were divided in opinion with the naturalists, but the bulk of them sided with the Frog-preference school. They said, with much plausibility, that in moral conduct (viz., in the adherence to rules best adapted to the health and welfare of the individual and the community) there could be no doubt of the vast superiority of the Frog. All history showed the wholesale immorality of the human race, the complete disregard, even by the most renowned amongst them, of the laws which they acknowledged to be essential to their own and the general happiness and wellbeing. But the severest critic of the Frog race could not detect in their manners a single aberration from the moral law tacitly recognised by themselves. And what, after all, can be the profit of civilisation if superiority in moral conduct be not the aim for which it strives, and the test by which its progress should be judged?

"In fine, the adherents of this theory presumed that in some remote period the Frog race had been the improved development of the Human; but that, from some causes which defied rational conjecture, they had not maintained their original position in the scale of nature; while the Ana, though of inferior organisation, had, by dint less of their virtues than their vices, such as ferocity and cunning, gradually acquired ascendancy, much as among the human race itself tribes utterly barbarous have, by superiority in similar vices, utterly destroyed or reduced into insignificance tribes originally excelling them in mental gifts and culture. Unhappily these disputes became involved with the religious notions of that age; and as society was then administered under the government of the Koom-Posh, who, being the most ignorant, were of course the most inflammable class —the multitude took the whole question out of the hands of the philosophers; political chiefs saw that the Frog dispute, so taken up by the populace, could become a most valuable instrument of their ambition; and for not less than one thousand years war and massacre prevailed, during which period the philosophers on both sides were butchered, and the government of Koom-Posh itself was happily brought to an end by the ascendancy of a family that clearly established its descent from the aboriginal tadpole, and furnished despotic rulers to the various nations of the Ana. These despots finally disappeared, at least from our communities, as the discovery of vril led to the tranquil institutions under which flourish all the races of the Vril-ya." [chapter 16]

■ Gender

In childhood [girls] perform the offices of work and labour impartially with the boys, and, indeed, in the earlier age appropriated to the destruction of animals irreclaimably hostile, the girls are frequently preferred, as being by constitution more ruthless under the influence of fear or hate. In the interval between infancy and the marriageable age familiar intercourse between the sexes is suspended. At the marriageable age it is renewed, never with worse consequences than those which attend upon marriage. All arts and vocations allotted to the one sex are open to the other, and the Gy-ei arrogate to themselves a superiority in all those abstruse and mystical branches of reasoning, for which they say the Ana are unfitted by a duller sobriety of understanding, or the routine of their matter-of-fact occupations, just as young ladies in our own world constitute themselves authorities in the subtlest points of theological doctrine, for which few men, actively engaged in worldly business have sufficient learning or refinement of intellect. Whether owing to early training in gymnastic exercises, or to their constitutional organisation, the Gy-ei are usually superior to the Ana in physical strength (an important element in the consideration and maintenance of female rights). They attain to loftier stature, and amid their rounder proportions are imbedded sinews and muscles as hardy as those of the other sex. Indeed they assert that, according to the original laws of nature, females were intended to be larger than males, and maintain this dogma by reference to the earliest formations of life in insects, and in the most ancient family of the vertebrata—viz., fishes—in both of which the females are generally large enough to make a meal of their consorts if they so desire. Above all, the Gy-ei have a readier and more concentred [*sic*] power over that mysterious fluid or agency which contains the element of destruction, with a larger portion of that sagacity which comprehends dissimulation. Thus they cannot only defend themselves against all aggressions from the males, but could, at any moment when he least expected his danger, terminate the existence of an offending spouse. To the credit of the Gy-ei no instance of their abuse of this awful superiority in the art of destruction is on record for several ages. . . .

They now bind themselves in wedlock only for three years; at the end of each third year either male or female can divorce the other and is free to marry again. At the end of ten years the An has the privilege of taking a second wife, allowing the first to retire if she so please. These regulations are for the most part a dead letter; divorces and polygamy are extremely rare, and the marriage state now seems singularly happy and serene among this astonishing people; —the Gy-ei, notwithstanding their boastful superiority in physical strength and intellectual abilities, being much curbed into gentle manners by the dread of separation or of a second wife, and the Ana being very much the creatures of custom, and not, except under great aggravation, likely to exchange for hazardous novelties faces and manners to which they are reconciled by habit. But there is one privilege the Gy-ei carefully retain, and the desire for which perhaps forms the secret motive of most lady asserters of woman rights above ground. They claim the privilege, here usurped by men, of proclaiming their love and urging their suit; in other words, of being the wooing party rather than the wooed. Such a phenomenon as an old maid does not exist among the Gy-ei. Indeed it is very seldom that a Gy does not secure any An upon whom she sets her heart, if his affections be not strongly engaged elsewhere. However coy, reluctant, and prudish, the male she courts may prove at first, yet her perseverance, her ardour, her persuasive powers, her command over the mystic agencies of vril, are pretty sure to run down his neck into what we call "the fatal noose." Their argument for the reversal of that relationship of the sexes which the blind tyranny of man has established on the surface of the earth, appears cogent, and is advanced with a frankness which might well be commended to impartial consideration. They say, that of the two the female is by nature of a more loving disposition than the male—that love occupies a larger space in her thoughts, and is more essential to her happiness, and that therefore she ought to be the wooing party; that otherwise the male is a shy and dubitant creature—that he has often a selfish predilection for the single state—that he often pretends to misunderstand tender glances and delicate hints—that, in short, he must be resolutely pursued and captured. They add, moreover, that unless the Gy can secure the An of her choice, and one whom she would not select out of the whole world becomes her mate, she is not only less happy than she otherwise would be, but she is not so good a being, that her qualities of heart are not sufficiently developed; whereas the An is a creature that less lastingly concentrates his affections on one object; that if he cannot get the Gy whom he prefers he easily reconciles himself to another Gy; and, finally, that at the worst, if he is loved and taken care of, it is less necessary to the welfare of his existence that he should love as well as be loved; he grows contented with his creature comforts, and the many occupations of thought which he creates for himself.

Whatever may be said as to this reasoning, the system works well for the male; for being thus sure that he is truly and ardently loved, and that the more coy and reluctant he shows himself, the more determination to secure him increases, he generally contrives to make his consent dependent on such conditions as he thinks the best calculated to insure, if not a blissful, at least a peaceful life. Each individual An has his own hobbies, his own ways, his own predilections, and, whatever they may be, he demands a promise of full and unrestrained concession to them. This, in the pursuit of her object, the Gy readily promises; and as the characteristic of this extraordinary people is an implicit veneration for truth, and her word once given is never broken even by the giddiest Gy, the conditions stipulated for are religiously observed. In fact, notwithstanding all their abstract rights and powers, the Gy-ei are the most amiable, conciliatory, and submissive wives I have ever seen even in the happiest households above ground. It is an aphorism among them, that "where a Gy loves it is her pleasure to obey." It will be observed that in the relationship of the sexes I have spoken only of marriage, for such is the moral perfection to which this community has attained, that any illicit connection is as little possible amongst them as it would be to a couple of linnets during the time they agree to live in pairs. [chapter 10]

A Gy wears wings habitually when yet a virgin—she joins the Ana in their aerial sports—she adventures alone and afar into the wilder regions of the sunless world: in the boldness and height of her soarings, not less than in the grace of her movements, she excels the opposite sex. But, from the day of her marriage she wears wings no more, she suspends them with her own willing hand over the nuptial couch, never to be resumed unless the marriage tie be severed by divorce or death. [chapter 20]

Art

I have said that [the Vril-ya's] dramas are of great antiquity. No new plays, indeed no imaginative works sufficiently important to survive their immediate day, appear to have been composed for several generations. . . . I could not help expressing to Aph-Lin my surprise that a community in which mechanical science had made so marvellous a progress, and in which intellectual civilisation had exhibited itself in realising those objects for the happiness of the people, which the political philosophers above ground had, after ages of struggle, pretty generally agreed to consider unattainable visions, should, nevertheless, be so wholly without a contemporaneous literature, despite the excellence to which culture had brought a language at once so rich and simple, vigourous and musical.

My host replied—"Do you not perceive that a literature such as you mean would be wholly incompatible with that perfection of social or political felicity at which you do us the honour to think we have arrived? We have at last, after centuries of struggle, settled into a form of government with which we are content, and in which, as we allow no differences of rank, and no honours are paid to administrators distinguishing them from others, there is no stimulus given to individual ambition. No one would read works advocating theories that involved any political or social change, and therefore no one writes them. If now and then an An feels himself dissatisfied with our tranquil mode of life, he does not attack it; he goes away." [chapter 17]

Threat and the Coming Race

Certainly I have no desire to insinuate, through the medium of this narrative, any ignorant disparagement of the race to which I belong. I have, on the contrary, endeavoured to make it clear that the principles which regulate the social system of the Vril-ya forbid them to produce those individual examples of human greatness which adorn the annals of the upper world. Where there are no wars there can be no Hannibal, no Washington, no Jackson, no Sheridan; where states are so happy that they fear no danger and desire no change, they cannot give birth to a Demosthenes, a Webster, a Sumner, a Wendell Holmes, or a Butler; and where a society attains to a moral standard, in which there are no crimes and no sorrows from which tragedy can extract its aliment of pity and sorrow, no salient vices or follies on which comedy can lavish its mirthful satire, it has lost the chance of producing a Shakespeare, or a Moliere, or a Mrs. Beecher-Stowe. But if I have no desire to disparage my fellow-men above ground in showing how much the motives that impel the energies and ambition of individuals in a society of contest and struggle—become dormant or annulled in a society which aims at securing for the aggregate the calm and innocent felicity which we presume to be the lot of beatified immortals; neither, on the other hand, have I the wish to represent the commonwealths of the Vril-ya as an ideal form of political society, to the attainment of which our own efforts of reform should be directed. On the contrary, it is because we have so combined, throughout the series of ages, the elements which compose human character, that it would be utterly impossible for us to adopt the modes of life, or to reconcile our passions to the modes of thought among the Vril-ya,—that I arrived at the conviction that this people—though originally not only of our human race, but, as seems to me clear by the roots of their language, descended from the same ancestors as the Great Aryan family, from which in varied streams has flowed the dominant civilisation of the world; and having, according to their myths and their history, passed through phases of society familiar to ourselves, had yet now developed into a distinct species with which it was impossible that any community in the upper world could amalgamate: and that if they ever emerged from these nether recesses into the light of day, they would, according to their own traditional persuasions of their ultimate destiny, destroy and replace our existent varieties of man.

It may, indeed, be said, since more than one Gy could be found to conceive a partiality for so ordinary a type of our super-terrestrial race as myself, that even if the Vril-ya did appear above ground, we might be saved from extermination by intermixture of race. But this is too sanguine a belief. Instances of such "mesalliance" would be as rare as those of intermarriage between the Anglo-Saxon emigrants and the Red Indians. Nor would time be allowed for the operation of familiar intercourse. The Vril-ya, on emerging, induced by the charm of a sunlit heaven to form their settlements above ground, would commence at once the work of destruction, seize upon the territories already cultivated, and clear off, without scruple, all the inhabitants who resisted that invasion. And considering their contempt for the institutions of Koom-Posh or Popular Government, and the pugnacious valour of my beloved countrymen, I believe that if the Vril-ya first appeared in free America—as, being the choicest portion of the habitable earth, they would doubtless be induced to do—and said, "This quarter of the globe we take; Citizens of a Koom-Posh, make way for the development of species in the Vril-ya," my brave compatriots would show fight, and not a soul of them would be left in this life, to rally round the Stars and Stripes, at the end of a week. [chapter 26]

SELECTIONS FROM *Mizora*

■ Inner Light

It was not a surprise to me that astronomy was an unknown science in Mizora, as neither sun, moon, nor stars were visible there. . . . They knew they occupied a hollow sphere, bounded North and South by impassable oceans. Light was a property of the atmosphere. A circle of burning mist shot forth long streamers of light from the North, and a similar phenomena occurred in the South.

The recitation of my geography lessons would have astonished a pupil from the outer world. They taught that a powerful current of electricity existed in the upper regions of the atmosphere. It was the origin of their atmospheric heat and light, and their change of seasons. The latter appeared to me to coincide with those of the Arctic zone, in one particular. The light of the sun during the Arctic summer is reflected by the atmosphere, and produces that mellow, golden, rapturous light that hangs like a veil of enchantment of the land of Mizora for six months in the year. It was followed by six months of the shifting iridescence of the Aurora Borealis.

As the display of the Aurora Borealis originated, and was most brilliant at what appeared to me to be the terminus of the pole, I believed it was caused by the meeting at that point of the two great electric currents of the earth, the one on its surface, and the one known to the inhabitants of Mizora. The heat produced by the meeting of two such powerful currents of electricity is undoubtedly the cause of the open Polar Sea. As the point of meeting is below the vision of the inhabitants of the Arctic regions, they see only the reflection of the Aurora. Its gorgeous, brilliant, indescribable splendour is known only to the inhabitants of Mizora. [25–26]

■ Selections from *The Smoky God*

In presenting the theme of this almost incredible story, as told by Olaf Jansen, and supplemented by manuscript, maps and crude drawings entrusted to me, a fitting introduction is found in the following quotation:

> "In the beginning God created the heaven and the earth, and the earth was without form and void." And also, "God created man in his own image." Therefore, even in things material, man must be God-like, because he is created in the likeness of the Father. A man builds a house for himself and family. The porches or verandas are all without, and are secondary. The building is really constructed for the conveniences within.

Olaf Jansen makes the startling announcement through me, an humble instrument, that in like manner, God created the earth for the "within"—that is to say, for its lands, seas, rivers, mountains, forests and valleys, and for its other internal conveniences, while the outside surface of the earth is merely the veranda, the porch, where things grow by comparison but sparsely, like the lichen on the mountain side, clinging determinedly for bare existence.

Take an egg-shell, and from each end break out a piece as large as the end of this pencil. Extract its contents, and then you will have a perfect representation of Olaf Jansen's earth. The distance from the inside surface to the outside surface, according to him, is about three hundred miles. The center of gravity is not in the center of the earth, but in the center of the shell or crust; therefore, if the thickness of the earth's crust or shell is three hundred miles, the center of gravity is one hundred and fifty miles below the surface.

In their log-books Arctic explorers tell us of the dipping of the needle as the vessel sails in regions of the farthest north known. In reality, they are at the curve; on the edge of the shell, where gravity is geometrically increased, and while the electric current seemingly dashes off into space toward the phantom idea of the North Pole, yet this same electric current drops again and continues its course southward along the inside surface of the earth's crust. [chapter 1]

According to Olaf Jansen, in the beginning this old world of ours was created solely for the "within" world, where are located the four great rivers—the Euphrates, the Pison, the Gihon and the Hiddekel. These same names of rivers, when applied to streams on the "outside" surface of the earth, are purely traditional from an antiquity beyond the memory of man.

On the top of a high mountain, near the fountain-head of these four rivers, Olaf Jansen, the Norseman, claims to have discovered the long-lost "Garden of Eden," the veritable navel of the earth, and to have spent over two years studying and reconnoitering in this marvelous "within" land, exuberant with stupendous plant life and abounding in giant animals; a land where the people live to be centuries old, after the order of Methuselah and other Biblical characters; a region where one-quarter of the "inner" surface is water and three-quarters land; where there are large oceans and many rivers and lakes; where the cities are superlative in construction and magnificence; where modes of transportation are as far in advance of ours as we with our boasted achievements are in advance of the inhabitants of "darkest Africa."

The distance directly across the space from inner surface to inner surface is about six hundred miles less than the recognized diameter of the earth. In the identical center of this vast vacuum is the seat of electricity—a mammoth ball of dull red fire—not startlingly brilliant, but surrounded by a white, mild, luminous cloud, giving out uniform warmth, and held in its place in the center of this internal space by the immutable law of gravitation. This electrical cloud is known to the people "within" as the abode of "The Smoky God." They believe it to be the throne of "The Most High." [chapter 1]

Olaf Jansen avers that, in the beginning, the world was created by the Great Architect of the Universe, so that man might dwell upon its "inside" surface, which has ever since been the habitation of the "chosen."

They who were driven out of the "Garden of Eden" brought their traditional history with them. The history of the people living "within" contains a narrative suggesting the story of Noah and the ark with which we are familiar. He sailed away, as did Columbus, from a certain port, to a strange land he had heard of far to the northward, carrying with him all manner of beasts of the fields and fowls of the air, but was never heard of afterward. [chapter 1]

But this dull-red, false sun, as we supposed it to be, did not pass away for several hours; and while we were unconscious of its emitting any rays of light, still there was no time thereafter when we could not sweep the horizon in front and locate the illumination of the so-called false sun, during a period of at least twelve hours out of every twenty-four.

Clouds and mists would at times almost, but never entirely, hide its location. Gradually it seemed to climb higher in the horizon of the uncertain purply sky as we advanced.

It could hardly be said to resemble the sun, except in its circular shape, and when not obscured by clouds or the ocean mists, it had a hazy-red, bronzed appearance, which would change to a white light like a luminous cloud, as if reflecting some greater light beyond.

We finally agreed in our discussion of this smoky furnace-colored sun, that, whatever the cause of the phenomenon, it was not a reflection of our sun, but a planet of some sort—a reality. [chapter 3]

■ People

There was not a single man aboard who would not have measured fully twelve feet in height. They all wore full beards, not particularly long, but seemingly short-cropped. They had mild and beautiful faces, exceedingly fair, with ruddy complexions. The hair and beard of some were black, others sandy, and still others yellow. The captain, as we designated the dignitary in command of the great vessel, was fully a head taller than any of his companions. The women averaged from ten to eleven feet in height. Their features were especially regular and refined, while their complexion was of a most delicate tint heightened by a healthful glow. [chapter 3]

We learned that the males do not marry before they are from seventy-five to one hundred years old, and that the age at which women enter wedlock is only a little less, and that both men and women frequently live to be from six to eight hundred years old, and in some instances much older. [chapter 4]

■ Technology

The ship was equipped with a mode of illumination which I now presume was electricity, but neither my father nor myself were sufficiently skilled in mechanics to understand whence came the power to operate the ship, or to maintain the soft beautiful lights that answered the same purpose of our present methods of lighting the streets of our cities, our houses and places of business.

It must be remembered, the time of which I write was the autumn of 1829, and we of the "outside" surface of the earth knew nothing then, so to speak, of electricity. [chapter 3]

We were taken overland to the city of "Eden," in a conveyance different from anything we have in Europe or America. This vehicle was doubtless some electrical contrivance. It was noiseless, and ran on a single iron rail in perfect balance. The trip was made at a very high rate of speed. We were carried up hills and down dales, across valleys and again along the sides of steep mountains, without any apparent attempt having been made to level the earth as we do for railroad tracks. The car seats were huge yet comfortable affairs, and very high above the floor of the car. On the top of each car were high geared fly wheels lying on their sides, which were so automatically adjusted that, as the speed of the car increased, the high speed of these fly wheels geometrically increased. Jules Galdea explained to us that these revolving fan-like wheels on top of the cars destroyed atmospheric pressure, or what is generally understood by the term gravitation, and with this force thus destroyed or rendered nugatory the car is as safe from falling to one side or the other from the single rail track as if it were in a vacuum; the fly wheels in their rapid revolutions destroying effectually the so-called power of gravitation, or the force of atmospheric pressure or whatever potent influence it may be that causes all unsupported things to fall downward to the earth's surface or to the nearest point of resistance. [chapter 3]

■ Inner World

The great luminous cloud or ball of dull-red fire—fiery-red in the mornings and evenings, and during the day giving off a beautiful white light, "The Smoky God,"—is seemingly suspended in the center of the great vacuum "within" the earth, and held to its place by the immutable law of gravitation, or a repellant atmospheric force, as the case may be. I refer to the known power that draws or repels with equal force in all directions.

The base of this electrical cloud or central luminary, the seat of the gods, is dark and non-transparent, save for innumerable small openings, seemingly in the bottom of the great support or altar of the Deity, upon which "The Smoky God" rests; and, the lights shining through these many openings twinkle at night in all their splendor, and seem to be stars, as natural as the stars we saw shining when in our home at Stockholm, excepting that they appear larger. "The Smoky God," therefore, with each daily revolution of the earth, appears to come up in the east and go down in the west, the same as does our sun on the external surface. In reality, the people "within" believe that "The Smoky God" is the throne of their Jehovah, and is stationary. The effect of night and day is, therefore, produced by the earth's daily rotation. [chapter 3]

About three-fourths of the "inner" surface of the earth is land and about one-fourth water. There are numerous rivers of tremendous size, some flowing in a northerly direction and others southerly. Some of these rivers are thirty miles in width, and it is out of these vast waterways, at the extreme northern and southern parts of the "inside" surface of the earth, in regions where low temperatures are experienced, that fresh-water icebergs are formed. They are then pushed out to sea like huge tongues of ice, by the abnormal freshets of turbulent waters that, twice every year, sweep everything before them. [chapter 4]

SELECTIONS FROM *At the Earth's Core*

■ Drilling Machine

[The "iron mole" was] a steel cylinder a hundred feet long, and jointed so that it may turn and twist through solid rock if need be. At one end is a mighty revolving drill operated by an engine which Perry said generated more power to the cubic inch than any other engine did to the cubic foot.

I remember that he used to claim that that invention alone would make us fabulously wealthy—we were going to make the whole thing public after the successful issue of our first secret trial—but Perry never returned from that trial trip, and I only after ten years. [chapter 1]

Theories of the Earth

One [geologist] estimates [that the earth's crust is] thirty miles, because the internal heat, increasing at the rate of about one degree to each sixty to seventy feet depth, would be sufficient to fuse the most refractory substances at that distance beneath the surface. Another finds that the phenomena of precession and nutation require that the earth, if not entirely solid, must at least have a shell not less than eight hundred to a thousand miles in thickness. [chapter 1]

"For two hundred and fifty miles our prospector bore us through the crust beneath our outer world. At that point it reached the center of gravity of the five-hundred-mile-thick crust. Up to that point we had been descending—direction is, of course, merely relative. Then at the moment that our seats revolved—the thing that made you believe that we had turned about and were speeding upward—we passed the center of gravity and, though we did not alter the direction of our progress, yet we were in reality moving upward—toward the surface of the inner world. Does not the strange fauna and flora which we have seen convince you that you are not in the world of your birth? And the horizon—could it present the strange aspects which we both noted unless we were indeed standing upon the inside surface of a sphere?"

"But the sun, Perry!" I urged. "How in the world can the sun shine through five hundred miles of solid crust?"

"It is not the sun of the outer world that we see here. It is another sun—an entirely different sun—that casts its eternal noonday effulgence upon the face of the inner world."[chapter 3]

"The earth was once a nebulous mass," [Perry said.] "It cooled, and as it cooled it shrank. At length a thin crust of solid matter formed upon its outer surface—a sort of shell; but within it was partially molten matter and highly expanded gases. As it continued to cool, what happened? Centrifugal force buried the particles of the nebulous center toward the crust as rapidly as they approached a solid state. You have seen the same principle practically applied in the modern cream separator. Presently there was only a small superheated core of gaseous matter remaining within a huge vacant interior left by the contraction of the cooling gases. The equal attraction of the solid crust from all directions maintained this luminous core in the exact center of the hollow globe. What remains of it is the sun you saw today—a relatively tiny thing at the exact center of the earth. Equally to every part of this inner world it diffuses its perpetual noonday light and torrid heat.

"This inner world must have cooled sufficiently to support animal life long ages after life appeared upon the outer crust, but that the same agencies were at work here is evident from the similar forms of both animal and vegetable creation which we have already seen. Take the great beast which attacked us, for example. Unquestionably a counter of the Megatherium of the post-Pliocene period of the outer crust, whose fossilized skeleton has been found in South America." [chapter 3]

■ The Inner World

[This was] a landscape at once weird and beautiful. Before us a low and level shore stretched down to a silent sea. As far as the eye could reach the surface of the water was dotted with countless tiny isles—some of towering, barren, granitic rock—others resplendent in gorgeous trappings of tropical vegetation, myriad starred with the magnificent splendor of vivid blooms.

Behind us rose a dark and forbidding wood of giant arborescent ferns intermingled with the commoner types of a primeval tropical forest. Huge creepers depended in great loops from tree to tree, dense under-brush overgrew a tangled mass of fallen trunks and branches. Upon the outer verge we could see the same splendid coloring of countless blossoms that glorified the islands, but within the dense shadows all seemed dark and gloomy as the grave.

And upon all the noonday sun poured its torrid rays out of a cloudless sky. [chapter 2]

As I looked I began to appreciate the reason for the strangeness of the landscape that had haunted me from the first with an illusive suggestion of the bizarre and unnatural—THERE WAS NO HORIZON! As far as the eye could reach out the sea continued and upon its bosom floated tiny islands, those in the distance reduced to mere specks; but ever beyond them was the sea, until the impression became quite real that one was LOOKING UP at the most distant point that the eyes could fathom—the distance was lost in the distance. That was all—there was no clear-cut horizontal line marking the dip of the globe below the line of vision.

"A great light is commencing to break on me," continued Perry, taking out his watch. "I believe that I have finally solved the riddle. It is now two o'clock. When we emerged from the prospector the sun was directly above us. Where is it now?"

I glanced up to find the great orb still motionless in the center of the heaven. And such a sun! I had scarcely noticed it before. Fully thrice the size of the sun I had known throughout my life, and apparently so near that the sight of it carried the conviction that one might almost reach up and touch it. [chapter 2]

We know that the crust of the globe is 500 miles in thickness; then the inside diameter of Pellucidar must be 7,000 miles, and the superficial area 165,480,000 square miles. Three-fourths of this is land. Think of it! A land area of 124,110,000 square miles! Our own world contains but 53,000,000 square miles of land, the balance of its surface being covered by water. Just as we often compare nations by their relative land areas, so if we compare these two worlds in the same way we have the strange anomaly of a larger world within a smaller one! [chapter 5]

"What is the Land of Awful Shadow?" I asked.

"It is the land which lies beneath the Dead World," replied Dian; "the Dead World which hangs forever between the sun and Pellucidar above the Land of Awful Shadow. It is the Dead World which makes the great shadow upon this portion of Pellucidar."

I did not fully understand what she meant, nor am I sure that I do yet, for I have never been to that part of Pellucidar from which the Dead World is visible; but Perry says that it is the moon of Pellucidar—a tiny planet within a planet—and that it revolves around the earth's axis coincidently with the earth, and thus is always above the same spot within Pellucidar. I remember that Perry was very much excited when I told him about this Dead World, for he seemed to think that it explained the hitherto inexplicable phenomena of nutation and the precession of the equinoxes. [chapter 15]

■ Monsters

The all-powerful Mahars of Pellucidar are great reptiles, some six or eight feet in length, with long narrow heads and great round eyes. Their beak-like mouths are lined with sharp, white fangs, and the backs of their huge, lizard bodies are serrated into bony ridges from their necks to the end of their long tails. Their feet are equipped with three webbed toes, while from the fore feet membranous wings, which are attached to their bodies just in front of the hind legs, protrude at an angle of 45 degrees toward the rear, ending in sharp points several feet above their bodies. [chapter 4]

Life within Pellucidar is far younger than upon the outer crust. Here man has but reached a stage analogous to the Stone Age of our own world's history, but for countless millions of years these reptiles have been progressing. Possibly it is the sixth sense which I am sure they possess that has given them an advantage over the other and more frightfully armed of their fellows; but this we may never know. They look upon us as we look upon the beasts of our fields, and I learn from their written records that other races of Mahars feed upon men—they keep them in great droves, as we keep cattle. They breed them most carefully, and when they are quite fat, they kill and eat them. [chapter 5]

Only the women and children fell prey to the Mahars—they being the weakest and most tender—and when they had satisfied their appetite for human flesh, some of them devouring two and three of the slaves, there were only a score of full-grown men left, and I thought that for some reason these were to be spared, but such was far from the case, for as the last Mahar crawled to her rock the queen's thipdars darted into the air, circled the temple once and then, hissing like steam engines, swooped down upon the remaining slaves. [chapter 8]

More amazing is the vocation that they discover for themselves, that not only of liberating the enslaved humans, but in giving them dominion over the other races of the underworld.

"Once the [Mahar] males were all-powerful, but ages ago the females, little by little, assumed the mastery. For other ages no noticeable change took place in the race of Mahars. It continued to progress under the intelligent and beneficent rule of the ladies. Science took vast strides. This was especially true of the sciences which we know as biology and eugenics. Finally a certain female scientist announced the fact that she had discovered a method whereby eggs might be fertilized by chemical means after they were laid—all true reptiles, you know, are hatched from eggs.

"What happened? Immediately the necessity for males ceased to exist—the race was no longer dependent upon them. More ages elapsed until at the present time we find a race consisting exclusively of females. But here is the point. The secret of this chemical formula is kept by a single race of Mahars. It is in the city of Phutra, and unless I am greatly in error I judge from your description of the vaults through which you passed today that it lies hidden in the cellar of this building.

"For two reasons they hide it away and guard it jealously. First, because upon it depends the very life of the race of Mahars, and second, owing to the fact that when it was public property as at first so many were experimenting with it that the danger of over-population became very grave.

"David, if we can escape, and at the same time take with us this great secret what will we not have accomplished for the human race within Pellucidar!" The very thought of it fairly overpowered me. Why, we two would be the means of placing the men of the inner world in their rightful place among created things. Only the Sagoths would then stand between them and absolute supremacy, and I was not quite sure but that the Sagoths owed all their power to the greater intelligence of the Mahars—I could not believe that these gorilla-like beasts were the mental superiors of the human race of Pellucidar.

"Why, Perry," I exclaimed, "you and I may reclaim a whole world! Together we can lead the races of men out of the darkness of ignorance into the light of advancement and civilization. At one step we may carry them from the Age of Stone to the twentieth century. It's marvelous—absolutely marvelous just to think about it."

"David," said the old man, "I believe that God sent us here for just that purpose—it shall be my life work to teach them His word—to lead them into the light of His mercy while we are training their hearts and hands in the ways of culture and civilization." [chapter 5]

Notes

CHAPTER 1

1. See, for instance, the works of Godwin and Kafton-Minkel. There are numerous Web sites with information on Ernst Zundel and Nazi hollow-Earth theories. See for instance: www.nizkor.org/hweb/people/zundel-ernst/flying-saucers/.
2. A. R. Becker begins her *Lost Worlds Romance* with the statement that the "lost worlds romance begins in the depths of the earth" (11), and she briefly reviews many of the works included in this anthology. Lauric Guillaud's *L'aventure mystérieuse de Poe à Merrit ou l'orphelin de Gilgamesh* begins with Symmes and Poe and the "rebirth of the imaginary voyage." Although Guillaud's first chapter deals looks at the hollow Earth in the early twentieth century, the book is not a study of the hollow-Earth theme. Walter Kafton-Minkel's *Subterranean Worlds: 100,000 Years of Dragons, Dwarfs, the Dead, Lost Races, & UFOs from Inside the Earth* deals mostly with the works of proponents of various hollow-Earth theories. His chapter 13, "The Inner World in Fiction," reviews many of the works dealt with here.
3. While Edward Bulwer-Lytton's *Coming Race* (1871) and Edgar Rice Burroughs's Pellucidar novels, beginning with *At the Earth's Core* (1914), are perhaps the best-known of these later works, dozens of novels with subterranean settings were published in the decades following Verne's novel. In *The Encyclopedia of Science Fiction*, Clute and Nicholls list some twenty additional utopian and fantasy novels from the late nineteenth and early twentieth centuries set in the inner world (579–580). Other works from this period often cited by critics include William Bradshaw's *Goddess of Atvatabar* (1892), John Uri Lloyd's *Etidorpha* (1895), and Willis George Emerson's *The Smoky God, or A Voyage to the Inner World* (1908). These and other lesser-known late-nineteenth- and early-twentieth-century works are discussed in the studies of Becker and Guillaud and are mentioned in the bibliographies of Bleiler, Lyman Tower Sargent, and Darko Suvin, and in the encyclopedias of Versins and of Clute and Nicols.
4. These are the only works that Garnier includes as "Voyages to the Underground," but this anthology also includes Lucian's *True History*, Cyrano's *Voyages*, *Gulliver's Travels*, Paltock's *Peter Wilkins*, and the utopias of Foigny, Veiras, and many others. Philip Gove provides an excellent discussion of the significance of the Garnier collection as well as a elaboration of the concept of the imaginary voyage (Gove, *The Imaginary Voyage*, 27–63). Yann Gaillard's *Supplé-*

ments au voyage de Bougainville (Paris: Lettres nouvelles, 1980), on the other hand, is little more than a synopsis of Garnier's anthology.

The only English-language equivalent to Garnier's collection is Henry Weber's one-volume anthology *Popular Romances: Consisting of Imaginary Voyages and Travels* (1812), which groups together *Gulliver's Travels*, *Robinson Crusoe*, and *Klim*, along with Robert Paltock's *Life and Adventures of Peter Wilkins* (1750) and Gibbon's *History of the Automathes*. The first four of these works were included in the Garnier collection. As Weber himself explains, in reference to Garnier's collection, "The intention of the present volume is far more limited, as it includes only five romances of the former description, all, excepting the second, of English growth" (Weber, *Popular Romances*, xxii).

5. In Sinbad's fourth voyage he finds himself in a land where, after the death of a spouse, the widow or widower is lowered into a cave from which there is no escape. This episode is explicitly copied by Mouhy in the first part of *Lamékis*. Gove explains that "the story of Sinbad the Sailor spread rapidly though Europe," and there was an English translation as early as 1706" (200–204). See Krappe, "The Subterraneous Voyage," 120–121.
6. In Tyssot de Patot's *Voyages et aventures de Jacques Massé*, Jacques Massé and two companions are shipwrecked on an island (usually identified as Australia) and then cross a lake and climb mountains before descending into a prosperous utopian kingdom. Later when they are forced to flee, they escape back to the seashore through an underground river, which may explain why it is sometimes described as a subterranean utopia. Other mistaken identifications of subterranean worlds include James Mc Nelis's reference to Kircher's *Mundus Subterraneus* as a "subterranean voyage" (Mc Nelis, introduction, xv), while Joscelyn Godwin refers to *Lamékis* as an "early novel on the theme of a Utopia beneath the surface of the earth" (Godwin, *Arktos*, 108). Neither of these descriptions is accurate.
7. In the *Dictionary of Literary Utopias*, G. Silvani describes the other world in much the same terms: "A violent storm drives the boat towards the North Pole; the merchant and his crew freeze to death, while the young lady, who is the only survivor, *lands on another planet that is next to the earth and linked to it through the poles*" (164; my italics). "A parallel world is another universe situated 'alongside' our own." This definition is taken from a lengthy discussion in Stableford, "Parallel Worlds," 907–908.
8. Raymond Bernard—the author of this and other books on the hollow Earth in the 1960s and 1970s—is given a chapter in Kafton-Minkel's *Subterranean Worlds* ("The Strange World of Dr. Bernard," 192–216), which includes extended discussions of various twentieth-century proponents of the hollow-Earth theory. See also Joscelyn Godwin's *Arktos: The Polar Myth in Science, Symbolism, and Nazi Survival,* particularly the chapter titled "The Hole at the Pole," 105–123.

There are numerous Web sites dealing with hollow-Earth theories. One place to begin is Craig Becker's "Bibliography of Flat, Hollow, and Inverted Earth Theories": www.bga.com/~beckers/craig/archives/hollow.html. Other sites include: www.ufomind.com/people/c/crenshaw and www.ufomind.com/para/conspire/hollow.

9. As we shall see, however, in some eighteenth-century defenses of the hollow Earth (in Halley and Casanova in particular), the idea is linked to the argument that God would not waste space! In *Subterranean Worlds,* Kafton-Minkel gives the outline of such a genealogy, beginning with legends and fables: from tales of dwarfs and gnomes and other mythic creatures from inside the Earth, to more general beliefs about the Earth as a figure for the womb and the birth process, as well as the many characterizations of the underworld as the home of the dead or of Hell (9–43). In his final chapter, Kafton-Minkel asks: "Why an Inner World?" and then offers four answers—"as a new world to discover," "as the longed-for Paradise," "as a sanctum for hidden secrets," and "as a Utopia"—before returning to the overall theme of "the return to the Earth Mother" (274–282).

CHAPTER 2

1. As Garnier writes in his introduction: "The next work will please by its oddness. . . . The traveller again passes through the interior of the globe and gives free rein to his imagination. . . . We do not know who the author of this second tale was" (Garnier, *Voyages imaginaires*, 19:xiii–xiv).

   There is little critical mention of this text apart from the references in Messac and Kafton-Minkel. My translation is based on Garnier, *Voyages imaginaires*, vol. 19. It is available online at gallica.bnf.fr. Here, for instance, is Camille Flammarion's description of the text: "This is the story of a subterranean voyage. A vast whirlpool carries a ship into the depths of the ocean and carries them under the sea itself: they are in the interior polar region where meteors and the aurora borealis are born. A long journey filled with marvelous adventures takes our travelers from island to island in this somber realm until one day, pushed by a south wind, *they ascend again to the surface of the earth* near the Cape of Good Hope" (Flammarion, *Les mondes imaginaires et les mondes réels*, 459; my italics). It is perhaps worth mentioning that Messac does not make this mistake, pointing out that "in truth, although the characters are supposed to have passed through the center of the earth, they do not give us many details about this truly unique place. . . . It is only after their arrival at the south pole that their adventures and the descriptions of strange beings begins" (Messac, "Voyages modernes, " 83).

3. It is early summer, and the longest night of the year takes place on June 21. During the eighteenth century it was widely assumed that the austral region was in a sort of perpetual night. See my discussion of *Peter Wilkins* in chapter 5.

4. Not until Captain Cook's voyages later in the eighteenth century did these austral lands begin to be known; as the narrator of Edgar Allen Poe's *Narrative of Arthur Gordon Pym* reminds us, "In January, 1773, [Captain Cook's] vessels crossed the Antarctic circle, but did not succeed in penetrating much further, for upon reaching latitude 67 degrees 15' they found further progress impeded by an immense body of ice. . . . In the November following he renewed his search in the Antarctic . . . [but] he was unable to go beyond 71 degrees 10'" (Poe, *Narrative*, 840–841 [chapter 16]). The polar regions continue to invite speculation, and one of the continuing claims by those who believe today in some version or another of the hollow Earth is based on an alleged suppressed record of Admiral Byrd's historic flight over the North Pole on February 19, 1947. For years rumors have persisted that Admiral Byrd actually flew beyond the Pole into an opening leading inside the Earth, where he met with advanced beings who had a sobering message for him to deliver to "Mankind and the Surface World" (see Godwin, *Arktos*).
5. Régis Messac points out that the idea of a subterranean passage between the poles was used by Poe in his "Ms. Found in a Bottle." Messac speculates that the note at the end of Poe's story, in which the author insists that he only became acquainted *afterward* "with the maps of Mercator, in which the ocean is represented as rushing, by four mouths, into the (northern) Polar gulf, to be absorbed into the bowels of the earth," was an attempt to conceal his knowledge of earlier works and in particular of the *Relation* (Messac, "Voyages modernes," 82–83). He does not mention the white stone structure, but Poe's *Narrative of A. Gordon Pym* also includes the unexplained hieroglyphs that Pym and Evans find in a cave and that are one sign of the existence of an underground race. See my discussion of *Pym* in chapter 11.

CHAPTER 3

1. The secret rites and religious ceremonies which take place beneath the Egyptian temple reinforce the secrecy of the proceedings and are associated with Masonic rites, as in the education of the king in the abbé Jean Terrasson's novel *Sethos: histoire ou vie tirée des monuments anecdotes de l'ancienne Egypte* (1731), and provide the stuff of various films and novels.

   There is little mention of this text apart from the references in Messac and Kafton-Minkel. My translation is based on Garnier, *Voyages imaginaires*, vols. 20–21. It is available online at www.gallica.bnf.fr.
2. In Sinbad's fourth voyage, he finds himself in a land where, after the death of a spouse, the widow or widower is lowered into a cave from which there is no escape.

CHAPTER 4

1. He is claimed by both countries, which were united at the time, and although he was born in Bergen (Norway), he spent most of his life in Copenhagen.

   There are complete Danish and Latin versions of the text of Klim available at the Danish Royal Library Web site: www.kb.dk/elib/lit/dan/old/authors/holberg/klim. The French edition is part of vol. 19 of Garnier, *Voyages imaginaires*, and is available online at www.gallica.bnf.fr.

2. Although Trousson explains that following the "austere and monotonous blueprints of Puritan utopias," the eighteenth century utopia "attempted to renew itself by means of the extraordinary" (*Voyages*, 96), he considers that *Klim* goes too far: "While the critique of customs, of morality and of politics is always implicit, presented indirectly as it were, it is nonetheless drowned in the outpourings of the imagination" (123).

3. Sigrid Peters argues that as satire, *The Journey of Niels Klim to the World Underground* should be understood in terms of a much more complex tradition. From the classics, Holberg takes the form of the "Menippean satire"; while from More and especially Erasmus, he takes the concept of *spoudogeloion* (itself derived from Menippean satire): the mixing of serious ideas and jokes (Peters, *Ludvig Holbergs Menippeische Satire*, 96.)

   The classical form of Menippean satire, as codified by Casuabon and Dryden (in his 1693 "Discourse on Satire," which Peters supposes Holberg to have read during his visit to the Bodleian library), is more than just the blend of wisdom and folly. It is as well the mix of prose and different kinds of verse, and it includes—and this is Peters's central point—the frequent and unmarked insertion into the text of citations from previous authors as a parodic and satiric strategy (65).

   While Paludan admirably situates *Klim* within the tradition of the imaginary voyage as satire, he overlooks the importance of Menippean satire, especially in terms of Holberg's frequent citations of classical authors without quotation marks in the text. In addition to pointing out that the mix of verse and prose present in the Holberg's original Latin (which disappears in the French and English translations I have consulted), the ability to appreciate this satirical technique has disappeared as well: "Through an analysis of the poetic quotations some of the fundamental structures of Holberg's citational procedure become clear, from which one can deduce the ways in which he was responding to particular authors. . . . The *Iter subterraneum* belongs to the tradition of the *spoudogeloion*, in which seriousness and frivolity are woven into a single unity, while the play presented by the manifold possibilities of citation prohibits any pedantic schematism" (Peters, *Ludvig Holbergs Menippeische Satire*, 133).

4. Here are two extreme examples of the complications involved in trying to

verify how much writers at the time were aware of each other's work. In the case of Holberg's *Journey of Niels Klim to the World Underground*, for instance, there is Eddy's claim that *Gulliver's Travels* was actually influenced by *Klim*, and not the contrary. More to the point, more than forty years after the book's appearance, Charles-Georges-Thomas Garnier wrote in his introduction to the novel that *Klim* was first written in Danish and then translated into Latin by an unknown hand.

CHAPTER 5

1. As an example of the misidentification of *Peter Wilkins*, see, for instance, Versins, who writes: "The hero discovers in the heart of an immense cavern a race of men who could fly" (*Encyclopédie de l'utopie*, 875). Since the title includes the phrase *His Shipwreck near the South Pole; His Wonderful Passage thro' a Subterraneous Cavern into a Kind of New World*, it may be the "passage through" that led Marjorie Nicolson to write that "we often forget . . . that we are in a subterraneous world" (*Voyages*, 139).
2. This involves not only translating and transcribing, but the manufacture of paper and ink (1990:371). The bringing of writing can be seen in Casanova's *L'Icosameron*, where Edouard improves on their method of writing down their musical language as well as introducing the printing press. The archetypal moment of the introduction of writing is described by Claude Lévi-Strauss in his account of his fieldwork in Brazil, in the chapter "The Writing Lesson" in *Tristes tropiques* (286–297). Even better known today is Jacques Derrida's critique of this episode in *Of Grammatology*.
3. There are similar, and more serious, references to clothing in *L'Icosameron,* although Edouard will not attempt to clothe the Megamicres.
4. During Wilkins's preparations for battle, for instance, he writes: "And then taking my Observation by a bright Star, for there was a clear Dawn all round the Horizon" (1990:295). The Antipodes were a favorite setting for fantastic voyages and utopias in the seventeenth and eighteenth centuries, until the voyages of Captain Cook in the late eighteenth century. For a discussion of Australia in this context, see Friederich, *Australia in Western Imaginative Prose Writings, 1600–1960*.

   In her 1948 *Voyages to the Moon,* Marjorie Hope Nicolson calls this section of *Peter Wilkins* a "subterraneous world" (139). In her discussion of subterraneous voyages (in the chapter titled "Variations on a Theme"), she briefly discusses Kircher, Burnet, and Holberg (as well as Burton's *Anatomy of Melancholy*; 224–230).

CHAPTER 6

1. Claeys explains that his excerpt "comprises most of the original," excepting

chiefly "The History of an Inhabitant of the Air" which is not part of the main story (xli). This digression takes up almost a third of the novel (pp. 116–194).

I have been unable to find any critical writing about this text. I have used the 1755 edition, which is available in microfilm in the ESTC series (Eighteenth Century Short Title Catalogue) as reel no. 9765, item 3.

2. Visitors are so frequent that while the narrator is in the Central World, he is visited by one of his acquaintances, who "tumbled into a vast hole" while climbing on Derby Peak (233). The magnetic attraction of the inner world will be an important theme in Collin de Plancy's *Voyage au centre de la terre.*
3. Born on Jupiter, he dies at the ripe old age of sixty years (nine hundred Earth years) after having murdered his wife and ascended to his father's throne. He is then imprisoned in a comet (as a serpent, 137), until he is killed when a horse steps on him and then is reborn as a slave on Saturn, where he lived for five hundred years until he was executed in a ceremony "in Honour of one of [the Emperor's] Concubines" (139). Next he is reborn on Earth, in Yorkshire, the son of a miller's wife, where he grows up and becomes a servant. When he resists the advances of his lady, she accuses him of robbery and he is again executed, soon to be reborn on Mars, a wonderful world, "filled with Heroes, Patriots and Lawgivers, and such as had formerly dy'd in their Country's Cause, or suffered an innocent and untimely Death" (184). After getting drunk with Alexander the Great, he falls sick, dies, and is then reborn in the inner world.
4. The trip from the inner world to the Earth's crust is accomplished in a fashion similar to that found in Klim's journey, for they are carried up and through the crust to London by giant birds.
5. For a discussion of these themes, see the listing for "Great and Small" in Clute and Nicholls, *The Encyclopedia of Science Fiction,* 518–520. While there are many earlier descriptions of the inhabitants of other worlds in the seventeenth and eighteenth centuries (Cyrano, etc.), the *Encyclopedia* states that the first instance of the microcosm was Fitz-James O'Brien's story "The Diamond Lens" in 1858, "in which a scientist discovers a tiny humanoid woman in a water drop" (519).

CHAPTER 8

1. "I had the fantasy of becoming the creator of a new world, a new race, new laws, a good religion . . . and of receiving the praise of the entire world. . . . Here is a book which will immortalize me" (quoted in Leibacher, "*L'Icosameron* de Casanova," 298). In the preface to volume 2 Casanova explicitly mentions Holberg: "Plato, Erasmus, Chancellor Bacon and Nicolas Klim are among those who made me want to publish this story" (2:iii). It was in fact so little known that in 1929 Régis Messac wrote that he was unable to find a copy of this "extremely rare" book for his survey of subterranean worlds (Messac, "Voyages

modernes," 82n 1). My translation is based on the original 1788 edition, available online at www.gallica.bnf.fr.

2. Not surprisingly, there are a number of abridged versions of the novel, including Rachel Zurer's 250-page English version (1986).
3. They had calculated that the diameter of [their] Sun was 672 *milles* [about 1.5 kilometers = approximately 1000 miles], and that from their Earth to its centre was a distance of three thousand and fifty-nine *milles* [= approximately 4500 miles], or 1/32 of the circumference of their world. Based on these figures, Edouard calculates that a distance of only 92.5 *milles* separates their world form ours—that is to say, the Earth's crust is about 140 miles thick (1:258).
4. Speaking of their language he mentions a "sixth sense": "Their language is truly music in prose . . . the beauty of their music . . . is not perceived by ears alone, and goes directly to the soul, by means of a sixth sense which we do not have and which God has placed all over their skin" (1:xvi).
5. Vegetarianism is a feature of a number of the peoples living in the underworld, from the anonymous 1755 *Voyage to the World in the Center of the Earth,* through the worlds of Seaborn and Collin de Plancy.
6. At one point Edouard says that the land is thirty thousand years old (3:180; four Megamicran years equal one Earth year, so 7500 years). At another point he describes how, under his influence, the Megamicres have developed a love of travel although "for the eight or nine thousand years that they have existed, they have never liked to travel" (5:237).
7. This is an essential part of Darko Suvin's definition of utopia: "Utopia is a verbal construction of a particular quasi-human community where sociopolitical institutions, norms, and individual relationships are organized according to a more perfect principle than in the author's community, this construction being based on estrangement arising out of an alternative historical hypothesis" (Suvin, *Metamorphoses*, 49).
8. Edouard's own explanation for his accumulation of weapons is worth repeating: at one point he says that he has 200,000 rifles and as many pistols as well as a number of cannons: "What is interesting is that when I began to accumulate these weapons I was not thinking at all about going to war . . . but because it was a beautiful act, one which in Europe was the exclusive right of princes, and because I was rich and loved spending money. . . . If this world had contained a sea I would have undertaken the construction of great ships, again for my pleasure rather than for the purpose of actually using them" (5:42–43). Of course he does go to war shortly afterward.
9. "Their flour, served without seasoning, is not only insipid, but so harmful that even the poor can only eat it boiled with greens. . . . This gruel is their food, and the milk that they give each other is their drink [since] drinking plain water

is forbidden them by divine law. And anyone who, having eaten the gruel, does not drink some milk, would be struck with a mortal indigestion" (1:27). Edouard describes their milk in rapturous terms: "What an exquisite taste . . . what a wonderful food. It filled our senses . . . awakening in us all the pleasurable sensations of which we were capable, all the pleasures we could desire, sensations which no other food had ever given us the least idea. We thought that the stories from mythology were not made up, that we were in the resting place of the immortals, and that this milk that we were sucking was the nectar, the ambrosia which would give us the immortality which seemed to belong to these creatures" (1:223–224).

10. "[In this book] you will find a human species/race which, in their perfection . . . were not divided into two sexes, and who do not need to sleep to regain their strength; who nourish themselves with their own milk, and do not need teeth to eat" (1:xiv).
11. He expounds the twelve basic precepts of his religion in the fourth volume (4:195–204).

CHAPTER 9

1. In his critical response to the negative review of McBride in the *American Quarterly Review* ("Symmes's Theory of Concentric Spheres," 1827), Reynolds writes: "That the earth is composed of five spheres, concentric with each other, and each sphere supplied with a 'mid plane space,' and that the water extends quite through the sphere, in some places, are points I shall not defend. I have never defended them. . . . But notwithstanding these concessions, I must still maintain, as a matter of pleasing speculation, if you please, that the earth we live on, may be a hollow sphere, and widely open at the poles" (Reynolds, *Remarks*, 5).
2. McBride's 1826 account should be considered the "official" one. The New York Public Library catalog notes that McBride's book was written "under the direction and with the revision of Captain Symmes" (NYPL catalog, "James McBride"). In the "Apology to Captain Symmes" with which McBride's book begins, he concludes by writing that "I hope that you will permit [this book] to pass as the Pioneer to a more complete demonstration of your Theory of Concentric Spheres" (McBride, *Symmes's Theory*, ix).
3. Walter Kafton-Minkel is one of the few critics who explicitly try to link Symmes's "discovery" with his reading: "We can be fairly certain that one of the books he read was Cotton Mather's *Christian Philosopher*, with its description of Halley's concentric-earths idea. Coming as he did from an educated family with a Puritan background—Mather had mentioned one of Symmes's ancestors in another of his books—the *Philosopher* could not have been unknown to him" (Kafton-Minkel, *Subterranean Worlds*, 58).

For a careful summary of the genealogy of these ideas, see Zirkle, "The Theory of Concentric Spheres." Zirkle is careful to admit that "there is some doubt as to where Symmes got his concept." She then goes on to establish that Cotton Mather's *Christian Philosopher* was inspired by Edmund Halley's "Account of the Cause of the Change of the Variation of the Magnetical Needle with an Hypothesis of the Structure of the Internal Parts of the Earth" (Zirkle, "The Theory of Concentric Spheres," 156). Paul Collins takes the opposite view about Symmes's awareness of the ideas of Halley and Mather: "Symmes was unlikely to have read these obscure works, and so his was an act of discovery made all the more impressive by his humble education. Moreover, his theory included a polar opening—Symmes Hole as it came to be widely known—and that meant that contact with the interior world could be made. In Halley's theory, the earth's outer shell was five hundred miles thick and had no hole, which gave his readers little reason to pursue the theory much further. Symmes, though, had offered them a gateway to new worlds" (Collins, "Symmes Hole," 58).

4. Although J. O. Bailey calls *Symzonia* the "first American utopia" (introduction, [vii]), Lyman Sargent has written me that "there are at least half a dozen US utopias predating Symzonia, going back to 1659." Of these, at least one is equal to *Symzonia*: John Lithgow's "Equality: A Political Romance" (1802), reprinted as *Equality; or, A History of Lithconia* (1827).
5. John Ross was a Scottish polar explorer who discovered the Boothian Peninsula near Baffin Island; his son, James Ross, continued in this tradition and discovered the magnetic North Pole in 1831. John Ross published *A Voyage of Discovery: Made under the Order of the Admiralty, in His Majesty's Ships Isabella and Alexander, for the Purpose of Exploring Baffin's Bay, and Enquiring into the Probability of a North-West Passage* in 1819. Lang and Lease suggest that Ross's book was one of the models for *Symzonia* (244n 14). They also cite this passage as an example of the book's satirical tone: "Ross's encounter with a tribe of Eskimos who pull their noses as a friendly gesture of greeting is transformed into burlesque in *Symzonia* when a native of the inner world reciprocates with a significant variation '. . . raising his hand to his forehead, he brought it down to the point of his nose, and waved it gracefully in salutation, with a slight inclination of the body, but without actually pulling the nose as I had done'"(244n 14). This admittedly ridiculous gesture becomes even more laughable when the internals "gracefully" thumb their noses in greeting, but this is immediately followed by other actions which turn the novel from humour to seriousness as he kneels and raises his arms to the sky, a gesture which convinces the internals of his good intentions—at least for a while: "Their suspicions of my being of the outcast tribe, were allayed by the testimony of reverence to the Supreme Being which I had given, by falling on my knees, and imploring the aid of heaven in my embarrassed situation; whereby they knew that

I could not be unworthy of their regard" (Seaborn, 133). I am not convinced that this passage is entirely satirical. Rubbing noses, for instance, is a traditional greeting in some aboriginal societies. It is important to read the entire passage. See the first selection of the "First Contact" section.

6. This need for little sleep is a familiar SF theme that marks superiority; it is also seen in H. G. Wells's Martians in *The War of The Worlds* (1898).
7. McBride devotes chapter 7 to this question as well: "Several objections made to the Theory of Concentric Spheres, answered, particularly the one that it convenes religious opinion; demonstrating that the earth, and the other orbs of the universe, are formed on the best possible plan for the maintenance and support of organic " life" (McBride, *Symmes's Theory*, ix).
8. David Seed cites an attribution to Symmes in the British Library catalog ("Breaking the Bounds," 95n 8), while J. O. Bailey writes that the "original card-catalogue in the [University of North Carolina] Library listed the book as by 'Symmes, J. C.' with no mention of Seaborn at all." Later someone entered on the card in pencil "'pseud. John Cleves Symmes, 1780–1829,' but with no indication of the source of this information" (Bailey, introduction, ix).
9. Dale Mullen wrote to William Stanton to ask him why *The Great United States Exploring Expedition* omitted any reference to *Symzonia*, "which seems to be universally regarded in SF circles as a document in the campaign [to win governmental support for a polar expedition to test his hollow-Earth theory]." Stanton replied that there had been some discussion of *Symzonia* in the original manuscript, but that he had been obliged to pare down the manuscript for publication.

   The most thorough consideration of Symmes and *Symzonia* remains Arie Nicholas Jan den Hollander's *De verbeeldingswereld van Edgar Allan Poe en enkele tijdgenoten* (1974), which, because it has not been translated, remains little known. There are six chapters in this short book, dealing with Symmes and his theory, "Jeremiah Reynolds in Antarctica," Reynolds and Melville, Reynolds and Poe, *Symzonia,* and the novel's later influence on Poe and science fiction. In the chapter on *Symzonia* (*De verbeeldingswereld van Edgar Allan Poe*, 83–99), Hollander deals primarily with internal arguments about why Symmes was almost certainly not the author. He begins, however, by agreeing with Bailey's comment that the Library of Congress catalog's description of the novel as a "burlesque" is simply wrong (Bailey, introduction to *Symzonia,* ix; Hollander, *De verbeeldingswereld van Edgar Allan Poe*, 95). Among the arguments against Symmes's authorship, Hollander (like Stanton and others) insists that Symmes's writing is so poor that it is "almost impossible that this novel could have been written by the same hand that wrote the Circular" (97). He also mentions the weaknesses and flaws in the character of Seaborn, which do not accord with Symmes's own certainties, and the fact that the hollow Earth of the novel and of the illustration show not a series of concentric worlds, but a single inner sphere (98).

10. Lang and Lease cite Henri Petter's *Early American Novel* (1971), which includes *Symzonia* in the chapter titled "Satirical and Polemical Fiction": it "combines a satire of John Cleves Symmes's 'Theory of Concentric Spheres' . . . with features strongly reminiscent of *Gulliver's Travels*" (149). Petter disputes Bailey's reading of the novel, writing that "the note of irony is sounded from beginning to end" (164n 118)—although Bailey himself called attention to the relationship to *Gulliver's Travels* (introduction, [viii]). In addition to the works of Holberg, Ross, and Swift, Neville Davies makes a strong case for Godwin's 1638 *Man in the Moone* as the key source for *Symzonia*—like Holberg's *Niels Klim*, again a utopian work.

CHAPTER 10

1. Collin de Plancy wrote under at least twenty pseudonyms (Roudaut, *Fonds*, 17n 33) The *Voyage* was published under the pseudonym Jacques Saint-Albin. The *Dictionnaire infernal* can be found online at numerous sites dedicated to the occult and the diabolical, such as www.heresie.com, www.deliriusrealm.com, and so on. The book began as a series of engravings of sixty-nine demons by Louis Breton, which Collin de Plancy then published with brief descriptions of each demon. (The images can be viewed at www.innuendocornecopria.com.) As the *Dictionnaire infernal* went through various editions, Collin de Plancy expanded and revised it, and after his conversion, he focused on heresies. Accordingly, the 1844 edition was titled *Dictionnaire infernal, ou Répertoire universel des êtres, des personnages, des livres, des faits et des choses qui tiennent aux apparitions, aux divinations, à la magie, au commerce de lenfer, aux démons, aux sorciers, aux sciences occultes, aux grimoires, à la cabale, aux esprits élémentaires, au grand oeuvre, aux prodiges, aux erreurs et aux préjugés, aux impostures, aux arts des bohémiens, aux superstitions diverses, aux contes populaires, aux pronostics, et généralement à toutes les fausses croyances, merveilleuses, surprenantes, mystérieuses ou surnaturelles.* The same year Collin de Plancy also published a *Dictionnaire des sciences occultes . . . ou, Répertoire universel des êtres, des personnages, des livres, des faits et des choses qui tiennent aux apparitions, aux divinations, à la magie, au commerce de l'enfer, aux démons, aux sorciers, aux sciences occultes . . . et généralement à toutes les fausses croyances, merveilleuses, surprenantes, mystérieuses ou surnaturelles* (Paris: Chez l'éditeur, 1846–1848).

2. I have found only a few critical references to the novel: briefly in Pierre Citron, and in an entry in the *Dictionary of Literary Utopias* by Nadia Minerva. Collin de Plancy's reference to Symmes is to be found in his preface: "There were numerous derisive comments a few years ago when an American announced that he

wanted to go to the North pole to find a great opening through which he hoped to reach the center of the globe in search of habitable lands" (1:vii–viii).

3. Before acknowledging that they are in fact inside the Earth, one of their number argues that instead they have landed on the moon! "While we were falling the whirlwind lifted us rather than throwing us down. Thus instead of being in a subterranean world, which would be impossible . . . we are on the moon. This explains why we can see the sun . . . and why we find people smaller than us since the moon is fifty-five times smaller than our earth" (2:13–14).

   Earlier, another of their number had insisted that they were approaching the gates of hell. "If I had only to fear wild animals, my whole body would not be trembling as it is now. As I said before, hell lies below us, and that is where our two friends have plunged, directly into the yawning maw of the devil which, as everyone knows, is always open" (1:176).

4. This is perhaps the first fictional example of this cliché, although these are not aliens from outer space.

5. These countries, despite references to the printing press, are not very advanced technologically. Of course, this novel was written in 1821; and the inhabitants of the underworld must do without iron.

6. My source is Jacques Collin de Plancy, *Voyage au centre de la terre ou aventures diverses de Clairancy et de ses compagnons dans le Spitzberg, au Pôle-nord, et dans des pays inconnus*, 3 vols. (Paris: Chez Callot et fils, 1821).

7. Holberg also describes a "natural" religion in the land of Potu.

8. "Animals flee death whereas the fruit of the tree falls into our hands when it is ripe" (2:102). Vegetarianism has been a frequent feature of the subterranean worlds we have seen.

9. If a league is three miles, this would give a circumference of 27,000 miles, although the Earth's circumference is actually about 24,900 miles. The thickness of the Earth's crust is usually estimated at about 25 miles, and not the 150–450 miles given here.

10. Or 2400 miles. The diameter of the earth is about 8,000 miles.

CHAPTER II

1. Paltock's novel is mentioned in "Hans Pfall," and Kircher in the "Descent into the Maelstrom." The narrator of "The Fall of the House of Usher" includes "the 'Subterranean Voyage of Nicholas Klimm' [*sic*] of Holberg" among his readings (Poe, *Tales and Poems*, 1:128).

2. Poe's works are readily available on the Internet (e.g., at the Project Gutenberg site: promo.net/pg/). The citations here are to Edgar Allan Poe, *The Tales and Poems of Edgar Allan Poe*, with a biographical essay by John H. Ingram, 4 vols. (New York: Scribner and Welford; London, John C. Nimmo, 1885). The critical

writing on Poe is immense, but the bibliography contains a number of articles dealing with the Symmes-Poe link.

There are a number of discussions of the Poe-Symmes link, most especially Arie Hollander, as well as J. O. Bailey's introduction to *Symzonia*, which begins with a discussion of "Poe's use of *Symzonia*." Bailey points out that Poe used seven hundred words of Reynolds's appeal to the U.S. Congress in 1834 in *Pym* (cited below). See also the discussions in David Seed and William Stanton.

3. Writing of the anonymous *Relation*, Régis Messac points out that the idea of a subterranean passage between the poles was used by Poe in his "MS. Found in a Bottle." Messac speculates that the note at the end of Poe's story, in which the author insists that he became acquainted only *afterward* "with the maps of Mercator," was an attempt to conceal his knowledge of earlier works and in particular of the *Relation* (Messac, "Voyages modernes," 82–83).
4. There have been several attempts to complete "Pym," including Jules Verne's *Le sphynx des glaces* (1897), H. P. Lovecraft's "At the Mountains of Madness" (1931), and Michel Bernanos's *La montagne morte de la vie* (1967). Rudy Rucker's 1990 science fiction novel *The Hollow Earth* also continues the uncompleted "Narrative of A. Gordon Pym" by making Poe the main character who travels through the passageway between the poles. Finally, an impressive treatment of this theme can be seen in a 1993 film from the Netherlands—*The Forbidden Quest*, directed by Peter Delpeut. This visually stunning film (which has strong overtones of Poe and Lovecraft) uses archival footage from various polar expeditions from the beginning of the twentieth century to relate the story of a doomed expedition that went to the South Pole in 1905 to find the subterranean passage to the North Pole.

CHAPTER 12

1. Numerous editions of the novel—in both English and French—are available both in print and online, so I have given chapter numbers rather than page numbers in citations. The Project Gutenberg has good editions at promo.net/pg/. Arthur Evans has pointed out the problems with some translations of Verne (*Jules Verne Rediscovered*, 1988). Two excellent editions of the *Voyage* in French, with notes and commentary, are those of Simone Vierne (Paris: Garnier-Flammarion, 1977) and Jean-Pierre Goldenstein (Paris: Presses Pocket, 1991). The latter includes more than 150 pages of notes. Goldenstein explains in detail the additions Verne made for the illustrated edition of 1867, all concerning prehistoric life: at the end of chapter 37 (in the scene describing the prehistoric graveyard—which includes a human skull), as well as for the reference to Boucher de Perthes's discovery of a human jawbone (chapter 38), and most importantly, for the herd of mastodons and the prehistoric man (437).

2. Arthur Evans reminds me that the episode of the giant prehistoric man and his flock was added several years later: "Those additions to VOYAGE (end of chap. xxxvii, some of chap. xxxviii, and all of chap. xxxix) were added in 1867. Most scholars believe that Verne added these episodes in order to 'update' the story with current events—e.g., reactions to the prehistoric discoveries of Boucher de Perthes (which JV mentions in the novel) and the controversial debates they caused in 1863–66—not to mention the fact that the first French translation of Darwin's *Origin of Species* appeared in 1863, triggering all sorts of evolutionary discussions—as well as to make the story more dramatic. It is interesting (and highly typical) that Verne never really says the giant and the mastodons are real: both Axel and his uncle are left wondering if perhaps it was all just a hallucination on their part" (Evans, private correspondence).
3. "Up to this time facts had supported the theories of Davy and of Liedenbrock; until now particular conditions of non-conducting rocks, electricity and magnetism, had tempered the laws of nature, giving us only a moderately warm climate, for the theory of a central fire remained in my estimation the only one that was true and explicable" (Evans, "Literary Intertexts," 42).
4. "There are a number of surprising parallels between Dumas's epic novel [*Isaac Laquédem*] and Verne's own *Voyage au centre de la Terre*" (Evans, "Literary Intertexts," 172). Evans specifically cites this passage as referring to Dumas's unfinished novel.
5. In her introduction to Verne's *Voyage*, Simone Vierne discusses more generally the question of influences, without citing predecessors, saying only that "the question of the internal makeup of our globe was a much debated topic at the time" (29).
6. They calculate that the Earth's radius, "the distance from the centre to the surface, is about 1,583 leagues; let us say in round numbers 1,600 leagues, or 4,800 miles" (chapter 26).

CHAPTER 13

1. Today, however, he is above all known for opening the 1830 novel *Paul Clifford* with the following sentence: "It was a dark and stormy night and the rain fell in torrents—except at occasional intervals, when it was checked by a violent gust of wind which swept up the streets (for it is in London that our scene lies), rattling along the housetops, and fiercely agitating the scanty flame of the lamps that struggled against the darkness." This led, in 1982, to the organization of the Bulwer-Lytton Fiction Contest, a literary competition sponsored by the English department at California's San Jose State University that challenges entrants to compose the worst opening sentence to the worst of all possible novels.

   Chapter and page references here are to Edward Bulwer-Lytton, *The Coming Race* (London: Routledge, 1888). The complete text is available at promo.net/pg/.

2. Nor do they know alcohol. This reminds us again of the inhabitants of *Symzonia*.
3. Kafton-Minkel is one of the more explicit of Bulwer-Lytton's critics in identifying the objects of the novel's satire: "[He] found the democratic pretensions and rabid patriotism of many of the Americans he had met irritating, and he made the protagonist of his story American to place in his mouth patriotic blusterings that would have done Marshall B. Gardner proud" (*Subterranean Worlds*, 260). He continues by arguing that the Vril-ya are a "satire on both feminism and socialism": the first in terms of the naiveté of contemporary "discussions on the equality of humanity, the dignity of the laborer, and the rights of women." In terms of the second, Kafton-Minkel sees the Gy-ei as "caricatures of nineteenth century feminists" (261). He also mentions that Bulwer-Lytton wrote afterward that the novel was intended to portray the "impracticality of utopias."

   Kafton-Minkel also discusses the popularity and some of the uses that the concept of *vril* was put to after the book's publication, from occultists to early versions of Viagra (*Subterranean Worlds*, 262).
4. *Mizora* first appeared anonymously in the *Cincinnati Commercial* in 1880 and 1881. Kristine Anderson has informed me that in the newspaper version, the editors described Mizora as "the land known to readers of the *Commercial* as Symmes Hole" (*Cincinnati Commercial,* December 15, 1880; cited by Kristine Anderson in a personal communication). The full title (as cited by Sargent, *British and American Utopian Literature*, 67–68) is *Mizora: A Prophecy; A Mss. Found Among the Private Papers of the Princess Vera Zarovitch* [pseudo.]*; Being a true and faithful account of her Journey to the Interior of the Earth, with a careful description of the Country and its Inhabitants, their Customs, Manners and Government. Written by Herself.* In one recent study, Robin Roberts asserts that *Mizora* is set in the Arctic and does not even mention its subterranean characteristics (Roberts, *A New Species: Gender and Science in Science Fiction* [Urbana: University of Illinois Press, 1993]).

   Several editions of *Mizora* are currently available. Chapter and page references here are to Mary Lane, *Mizora: A Prophecy*, ed. and with a critical introduction by Jean Pfaelzer (Syracuse: Syracuse University Press, 2000).
5. In the "Author's Afterword" he takes a more modest position: "It is impossible for me to express my opinion as to the value or reliability of the wonderful statements made by Olaf Jansen."

   Chapter and page references here are to Willis George Emerson, *The Smoky God, or A Voyage to the Inner World* (Chicago: Forbes, 1908). The original edition is available online at promo.net/pg/.
6. Burroughs's novels are readily available online. Chapter and page references here are to Edgar Rice Burroughs, *At the Earth's Core* (New York: Doubleday, 1977).

Bibliography

Adams, Frank Dawson. *The Birth and Death of the Geological Sciences*. New York: Dover, 1954.

Anonymous. *Relation d'un voyage du Pôle Arctique, au Pôle Antarctique, par le centre du monde, avec la description de ce périlleux passage, & des choses merveilleuses & étonnantes qu'on a découvertes sous le Pôle Antarctique*. In Charles-Georges-Thomas Garnier, ed., *Voyages imaginaires, songes, visions, et romans cabalistiques*. Vol. 19. À Amsterdam, et se trouve à Paris: Rue et Hôtel Serpente, 1788.

Anonymous. *A Voyage to the World in the Center of the Earth Giving an Account of the Manners, Customs, Laws, Government, and Religion of the Inhabitants, Their Persons and Habits Described with Several Other Particulars: In which Is Introduced the History of an Inhabitant of the Air, Written by Himself, with Some Account of the Planetary Worlds*. London: S. Crowder and H. Woodgate, 1755.

Bailey, J. O. "An Early American Utopian Fiction." *American Literature* 14, no. 3 (November 1942): 285–293.

——. Introduction to *Symzonia*. In Adam Seaborn [John Cleves Symmes?], *Symzonia: A Voyage of Discovery*, iii–x. Edited by J. O. Bailey. Gainesville, Fla.: Scholars' Facsimiles and Reprints, 1965.

Becker, A. R. *The Lost Worlds Romance: From Dawn to Dusk*. Westport, Conn.: Greenwood Press, 1992.

Bentley, Christopher. Introduction to Robert Paltock, *The Life and Adventures of Peter Wilkins*, edited by Christopher Bentley. Oxford: Oxford University Press, 1973.

Bernard, Raymond. *The Hollow Earth: The Greatest Geographical Discovery in History; Made by Admiral Richard E. Byrd in the Mysterious Lands beyond the Poles—the True Origin of the Flying Saucers*. New York: Bell, 1979.

Bleiler, E. F. *Science Fiction: The Early Years*. Kent, Ohio: Kent State University Press, 1990.

Bousquet, J. "Lesuire." In *Le dix-huitième siècle romantique*. 332–343. Paris: Pauvert, 1972.

Bulwer-Lytton, Edward. *The Coming Race*. London: Routledge, 1888.

Burnet, Thomas. *The Sacred Theory of the Earth*. [1691.] London: Centaur, 1965.

——. *The Sacred Theory of the Earth: Containing an Account of the Original Creation, and of All the General Changes Which It Hath Undergone, or Is to Undergo, until the Consummation of All Things*. 7th ed. [1691.] London: Printed for T. Osborn [et al.], 1759. [Available on microfilm in the ESTC (Eighteenth Century Short Title Catalogue) series, reel no. 6330, item 6.]

Burroughs, Edgar Rice. *At the Earth's Core*. New York: Doubleday, 1977.

Casanova, Giovanni Giacomo. *L'Icosameron, ou Histoire d'Edouard et d'Elisabeth qui passèrent quatre vingts ans chez les Mégamicres habitans aborigènes du Protocosme dans l'intérieur de notre globe, traduite de l'anglois par Jacques Casanova de Seingalt Vénitien*. 5 vols. Prague: Imprimerie de l'école normale, [1787].

Cavendish, Margaret. *The Description of a New World, Called the Blazing World*. Edited by Kate Lilley. London: William Pickering, 1992.

Citron, Pierre. "Sur quelques voyages au centre de la terre." In *Colloque d'Amiens: nouvelles recherches sur Jules Verne et le "Voyage,"* 67–80. Paris: Minard, 1978.

Claeys, Gregory, ed. *Utopias of the British Enlightenment*. Cambridge: Cambridge University Press, 1994.

Clark, P. "The Symmes Theory of the Earth." *Atlantic Monthly*, April 1873, 471–480.

Clute, John, and Peter Nicholls. *The Encyclopedia of Science Fiction*. London: Orbit, 1993.

Cohen, I. Bernard. "Notes and Correspondence." *Isis* 35 (1944): 333–334.

Collier, Katharine Brownell. *Cosmogonies of Our Fathers: Some Theories of the Seventeenth and Eighteenth Centuries*. New York: Columbia University Press, 1934.

Collin de Plancy, Jacques. *Voyage au centre de la terre ou Aventures diverses de Clairancy et de ses compagnons dans le Spitzberg, au Pôle-nord, et dans des pays inconnus*. 3 vols. Paris: Chez Callot et fils, 1821.

Collins, Paul. "Symmes Hole." In *Banvard's Folly: Thirteen Tales of Renowned Obscurity, Famous Anonymity, and Rotten Luck*. New York: Picador, 2001.

Crossley, Robert. "Ethereal Ascents: Eighteenth-Century Fantasies of Human Flight." *Eighteenth-Century Life* 7, no. 2 (January 1982): 55–64.

Davies, H. Neville. "Symzonia and *The Man in the Moone*." *Notes and Queries* 15 (September 1968): 342–345.

Derrida, Jacques. *Of Grammatology*. Translated by Gayatri Chakravorty Spivak. Corrected ed. Baltimore: Johns Hopkins University Press, 1998.

De Quincy, Thomas. *Niles Klim, Being an Incomplete Translation from the Danish of Ludvig Holberg, Now Edited from the Manuscript by S. Musgrove*. Auckland University College, Bulletin no. 42, English Series no. 5, 1953.

Eddy, William. *Gulliver's Travels: A Critical Study*. Princeton: Princeton University Press, 1963.

Ellenberger, Francois. *Histoire de la géologie*. 2 vols. Paris: Lavoisier, 1994.

Elliot, Robert. *The Shape of Utopia*. Chicago: University of Chicago Press, 1970.

Emerson, Willis George. *The Smoky God, or, A Voyage to the Inner World*. Chicago: Forbes, 1908.

Evans, Arthur B. *Jules Verne Rediscovered: Didacticism and the Scientific Novel*. New York: Greenwood Press, 1988.

———. "Literary Intertexts in Jules Verne's *Voyages extraordinaires*." *Science-Fiction Studies* 23, no. 2 (July 1996): 171–187.

Fitting, Peter. "Buried Treasures: Reconsidering Holberg's *Niels Klim in the World Underground*." *Utopian Studies* 7, no. 2 (1996): 93–112.

———. "Imagination, Textual Play, and the Fantastic in Mouhy's *Lamékis*." *Eighteenth-Century Fiction* 5 (July 1993): 311–329.

Flammarion, Camille. *Les mondes imaginaires et les mondes réels: voyage pittoresque dans le ciel et revue critique des théories humaines scientifiques et romanesques, anciennes et modernes sur les habitants des astres*. 19th ed. Paris: C. Marpon et E. Flammarion, 1884.

Fortunati, Vita, and Raymond Trousson, eds. *Dictionary of Literary Utopias*. Paris: Honoré Champion, 2000.

Friederich, Werner P. *Australia in Western Imaginative Prose Writings, 1600–1960: An Anthology and a History of Literature*. Chapel Hill: University of North Carolina Press, 1967.

Gardner, Martin. "Flat and Hollow." In *Fads and Fallacies in the Name of Science*, 16–27. 2nd ed. New York: Dover, 1957.

Garnier, Charles-Georges-Thomas, ed. *Voyages imaginaires, songes, visions, et romans cabalistiques*. 36 vols. À Amsterdam, et se trouve à Paris: Rue et Hôtel Serpente, 1787–1789.

Godwin, Joscelyn. *Arktos: The Polar Myth in Science, Symbolism, and Nazi Survival*. London: Thames and Hudson, 1993.

———. *Athanasius Kircher: A Renaissance Man and the Quest for Lost Knowledge*. London: Thames and Hudson, 1979.

Gohau, Gabriel. *Les sciences de la terre aux XVIIe et XVIIIe siècles*. Paris: Albin Michel, 1990.

Goubier-Robert, Geneviève. "'L'année merveilleuse' ou l'utopie dans *L'aventurier françois* de Robert-Martin Lesuire." *Utopie et fictions narratives*. Special issue, *Parabasis* 7 (1995): 211–221.

Gove, Philip Babcock. *The Imaginary Voyage in Prose Fiction: A History of Its Criticism and a Guide for Its Study, with an Annotated Check List of 215 Imaginary Voyages from 1700 to 1800*. New York: Columbia University Press, 1941.

Guillaud, Lauric. *L'aventure mystérieuse de Poe à Merrit ou l'orphelin de Gilgamesh*. Liège: Editions de Céfal, 1993.

Hallam, A. *Great Geological Controversies*. 2nd ed. Oxford: Oxford University Press.

Halley, Edmund. "A Theory of the Magnetic Variations." Reprinted in John Lowthorp, *Philosophical Transactions and Collections, to the End of the Year 1700*,

Abridg'd and Dispos'd under General Heads, 2:610–620. 3 vols. 3rd ed. London: Printed for J. Knapton, 1722.

Hammer, Simon C. *Ludvig Holberg: The Founder of Norwegian Literature and an Oxford Student*. Blackwell: Oxford, 1920.

Holberg, Ludvig. *A Journey to the World Underground by Nicholas Klimius*. In *Popular Romances, Consisting of Imaginary Voyages and Travels, Containing* Gulliver's Travels, Journey to the World Underground, The Life and Adventures of Peter Wilkins, The Adventures of Robinson Crusoe, *and* The History of the Automathes, *to which Is Prefixed an Introductory Dissertation*, edited by Henry Weber, 117–200. Edinburgh: James Ballantyne, 1812.

———. *The Journey of Niels Klim to the World Underground*. Introduced and edited by James I. Mc Nelis Jr. Westport, Conn.: Greenwood Press, 1960.

Hollander, Arie Nicholas Jan den. *De verbeeldingswereld van Edgar Allan Poe en enkele tijdgenoten*. Amsterdam: Polak and Van Gennep, 1974.

Hougaard, Jens. *Ludvig Holberg: The Playwright and His Age up to 1730*. Translated by Jean and Tom Lundskær-Nielsen. Odense: Odense University Press, 1993.

Humboldt, Alexander von. *Cosmos: A Sketch of a Physical Description of the Universe*. Translated by E. C. Otté. 2 vols. London: Henry G. Bohn, 1848.

Jansen, F. J. Billeskov. *Ludvig Holberg*. New York: Twayne, 1974.

Jones, James F. "Adventures in a Strange Paradise: Utopia in 'Nicolai Klimii Iter subterraneum.'" *Orbis Litterarum* 35 (1980): 193–205.

Kafton-Minkel, Walter. *Subterranean Worlds: 100,000 Years of Dragons, Dwarfs, the Dead, Lost Races, & UFOs from Inside the Earth*. Port Townsend, Wash.: Loompanics Unlimited, 1989.

Kircher, Athanasius. *Mundus Subterraneus, in XII Libros digestus; quo Divinum Subterrestris Mundi Opificium*. Amsterdam: Apud Joannem Janssonium à Waesberge & filios, 1678.

Krappe, Alexander. "The Subterraneous Voyage." *Philological Quarterly* 20, no. 2 (April 1941): 119–130.

Lane, Mary. *Mizora: A Prophecy*. Edited and with a critical introduction by Jean Pfaelzer. Syracuse: Syracuse University Press, 2000.

Lang, Hans-Joachim, and Benjamin Lease. "The Authorship of *Symzonia*: The Case for Nathaniel Ames." *New England Quarterly* 18, no. 2 (June 1975): 241–252.

Leibacher, Lise. "*L'Icosameron* de Casanova: nature et culture de l'ambiguité." *Utopia 2*. Special issue, *EMF: Studies in Early Modern France* 5 (1999): 103–126.

Lesuire, Robert-Martin. *L'aventurier françois, ou Mémoires de Grégoire Merveil*. 2 vols. Paris: Quillau l'ainé [and] LaVeuve Duchesne, [1782].

———. *Première suite*. 2 vols. Nouvelle éd. Paris: Quillau et al., 1787.

Lévi-Strauss, Claude. *Tristes tropiques*. Translated by John Russell. New York: Atheneum, 1967.

Lewis, A. "Symzonia." In *Dictionary of Literary Utopias*, edited by Vita Fortunati and Raymond Trousson, 592–593. Paris: Champion, 2000.

Lucian. *True History*. Translated by Paul Turner. Bloomington: Indiana University Press, 1958.

Manguel, Alberto and Gianni Guadalupi. *The Dictionary of Imaginary Places*. Expanded ed. Toronto: Lester and Orpen Dennys, 1987.

Mather, Kirtley, and Shirley L. Mason. *A Source Book in Geology, 1400–1900*. Cambridge: Harvard University Press, 1970.

McBride, James. *Symmes's Theory of Concentric Spheres, Demonstrating that the Earth Is Hollow, Habitable Within and Widely Open about the Poles; By a Citizen of the United States*. Cincinnati: Morgan, Lodge and Fisher, 1826.

Mc Nelis, James. Introduction to Ludvig Holberg, *The Journey of Niels Klim to the World Underground*, edited by James Mc Nelis, vii–xxvii. Westport, Conn.: Greenwood Press, 1960.

Messac, Regis. "Voyages modernes au centre de la terre." *Revue de littérature comparée* 9 (1929): 74–104.

Miller, Wm. Marion. "The Theory of Concentric Spheres." *Isis* 33 (1941): 507–514.

Minerva, Nadia. *Jules Verne aux confins de l'utopie*. Paris: L'Harmattan, 2001.

———. "Utopia e speleologia." In *Utopia e . . . : amici e nemici del genere utopico nella letteratura francese*. Ravenna: Longo, 1995.

———. "Voyage au centre de la terre." In *Dictionary of Literary Utopias*, edited by Vita Fortunati and Raymond Trousson. Paris: Honoré Champion, 2000: 669–670.

Mouhy, Charles de Fieux. *Lamékis, ou Les voyages extraordinaires d'un Egyptien dans la terre intérieure*. In *Voyages imaginaires, songes, visions, et romans cabalistiques*, edited by Charles-Georges-Thomas Garnier. Vols. 19–20. À Amsterdam, et se trouve à Paris: Rue et Hôtel Serpente, 1788.

Mullen, R. D. "The Arno Reprints." *Science-Fiction Studies* 2, no. 2 (July 1975) 179–185.

———. "The Authorship of Symzonia." *Science-Fiction Studies* 3, no. 1 (March 1976): 98–99.

Nelson, Victoria. "Symmes Hole, or the South Polar Grotto." In *The Secret Life of Puppets*, 138–161. Cambridge, Mass.: Harvard University Press, 2001.

Nicolson, Marjorie Hope. *Voyages to the Moon*. New York: MacMillan, 1948.

Norman, Daniel. "Notes and Correspondence." *Isis* 34 (1942): 29–30.

Nydahl, Joel. "Early Fictional Futures: Utopia, 1798–1864." In *America as Utopia*, edited by Kenneth M. Roemer, 254–291. New York: Burt Franklin, 1981.

Paltock, Robert. *The Life and Adventures of Peter Wilkins*. Edited by Christopher Bentley. Oxford: Oxford University Press, 1973.

———. *The Life and Adventures of Peter Wilkins*. Edited by Christopher Bentley, with a new introduction by James Grantham Turner. Oxford: Oxford University Press, 1990.

———. *The Life and Adventures of Peter Wilkins, a Cornish Man, Taken from His Own Mouth, in His Passage to England, from off Cape Horn in America, in the Ship Hector, by R. S., a Passenger in the Hector*. In *Popular Romances, Consisting of Imaginary Voyages and Travels, Containing* Gulliver's Travels, Journey to the World Underground, The Life and Adventures of Peter Wilkins, The Adventures of Robinson Crusoe, *and* The History of the Automathes, *to Which Is Prefixed an Introductory Dissertation*, edited by Henry Weber, 201–348. Edinburgh: James Ballantyne, 1812.

Paludan, Julius. *Om Holbergs "Niels Klim," med saerligt Hensyn til tidligere Satirer i Form af opdigtede og vidunderlige Reiser*. Copenhagen: Wilhelm Priors, 1878.

Peck, John Wells. "Symmes's Theory." *Ohio Archaeological and Historical Quarterly* 18 (1909): 28–42.

Peters, Sigrid. *Ludvig Holbergs Menippeische Satire: Das "Iter Subterraneum" und seine Beziehungen zur antiken Literatur*. Frankfurt: Peter Lang, 1987.

Petter, Henri. *The Early American Novel*. Columbus: Ohio State University Press, 1971.

Poe, Edgar Allan. *The Complete Tales and Poems of Edgar Allan Poe*. New York: Modern Library, 1938.

———. *The Tales and Poems of Edgar Allan Poe*. 4 vols. New York: Scribner and Welford, 1885.

Reynolds, J. N. *Remarks on a Review of Symmes' Theory which Appeared in the American Quarterly Review, by a "Citizen of the United States."* Washington: Gales and Seaton, 1827.

Roberts, Robin. *A New Species: Gender and Science in Science Fiction*. Urbana: University of Illinois Press, 1993.

Robinson, Christopher. *Lucian and His Influence*. London: Duckworth, 1979.

Rollins, James. *Subterranean*. New York: Avon, 1999.

Rossel, Sven, ed. *Ludvig Holberg: A European Writer*. Amsterdam: Rodopi, 1994.

Roudaut, François. *Le fonds de Collin de Plancy*. Geneva: Slatkine, 1994.

Sargent, Lyman Tower. *British and American Utopian Literature, 1516–1985*. New York: Garland, 1988.

Seaborn, Adam [John Cleves Symmes?]. *Symzonia: A Voyage of Discovery*. New York: Printed by J. Seymour, 1820.

———. *Symzonia: A Voyage of Discovery*. Facsimile reproduction with an introduction by J. O. Bailey. Gainesville, Fla.: Scholars' Facsimiles and Reprints, 1965.

Seed, David. "Breaking the Bounds: The Rhetoric of Limits in the Works of Edgar Allan Poe, His Contemporaries and Adaptors." In David Seed, *Anticipations: Essays on Early Science Fiction and Its Precursors*, 75–97. Syracuse: Syracuse University Press, 1995.

Silvani, Giovanna. "The Description of a New World, Called the Blazing World." In *Dictionary of Literary Utopias*, edited by Vita Fortunati and Raymond Trousson, 164–167. Paris: Champion, 2000.

Stableford, Brian. "Parallel Worlds." In *The Encyclopedia of Science Fiction*, edited by John Clute and Peter Nicholls, 907–909. London: Orbit, 1993.

Stanton, William. *The Great United States Exploring Expedition of 1838–1842*. Berkeley: University of California Press, 1975.

Suvin, Darko. *Metamorphoses of Science Fiction: On the Poetics and History of a Literary Genre*. New Have: Yale University Press, 1979.

———. *Victorian Science Fiction in the UK: The Discourses of Knowledge and of Power*. Boston: G. K. Hall, 1983.

Symmes, Americus. *The Symmes Theory of Concentric Spheres, Demonstrating that the Earth Is Hollow, Habitable Within, and Widely Open about the Poles: Compiled by Americus Symmes from the Writings of His Father, Capt. John Cleves Symmes*. 2nd ed. Louisville, Ky.: Bradley and Gilbert, 1885.

Symmes, John Cleves. *Declaration that the Earth Is Hollow, Containing a Number of Solid Concentric Spheres, and Open at Both Poles, and an Invitation for 100 Brave Companions to Undertake an Expedition to Prove It*. [St. Louis, Mo.?]: N.p., 1818.

"Symmes and His Theory." *Harper's Monthly*, September 1882, 740–744.

"Symmes's Theory of Concentric Spheres; Demonstrating that the Earth Is Hollow, Habitable Within, and Widely Open about the Poles" [review of McBride, *Symmes's Theory of Concentric Spheres*]. *American Quarterly Review* 1 (March 1827): 235–253.

Trousson, Raymond. *Voyages aux pays de nulle part: histoire littéraire de la pensée utopique*. Bruxelles: Editions de l'université de Bruxelles, 1975.

Turner, James Grantham. Introduction to Robert Paltock, *The Life and Adventures of Peter Wilkins*. Edited by Christopher Bentley, with a new introduction by James Grantham Turner. Oxford: Oxford University Press, 1990.

van Herp, Jacques. *Panorama de la science fiction: les thèmes, les genres, les écoles, les problèmes*. Verviers, Belgium: Gérard, 1973.

Verne, Jules. *Voyage au centre de la terre*. Paris: Garnier-Flammarion, 1977.

Versins, Pierre. *Encyclopédie de l'utopie, des voyages extraordinaires, et de la science fiction*. Lausanne: L'age d'homme, 1972.

Vierne, Simone. Introduction to Jules Verne, *Voyage au centre de la terre*, 2–35. Paris: Garnier-Flammarion, 1977.

"A Voyage to the Internal World" [review of Symmes, *Symzonia*]. *North American Review*, n.s. 13 (July 1821): 134–143.

Weber, Henry, [ed.]. *Popular Romances, Consisting of Imaginary Voyages and Travels, Containing* Gulliver's Travels, Journey to the World Underground, The Life and Adventures of Peter Wilkins, The Adventures of Robinson Crusoe, *and* The

History of the Automathes, *to Which Is Prefixed an Introductory Dissertation*. Edinburgh: James Ballantyne, 1812.

Welcher, Jeanne K., ed. *Gulliveriana VIII: An Annotated List of Gulliveriana, 1721–1800*. Delmar, N.Y.: Scholars' Facsimiles and Reprints, 1988.

Zirkle, Conway. "The Theory of Concentric Spheres: Edmund Halley, Cotton Mather, & John Cleves Symmes." *Isis* 37 (1947): 155–159.

Zurer, Rachel. *Casanova's "Icosameron."* Translated and abridged from the original French by Rachel Zurer. New York: Jenna Press, 1986.

Index

About the Editor

Peter Fitting is director of the Department of Cinema Studies at the University of Toronto. He is also former chairman of the Society of Utopian Studies.